Death In The Garden

Elizabeth Ironside

NEW ENGLISH LIBRARY
Hodder and Stoughton

Copyright © Elizabeth Ironside 1995

The right of Elizabeth Ironside to be identified as the author of
the work has been asserted by her in accordance with the
Copyright, Designs and Patents Act 1988.

First published in Great Britain in 1995 by
Hodder and Stoughton

First published in paperback in 1996 by
Hodder and Stoughton
A division of Hodder Headline PLC

A New English Library paperback

10 9 8 7 6 5 4 3 2

A CIP catalogue record for this title is available
from the British Library.

ISBN 0 340 64035 9

Typeset by
Letterpart Limited, Reigate, Surrey
Printed and bound in Great Britain by
Mackays of Chatham PLC, Chatham, Kent

Hodder and Stoughton
A division of Hodder Headline PLC
338 Euston Road
London NW1 3BH

Elizabeth Ironside has travelled widely and lived in France, India and Russia and now lives in London. Her first novel, *A Very Private Enterprise*, won the Crime Writers' Association John Creasey first novel award and was also shortlisted for the Betty Trask Award.

Also by Elizabeth Ironside

A Very Private Enterprise

For M.

Et In Arcadia Ego

Inscription upon a tomb, usually translated:
'And I too (the occupant of the tomb) was in Arcadia.'
But perhaps rather,
'I too (the tomb) am in Arcadia';
that is, 'even in Arcadia there am I, Death.'

CONTENTS

Part One

A LIFE

Friday 4th December 1925

Today at half-past two in the afternoon I was acquitted of the murder of my husband.

Five minutes earlier I had known I was to die. The certainty was absolute that what I have lived through in the last half year could only lead to death and a death timed, certain, ritualised. The members of the jury whose faces I had studied so often and so carefully over the last few days looked uneasy, even guilty, as they came through the archaic door and back into their panelled pen, the counter-part of mine. I knew then that what I expected, and had prepared for, would be. Not one of them had ever met my gaze, though they had watched me, as I them, their lids lowering, their eyes sliding away like fish through muddy water as our glances were about to clash. How can you look someone in the eye who is claiming her life from you? Not begging a ha'penny or a glass of water, but a life. Most of them had the appearance of those who would easily refuse a ha'penny and counted my life worth little more. I knew what I was about to hear. I had prepared myself to listen without a sign as if to the words of a psalm.

'. . . and that you be there hanged by the neck until you be dead;

that your body be buried within the precincts of the

3

prison in which you shall be confined; and may the Lord have mercy on your soul.

'Amen.'

It was as solemn as a service, the start of the burial of the dead; they came in like the choir ready to chant the responsals.

Gentlemen of the Jury, are you agreed upon your verdict?

We are, my lord.

Are you all agreed upon your decision?

We are, my lord.

Gentlemen of the Jury, do you find the accused, Athene Pollexfen, guilty or not guilty?

Not guilty, my lord.

Such formality suppresses emotion, contains it. I suppose it is one reason why men use ritual at such moments, which would otherwise be too terrible. The congregation did, however, exhale a long, hushing breath. Even then I did not understand what had been said. I had been rehearsing the exchanges in my mind for so long, in order to be able to hear the word 'guilty' without fainting, that I did not believe what I had heard and the strict control of my features which I had been willing since the moment that I had entered the courtroom did not relax at all. The foreman spoke in iambics, 'Not *guilty*, my *lord*,' and the misplaced stress distracted my ear from that essential negative, the negation that gave me back my life.

Wallace turned to me, triumphant. His smooth, pale face flushed slightly as he shook my hand. And my first words were to thank him, which I tried to do with all my heart. He undoubtedly saved me and his skill persuaded those men (not gentle) of the jury to see that – whatever they thought – whatever they felt about me – the rules did

4

not permit my death. He will be well rewarded by his victory, even if my thanks could not come from my heart. I cannot like or respect my saviour. I know he thinks me guilty and he never persuaded himself of what he convinced the jury. He manipulated the facts of the case, the emotions of the jury, the humours of the judge. He did not care for truth. And why should I care since he has saved my life? We have parted with the gains of our victory and deep reservations about one another's integrity.

All this time my only thought has been to live, to evade that squalid and certain death, the date known, the time known, and to live for a death free and uncertain. And now that the line of a fixed death has been withdrawn I wonder what I shall live for and how I shall live at all. For Peter, of course, but he has managed without me all these months and when I see him tomorrow, today, I write this very late, will he know me when we meet? Death is a huge cliff and when you are about to be thrown off it, like an Aztec sacrifice, other problems on the valley floor look very small, but once on the ground with the rest of the world they become again of dominating proportions.

Part Two

A BIRTHDAY

1

Pia Novikoff and her husband sat opposite one another in the window seats of an empty third-class carriage. Arkadi was looking out at the landscape that moved with jolting slowness past his gaze. A newspaper lay on his lap, folded open at an obituary according to a complex origamatic scheme. His attention, though apparently divided between the view and the death, was, in fact, fixed on his wife. Pia was leaning forward, her hands clasped between her knees and her mobile, triangular face concentrated on Arkadi.

Husband and wife had not seen one another for some two weeks before their meeting an hour earlier on the platform of St Pancras Station. Pia had chosen the train, a stopping one, in order to have time to talk to Arkadi. Their separation was perfectly normal; Pia spent most of her time in Oxfordshire where she rented a cottage on a hillside above a grey stone village, while Arkadi, whose toleration of English country life was exceedingly low, continued to occupy the rooms in Chelsea that he had lived in since before their marriage. They met irregularly, more often in London than elsewhere, as Pia was ultimately the more conciliating and, in this, adaptable of the two. She would arrive, without announcement, at Justice Walk and stay until, a few days later, her need for an open panorama, her animals and her painting drew her back to the country.

She was now busy recounting events of the last ten days to her seemingly abstracted husband. Her eyes were focused unswervingly on his face as she told a tale of murder, the criminal one of her dogs, the victim a Christmas turkey belonging to her neighbour. She knew the story held no intrinsic interest for him: he could barely remember the faces of the people he met every day, still less the personalities of her animals. But she knew, too, that her recounting was essential to him, as a tether holding him to the ground, a link to ordinary life without any need for him to take part. It was only her turning the quotidian into a story that gave it any reality in his consciousness. She sometimes wondered what did exist for him in the present, whether she herself was as ghostly and contingent as the rest of the world. She secretly feared that he had married her in a dream from which he would one day wake up.

Arkadi's own reality was in the head and in the past. He had been brought up in Moscow, an utterly beloved only child of a wealthy and talented Jewish family. He spoke only rarely about that world that had ended finally seven years ago in 1918 when he and a cousin had sailed from the Crimea for Turkey, leaving behind their futures.

Pia had occasional glimpses of his mother, a mathematician and pianist, educated in Vienna and Paris, speaking five languages, who after her marriage divided her powerful love between her music and her son. In the mansion which the family had built for itself on Povarskaya Ulitsa there had been a neo-gothic music room where in the dark afternoons of the Russian winter Irina Yakovlevna had played to her child. Pia's imagination was entirely visual and she could not hear the Barcarolle; she could only see the masses of dark, coiled hair and swelling skirts, the slender, stemlike golden neck bent over the arching wrists. How Arkadi had conveyed that chiaroscuro, weight and slenderness she could not remember; and for a time she doubted the truth of her vision, until one day, opening the top left-hand drawer of his tallboy in Chelsea in order to put away some laundry, she had found a photograph of a woman sitting on a terrace with exactly that fragile neck balancing hat and hair; behind her lay the lawns and sunshine of the pre-war world. Pia had shut the drawer hastily, shuddering, leaving the linen on the bed. Who could ever compare with a mother so beautiful, cultivated, clever and dead, shot by a sniper's bullet in December 1917?

Pia Yaldwyn had met and married Arkadi knowing almost nothing about his past and his family, priding herself on not caring about those details by which a marriage was normally judged suitable or desirable. She had given herself credit for her unworldliness; underneath this insouciance she had later discovered her complacent belief in the superiority not just of her own family but her own race. She had been ashamed of her own amazement as she gradually learned, partly from her cousin Jono and partly from Arkadi himself, of the wealth and cultivation of his world: the performances by Scriabin, Chaliapin and Rachmaninov in that gothic music room; the canvases by Matisse commissioned by Arkadi's father for his wife's sitting-room; the manuscripts of eighteenth-century musicians collected by his mother.

Her own family's pre-Raphaelite connections seemed minor and provincial in comparison; her own high-minded ignorance of his background, ridiculous. There had been no way of knowing the shabby figure she had first met consuming tea and buns with Diana at Lyons' had been made by all that and, beyond the secular generations of his parents and grandparents, by centuries of rabbinical learning. He had looked foreign, poor, vulnerable. Pia had loved him at once, entirely, without hope and without envy. Diana was so extraordinary, so fascinating, that Pia was not sufficiently unreasonable to expect that Arkadi would notice her as anything other than her friend's friend. It was her luck that Diana's ambitions did not comprehend Arkadi and that he was left to her.

The story of the neighbours' turkey and the murdering but provoked mongrel was finished. The train was passing a row of grimy back gardens, each one containing a shack made of old sleepers nailed together in uncarpenterly fashion. A woman emerged from one of them, blotting the palm of her hand on her apron, leaving a bloody handprint on the washed-out cloth.

'Who will be there today?' Arkadi asked before Pia could begin her next tale.

'At Laughton? George and Diana and us and Diana said Gaëtan was in England. I suppose that's why we've been asked. And Diana mentioned that Fanny might be there: she's that awful cousin of George's.'

'It's Diana's birthday. I imagine that's why we've been asked.'

'Of course, how could I have forgotten. I haven't brought a present, how awful of me.'

'Fortunately I have. I have a new novel. We can give her that.'

'Darling Arkadi, how clever and thoughtful you are. It would have been appalling to have had nothing to give.' Pia's praise of her husband was bestowed and received without the slightest undertone of irony, though it was she who normally remembered every birthday, every social engagement and obligation, bought every present and maintained all their correspondence.

'How lovely to be all together again. Perhaps Jono and Edith will come over from Cambridge. It's such a long time since we met. It must be at least six years ago, in Paris. Do you remember? Jono and I were there with Edith and we met you quite by accident in the rue du Bac and we walked together towards the boulevard and on the corner of Paul Louis Courrier I suddenly saw Diana. We all had dinner at the Bon Accueil. That was the last time. And I had salade aux gésiers, so delicious. Why can't we do wonderful things with turkey gizzards, no it's goose, isn't it? And you had an andouillette which looked like a section of veined marble. Oh I remember it so well. It was such a lovely evening.'

Arkadi had turned his absent gaze from the dense greenness of the landscape to look at his wife's face, her eyes slightly glazed as she thought about the past.

'I remember it so well because you sat next to me, darling Arkadi, and during dinner you leaned over and touched my arm and I knew that, for the first time, you had seen me.'

Arkadi had often had occasion to remark and to bless Pia's acute and sensitive observation of the actual and her lack of interest in making any deduction from what she had seen; she was incapable of putting two and two together. Meeting him and Diana, the lined, creamy pinkness of the sausage, the touch on her arm, each event was received in the same way. Her eye caressed the surfaces, absorbing colour and texture unnoticed by others, and went no further. Arkadi, whose mind constantly made connections between the most distant and apparently unrelated facts and objects, found Pia's view profoundly strange. It was one of her traits that in the end had made her attractive to him: he could not really believe that this was the way she saw the world. He felt she must secretly see the relationships that

13

were there, interwoven beneath those surfaces, but not mention them, perhaps out of English good manners. One day she would say something that would show that she knew why he and Diana were met within a quarter of a mile of one another that evening in Paris.

'I was always afraid, no, I just always thought you would marry Diana,' Pia was saying. 'It was strange because you often seemed not even to like one another much in those days. You get on better now she is married. You just seemed to go together somehow.'

'You mean we were similar because we were both different, outsiders.'

Pia looked for a moment like someone who has been woken up. Arkadi so rarely intervened in the monologues that she ran for his benefit. 'Outsiders? In what way outsiders? You two were central to everybody; neither of you was ever on the outside of anything.'

But they had been outsiders, Arkadi and Diana, in different ways and that had made them attractive to their English contemporaries and slightly hostile to one another. Arkadi, in spite of having been to Cambridge, was an outsider because he was ineradicably a foreigner. Though his clothes, manner, upbringing were all as they should have been, they were placed, like a bowler hat on a medieval icon, on someone with the cropped dark hair, aquiline nose and chocolate-brown eyes that could not have been English.

Diana on the other hand was a social outsider. Her speech, which had once marked her clearly as a colonial, she had faultlessly corrected to an echo of Pia's own, but there was always something exaggerated about her that suggested she was playing, rather than being, herself. She was too slim, her hair too neat, her clothes, even in her wildest Bohemian period, too elegant or too striking. And underneath that smooth surface Pia was always aware of an anarchic will.

Diana didn't give a damn; she had no preconceived ideas of order or authority or tradition, for all her interest in classical Greece. Her ideas about sex and social relations had been radical, revolutionary. Pia had watched, fascinated, the verbal constructions of a new world in human relations propounded by Diana over cups of cocoa when they were both at the Slade. She had followed Diana to meetings in support of women's suffrage, and left early with her, too. Diana had had little time for politics, still less for the real Revolution that had been happening then. Pia had been excited by events in Russia, had been filled with Bolshevik enthusiasm; Diana had dismissed it all as men fighting over power and land and had taken little interest in what occurred. When Arkadi arrived, his contempt for the Bolsheviks, his stories of what was happening in Russia, had turned Pia round to his view. Diana had not had to change her mind. Pia saw that Diana, with her lack of political fervour, made her judgements of people and events without the little adjustments that went on unconsciously in Pia's own mind, the placing of people in social and intellectual categories that she had not made herself but inherited or acquired; the observations of accent, moustache, hands, boots, phrasing and the judgements thereon she could not avoid making; Diana made them too, on different grounds, and reached different conclusions.

'If anyone was outside it was me. I was always hanging on, not really knowing what you were all doing, just wanting to come too, like when I was little, tagging along after the boys on holidays in Scotland.'

Pia suddenly saw her brothers on the moors ahead of her, running with that high-legged bound demanded by the rough, springy heather. She could see the wiry stems with their run of tiny oval flowerheads and hear the warning cry, 'G'back, g'back,' as a grouse, put up by the boys' yells, rose clumsily into the air. Now they lay in France: Charles Yaldwyn, gassed at La Bassée Canal, July 1915; Francis Yaldwyn, missing at High Wood, 14th July 1916, the battle of the Somme; Arthur Yaldwyn, dead of his wounds at a casualty clearing station at Montfaucon, 1st November 1918. Whenever her thread of thought brought her to that triple loss, Pia's mind swerved violently and returned to an earlier path.

'I thought you would marry Diana not because you were both outsiders but because you were – are – so striking.' It would have been only fitting that two such people should have married. And who else would have been able to accommodate Diana's views about men and women and marriage? How was she to know Diana would apostasise and turn into a gracious political hostess, conventionally married to a conventional man? 'I hope that Jono and Edith and even the boring cousin are there. I like George Pollexfen heavily diluted,' she said.

'I don't know why you are so down on him; as far as he is concerned you, and perhaps Jono, are the only tolerable old friends Diana has. The rest of us are all Jews and Dagos.'

Pia flinched; she detested hearing such formulations even in irony. 'I can't help it. There are very few people I dislike but George Pollexfen is one of them. I find it hard to look him in the face. I think it is because he had such a good war. He obviously enjoyed it: no nerves, no feelings. In any case, it was not difficult to enjoy on Haig's staff.'

'Be fair, Pia. He served in the trenches; he was decorated for bravery. You can't pretend he spent four years on the Staff.'

Arkadi had no great liking for Diana's husband, but his reasonableness and an atavistic male loyalty always made him defend Pollexfen against Pia's criticisms. There was also a perverse amusement in his defence of someone who would never know he was being championed and would reject Arkadi's partisanship if he did. The Englishman's prejudice against foreigners, against ideas, set George in automatic opposition to Arkadi. His sense of racial superiority was reinforced by the sexual: he had carried off Diana in a few months when Arkadi, who had known her for several years, had had no success.

Fairness was not a virtue that Pia practised much. No theoretician, she was easily susceptible to ideas of social justice and would from time to time argue passionately with Arkadi in favour of socialism. However, in her own life uneven distribution was the rule. She would empty her pockets on one occasion and set her dogs loose on another. Her claim to dislike few people was an instance of her lack of self-knowledge: her loves and hates were passionate and arbitrary.

She had moved her gaze to the window and with thoughts of George Pollexfen her expression had grown gloomy. Arkadi watched her for a while before saying consolingly, 'He'll be much outnumbered by all of us. This is obviously Diana's weekend. She has been allowed to invite us for her birthday. You'll enjoy it.'

Jonothon Pybus and Edith Scrafton were the first to arrive at Laughton; Diana had sent a car to Cambridge and it returned with them at tea-time. Though Pybus and Edith lived within a few miles of one another, and Pybus worked in the same laboratory at which Edith's father had formerly presided, they met infrequently, usually by chance in the street, Pybus on foot, Edith on her bicycle. Edith, who could pick Jono out in a crowd of thousands, would always recognise his distinctive limping gait and stop to greet him, standing with one foot still poised on a pedal, to ask news of Diana or Pia, which he rarely had, or of his health, which he would rarely give.

The journey from Cambridge had passed more successfully than their casual encounters. Edith was not gifted with small talk, though, like many austere people, she enjoyed listening to it and could absorb Pia's chatter for hours. She always used the same conversational technique, questions about his work, when she was alone with Pybus, who was convinced that he did not know how to talk to women, as if there were a special language for that foreign tribe. Jono was reassured by this habit and was usually able to ignore her sex and talk comfortably about his plans to work in Göttingen in the autumn. He was going to Berlin in July, he said, for a holiday.

Edith sat with her eyes on the chauffeur's neck, her face inclined towards Jono to indicate her attention. She did not, of course, hold individual Germans responsible for the war, she was too reasonable for that, but she was not sure that she would want to go to Germany for either work or pleasure. And for Jono, after all he had been through, to be so filled with enthusiasm for things German was odd.

Though Edith's appearance was archetypally that of the unworldly Cambridge bluestocking, she was as subtle as Diana in her dealings with people. She had to be; she lived with a neurasthenic mother and tyrannical father outside Cambridge, running the house, handling the servants and the money and, in the interstices, working on the language and poetry of the troubadours. A book was promised, one day. Only the utmost tact and skill allowed her to live among the seething discontents and selfishness of her home without being entirely overwhelmed.

The car slid between the thick yew hedges at the entrance to Laughton. Edith caught sight of Diana in the garden and by the time they drew up in front of the house their hostess was standing under the pagoda-roofed porch waiting to embrace them. Diana had changed a great deal since Edith first met her at the beginning of the war. Then, she had been deliberately outrageous with her cropped hair, her skimpy, masculine clothes and her defiant views on any subject, designed to shock their parents' generation. She was now everything that a rich young married woman should be. She kissed Edith affectionately, shook hands with Jono and led them indoors.

They had tea in Diana's white sitting-room on the first floor looking out over the garden. She sat on the floor beside the heavy silver tray and poured for each of them without needing to ask what they liked. Through the window, open behind half-drawn blinds to protect them from the still powerful glare of the obliquely shining sun, came bird-song and, fainter, the high call of a child at play. The exterior cries and interior silence went on just a few seconds longer than was comfortable, until Diana replaced her cup in its saucer and said, 'So, Edith, before I ask about *amou-ou-our* and the troubadours and the really important things in life, tell me about the witch and the bully. How are the old horrors? How did you succeed in getting them to give you up for three days?'

'It's not that difficult. I manage it from time to time. I even had two weeks away at Easter to go climbing at Chamonix. Mother was convinced that I would break my leg, or even worse, my neck and then "What would become of Father and me?" she wanted to know.'

'They are quite impossible. They are eating you up. Devouring you. You should leave them; divorce your parents. Wicked old people should be exposed on hillsides like unwanted children. I am making arrangements for Peter to dispose of me when I'm . . . perhaps sixty, another thirty years to go. I once thought thirty would be old enough to die; now I reach that age I feel I may want to linger on a few years yet.'

Edith had a theory that very often when people spoke about one thing, there was an alternative series of references that they were not always aware of but which framed their subject matter and way of speech. She had often wondered about her friend's marriage.

Pybus lay back in his chair, balancing his teacup on his incipient paunch; high table was rounding him out. Edith could see him listening abstractedly to their conversation, women's talk which had not the slightest resonance for him. The college and his gyp between them looked after his routine needs and there was no one, parent, sister or spouse, to make demands on his time or emotion. To his friends his kindness and generosity were unstinting, but almost never did he permit them to interrupt his pattern of study, teaching, riding and conversation.

The door opened and the talk ceased abruptly. George Pollexfen stood in the entrance. Though above middling height, he gave the impression of stockiness. His importance was stressed in a breadth of chest and width of brow. He filled the doorway, solidly, compactly, with almost too much emphasis. His fair hair, now receding slightly, was impeccably smoothed away from his reddish face; his eyes, unexpectedly, were dark brown, and with their slightly downcast corners saddened and weakened his face.

'No, no, don't move,' he said just too late to stop Pybus from awkwardly levering himself out of his chair. 'How nice to see you. You've beaten your host. I meant to be here earlier; I was delayed in town and had to catch a later train.' He shook hands with Edith. Diana did not move from her graceful, mermaid position on the floor. Pybus was now upright and they shook hands. Pollexfen put his hand on his wife's head, not exactly caressingly, resting it heavily on her smooth, dark hair. 'Fanny came down with me. Will you have tea sent to her room? You've met my cousin Frances, haven't you? She's a bit tired and won't appear before dinner. You'll want to talk a bit longer, so I'll leave you. Where's Peter, my dear?'

Diana glanced at the little enamel clock on the mantelshelf. 'He should be upstairs by now. If you want to go to see him I should wait until after Nurse has given him tea.'

'Oh, I might go up anyway.'

'Very well. Tell him I shall come at seven to read to him as usual. If you wouldn't mind ringing before you go, I'll do something about Fanny's tea.' Diana continued to sit quite still in the centre of the floor while her husband made a small performance of remembering where the bell-push was and finally retired from the room.

Edith wondered whether she had imagined Diana's momentarily held breath and the slow release of air through parted lips as the door at last closed.

Pia had sent a telegram from St Pancras Station while she waited for Arkadi, giving the time of arrival of their train, so she was not surprised to see a car waiting for them as they alighted from their carriage. Beyond the flower beds thick with peonies, an idiosyncratic passion of the deputy station master, and the roses which entangled the railings, she could see the sleek, black shape of one of the more important Pollexfen cars; then the rear door opened and Diana herself appeared, waving.

She sat between them for the few miles to the house, alternately clasping Pia's hand in both of hers and gesticulating with a characteristic fluid flexing of wrist and knuckle. Arkadi was silent as the two women's conversation swooped from topic to topic.

'How are you? What are you working on now? Why are you never in London? And when will be your next exhibition? You are so lucky, Pia; you have the ideal arrangement, separate houses, freedom to work. Why is it not the normal form of marriage? Don't you think, Arkadi?'

'It suits us, yes.'

'It would suit everyone. What married woman would not like to live an independent life? And Englishmen would prefer it. They don't even like women; they would much rather spend their time with other chaps, telling jokes, haw haw.'

Pia was beginning to feel distressed. She hoped that the glass partition fitted tightly enough for the chauffeur not to hear about what for her and Arkadi was perfectly natural behaviour, which, extolled by Diana, became a marital disloyalty and a sign of unhappiness that she did not want to see.

Diana may have observed her constraint for she left the topic to say, 'Jono and Edith have already arrived. They are both as ever, though Jono is getting fatter. Edith is still masochistically dedicated to the happiness of the two old horrors, the study of courtly love and the worship of Jono.'

'Edith likes her love unrequited. It was the war. All those terrible things she saw at the Front. We envied her, do you remember, for seeing Life.'

'You did; I, never.'

'But now she has had enough of Life; she prefers libraries. Who can blame her; she's happy, I think.'

'Is she? How can we tell? How can we know who is happy, or if we would not be happier ourselves in another way of life that we hardly even know about?'

'Edith is still recovering from the war. She'll surprise you two yet.' Arkadi's intervention provoked astonishment, the convention being that he took no part in Pia's and Diana's discussions of emotions and relationships.

'And your photographs, Diana? You're becoming so grand. We saw the photograph of the Duchess in last month's *Queen*.'

The car was coming to a halt at the front door as she spoke. Diana leaned forward. 'Stanley, go straight into the yard and get someone to take in the bags and oh, ask for tea as well.' The car slid on round the side of the house and through an arch into a courtyard. 'Before we go inside, come and see what I've had done in the stables.'

They had arrived at the business side of the house and leaving the chauffeur to unload the cases and take them in through the back door, Diana led them across the stone-flagged yard past the old coach house where the open doors displayed two more Pollexfen motors. She stopped half-way, hesitating. 'Arkadi, do you really want to come? Would you rather go in and wait for tea? Or go to your room and rest?'

Pia, standing between them, glanced at their faces, assessing Diana's need to talk to her alone, Arkadi's level of boredom.

Arkadi said at once, hardly breaking his stride, 'No, no. I'll come with you.' Pia followed them, wondering whether his decision was taken on the risk of having to have tea with Pollexfen without her protection or the attraction of Diana's secret.

On their left, from the range of buildings opposite the house, came the rustling of straw and snickering of horses. A strapper stepped into the yard carrying some tack. Diana waved to him and entered one of the green-painted

23

doors opposite them. Inside, bins of corn stood around the edge of the dimly lit space; above, on shelves, jars and boxes were neatly ordered. A newly constructed staircase rose over a table on which stood a gas ring and a large boiling pan. They climbed the steep stairs, halting at the small landing at the top while Diana unhooked a key hung high up on the jamb and opened the door. She walked in ahead of them.

'Isn't it wonderful? I have just had it done. Even George hasn't seen it yet. I only discovered this place last year. I've never had so much space since I was at Madame Labernadie's in Paris.'

The room lay under the slope of the rafters and had once evidently been partitioned into several small cubicles. These had been removed, leaving space for two trestle tables in the centre, lit by three dormer windows and electric lights hanging from the highest beam. At the far end two deep sinks were set under shelves of tins and glass jars. She led them to where part of the space had been partitioned off to form a dark-room. It was neatly, almost clinically, ordered with two deep sinks and a long draining board. Above were narrow shelves with glass jars ranged on them.

Arkadi strolled towards one of the tables and began to leaf through the folders in an album stand. Pia went straight to the rail that hung almost the length of the room from the lowest part of the roof slant, supporting what looked like a collection of imperial rags. She seized at once an austere black silk coat, fastened down the front with innumerable jet buttons, its sleeves longer than any human arm, holding it up against herself.

'Your costumes, Diana. What's this one? Is it me? When I think what you used to do with Ma's sable coat and a few cashmere shawls.'

'Now I buy them anywhere I can, flea markets, country-house sales. That is a Russian kaftan. Look, Arkadi, would your ancestors have worn that? It's ideal for you, not Pia. I shall photograph you in it.'

Arkadi glanced at his wife, but made no response, continuing to sort the folders according to some private criterion. Pia dropped the kaftan on the floor and took up a piece of golden cloth embroidered with blue, green and red butterflies, birds and flowers.

'This is for me then. I love this. The colours are so wonderful. And hats.' She bent down to open one of the boxes stacked under the clothes rail, bringing out a toque made of blue and silver damask and, flinging off her velvet beret, perched it on her wild curls.

'No, no.' Diana crouched beside her, rummaging. 'That would be for Edith; the only thing to do with her face is to expose it as sharply as possible, while you need something fluffy, rococo. No, all right, baroque. You don't think you're rococo but you are. Pleasure, pleasure; you are pleasure for us all. Now, what else? Perhaps I shall mark my birthday by photographing each one of you. Will you submit?'

Pia had flung several more clothes on to the floor, spreading them out to display their pattern or colour, trying them out. 'If I can choose my own costume. You will never get Arkadi to dress up.'

'It's not dressing up; and you certainly can't choose. It's perhaps one thing, a hat, a shawl, a flower which does something for a face, reveals an expression, emphasises a feature, gives significance.'

Arkadi had pulled several of the paper folders from the stand and had opened them on the table, shuffling the photographs out of them, placing some of them in a row at one end according to some system of his own. 'These you took in Paris.'

Diana glanced at them, shifting them gently with her fingertips. 'They're very old. That one I took in August 1914, look.' She picked out a print of two figures turning away from a newspaper stand, a young man and behind him a middle-aged woman. Both had their eyes on the newspapers they had just bought, the boy's drawn and haunted by his future, the woman's brisk and smiling. At their feet a billboard: '*La Guerre.*'

'Technically it's not very good and it's so . . . obvious, don't you find?'

'Technically? How do I know? And it wasn't obvious in 1914. Most of the young were cheering enthusiastically.' He picked out several others. 'And they seem good, visually. Taken from farther away, more restrained. These are harder, less involved than the portraits you do now.'

'You like the old ones better.'

'Yes.'

Pia, crouched on the floor by the hats, was watching them again. Arkadi's face was as opaque as it always was; Diana was smiling, relaxed.

'I like to be more intimate now. I've left buildings and taken on humans.'

'They're not intimate, the sort of thing you're doing for these magazines; they're idealised, fluffy, romantic, soft-hearted.'

Diana, whom Pia would have expected to defend her work with vigour, even savagery, simply nodded, still smiling. Pia felt uneasy again. Diana's reactions had always been exaggerated and this smiling acceptance of criticism of her work was unnatural in its patience. She waited. Arkadi said nothing more.

'I shall take a very hard-hearted photograph of you tomorrow, Arkadi. Now you must want to change, and if there is time, Pia must come up and see Peter before dinner.'

After tea Jonothon Pybus removed his false leg and sat down in his room with a recent scientific journal to pass the time until dinner. He had refused an invitation to sit on the terrace while Edith walked in the garden with George and had returned to his room on the second floor to find his suitcase unpacked, his clothes laid out and his book beside his bed. He had sighed with pleasure at being in Diana's well-conducted house.

He first removed his jacket, hanging it in the handsome mahogany wardrobe. Turning his back on an image he was not in the habit of regarding, he dropped his braces and applied himself to what he called his live shoe, then the dead one. He placed them at the end of the bed and began to unbutton. He folded the trousers and hung them up before sitting on the edge of the chair, releasing the catches that allowed the limb to be bent and then unbuckling the leather socket that held the whole apparatus in place. Finally he swung his good leg on to the stool and lay back, leaving the prosthesis propped up beside him wearing a long grey sock wrinkled to the ankle by the fall of the trousers. The journal was still on the bedside table. He levered himself up and hopped over to fetch it, reclined once again with another contented sigh.

Pybus enjoyed coming to Laughton which he did more frequently than any of the others not only for Diana's weekends but for George's, too, and probably he, of all the guests and inhabitants of the house, was looking forward to the next few days with the keenest pleasure. The only small discomfort as far as he was concerned was the presence of Edith, who was an insistent reminder of a guilt which he normally forgot. He told himself that the guilt was unjustified; he had never said or done the least thing to lead her to expect anything from him. Indeed, Edith expected nothing, which made it worse. And quite apart from what Edith felt for him, or he thought she felt, or others thought she felt, there was between them the ineradicable moments of the journey from the dressing station to Hospital Number 8 in the ambulance which she drove and in which he lay with six others, his right leg mangled, a tourniquet in the groin.

The only thing he could remember about that night, as distinct from what he guessed must have happened, having seen it endured by others innumerable times, was Edith's face, filthy, pale, worn, but unmistakably Edith beneath the blue uniform cap. At the time it had been an extraordinary sign of hope, a signal he would survive, so unexpectedly to be found by her. Now, he thought of it with revulsion. Seeing her reminded him of all the carnage that she must have witnessed, the bodies, vomit, urine, faeces, blood, blood, blood, that she had driven around for eighteen months. Women, Pybus felt, should have nothing to do with such horrors. The fact that Edith had known them made them more real, harder to suppress. Edith colluded, never mentioned what she knew, never recalled the comradely past, as Pia and Diana the pacifists did. But she knew.

Pybus dismissed Edith and concentrated on amusement to come: good food, wine, conversation. George and Diana kept an excellent table, something he was used to and coming now to demand.

Arkadi, who, in as much as he worked at all, wrote and edited the literary section of a cultural review, would be good for news of literary and intellectual London; Gaëtan, who did not work, at least for money, for news of all aspects of Parisian life. Pybus liked gossip, but only men's:

women's rarely yielded those treasures which he sought and which, when he found them, he hoarded until he was ready to display them alongside others acquired elsewhere, to astonish his audience. Power in any manifestation was what really interested him. He had no wish to exercise it; he liked to be near it, to observe it, to laugh at it and sometimes to nudge it with an elbow. George's weekends were more interesting, from this point of view, for he invited MPs, ministers, judges, great industrialists, civil servants of the higher and more influential kind. Diana's friends were the witty, the smart, the artistic but not necessarily as powerful as George's less beautiful and less amusing acquaintance. They were usually judiciously dosed with George's. There must be some reason that he had not yet penetrated for such an assemblage of Diana's oldest friends all pre-dating her marriage, and poor George supported only by his cousin; perhaps he would count Jono himself as partly on his side.

Thinking of the faces that would shortly assemble in the grey drawing-room and process, with a formality never known before George appeared among them, into the dining-room, Pybus felt himself at his most protean, linked to each by a different event or phase in his life. Now Diana was the centre of the disparate worlds which would be represented there but originally it had been he.

Jonothon Pybus was Pia's cousin and tied to her by more than a mutual grandparent. He had volunteered in 1914 with Charles Yaldwyn, Charles abandoning his last year at Cambridge, Jono his plans for a Fellowship and research, to disappear together to a training camp in Wales in a blaze of martial enthusiasm. Why Pia's brother had volunteered Jono was never clear; Jono had done so because he loved Charles and could not let him go alone. In the end they were parted early on, sent off to different regiments.

Charles had fallen distressingly in love with Diana whom he met on his last leave before his departure for France in 1915. She had kissed him and given him a photograph which he carried until his death four weeks later. Jono, too, had kissed her, chastely, as Pyramus had kissed the Wall, which she still represented for him, dividing him from and uniting him with the golden Charles who had ridden off to war like one of Edith's troubadours, carrying Diana's favour in his breast.

In France Jono had come across George, during the latter's time at the Front, near Loos in 1915. They had been separated by George's move, first to Headquarters and then on to the Staff, but after demobilisation they had met again in London and found they had a number of friends in common. George was ten years older than Jono, already deeply immersed in politics before the war, getting himself returned to Parliament in a by-election in 1920 as one of England's heroes. He had just been elected, was bathed in a double radiance as soldier and legislator, when Jono met him again at a Monday to Friday in Oxfordshire. Here, to his surprise, he found Diana was also present, as a decorative addition and discovery of the hostess, whose photograph she had taken. Jono could see that the host, a senior political figure, was fascinated by Diana who handled him with superlative skill. She had already begun her metamorphosis from the socially *épatante* to the socially desirable and she understood that it is approval from hostesses not admiration from hosts which obtains invitations. The older man had sportingly resigned his gallantries when Pollexfen came on the scene.

George, Pybus recalled, had been instantly overwhelmed by this example of the New Woman, by her beauty, her forceful personality, her independence and the nervous deference produced in other men by her professional skills. At that time, still so soon after the war and his own terrible injuries, Jono had yet less interest, even as an observer, in the attraction between male and female. He accepted the pairing off of his friends without speculation on cause or consequence; in this case, it had occurred to him to wonder if Pollexfen knew what he was getting, or Diana what she was taking on. George came with so much in the way of background, all the baggage that had been with him since his birth; Diana travelled very light indeed.

Would not Arkadi have been a more suitable, or at least a more likely, husband for her? Jono had known Arkadi longer than George, though not well. They had been at Cambridge before the war, at the same college, and Jono, whose quiet, chameleon personality allowed him into many different societies, was one of the few Englishmen who had penetrated the world of rich young Russians who lived in their own manner, as if in a gothic St Petersburg. Arkadi then was still recognisable in the Arkadi of today. If Jono himself had fought a war, seen unspeakable deaths, lost a leg and lost Charles, Arkadi had been through a revolution and lost his country, his fortune and his whole family. On the evidence, of the two of them, Arkadi's lot was the harder to bear. His adjustment to his new circumstances was less complete than Jono's, at least so Jono thought. And yet in many ways Arkadi was the same: in his overriding interest in things of the mind, his lack of concern for money and how he would live, he had not changed. Before, he had seemed to survive on Bollinger and caviar, now on tea and buns and, for all the pleasure he showed, one might have been the other all along.

Jono had introduced George to Diana; Arkadi, however, had found her without his help. They were already friends when he had re-established contact with Arkadi in the year after the war, during the long twilight period during which his body gradually realised that loud noises were not necessarily attempts to kill him, and his mind, except in sleep, came to terms with a new sort of physical normality. Arkadi in 1919 had been very isolated, existing by teaching French and writing an occasional article on Russian and French art or poetry for evanescent reviews. He had been reluctant in his impoverished condition to reclaim his friendships with the Englishmen he had known at Cambridge and only the most persistent, like Jono, had succeeded in enticing him out for dinner or a drink. Pybus had felt, obscurely, a sense of rejection when he discovered that Arkadi went willingly and frequently to the Yaldwyn house, evidently drawn there by Pia, he supposed.

Gaëtan, too, whom Jono had known since before the war when he used to go to Chamonix to climb, had been adopted into the Yaldwyn household, had become Pia's friend and Diana's. Although, Pybus noted with satisfaction, he at least had not allowed his friendship with the girls to be overtaken by love, desire or whatever word men used to describe the absurd and unpredictable diversion of their relations with the opposite sex from comfortable companionship to that obsessive pursuit that undermined all other connections. Gaëtan, that rarity, an Anglophile, Anglophone Frenchman, had a different attitude to women from Pybus. He frankly enjoyed their company, company of all kinds. Jono knew that his aunt and cousin, though perhaps not Diana, for all their high Bohemianism, would be shocked by the members of the demi-monde whom Gaëtan entertained, and even maintained, under his roof at Chantilly, where he had now settled to follow his third passion, after alpinism and women: the horse. This remained their common interest; Jono could no longer climb and had never found the society of soubrettes interesting. He often visited Gaëtan's stud and in return put up his friend in Cambridge when he came over to Newmarket for races or sales. Jono, his head nodding over his journal, looked forward to arranging his next visit to France.

Fanny Pollexfen was dressed for dinner before anyone else and took herself down to the drawing-room when she knew everyone would still be upstairs. An Edwardian routine lingered on at Laughton, many of the servants dating back to the grand days of George's aunt, and George, at least in the country, had not taken to serving cocktails before dinner. Fanny, however, did not resort to the little flask in her room except in the direst circumstances, for it was her method of life to live off the land and the land here was a rich one and easily picked. Tullet, the butler, she had known since she was tiny and, though she had to tolerate his avuncular disapproval as the price, she could always persuade him to mix her up something. She had, after all, taught him some concoctions which were not part of an old butler's training.

Her glass in her hand, Fanny sat down and reviewed her diary. The next few days were not promising to be among the most amusing of the year and it was rather shaming to have to spend the middle of June at a boring house party at her cousin's; better things promised for the following week and in the meantime, who knew, an unknown Frenchman might still produce more amusement than Diana's tedious intellectual friends or even dear George.

Fanny's adoration for George from an early age was taken for granted by her cousin and repaid with open house in London and Laughton. She had adored him, certainly, once; since those days of her early teens she had learned a lot about men and the world, and now rated George rather lower than when he was, with John, her brother, about the only young man she knew. However, George was rich and Fanny continued to adore him for that reason if for no other. Fanny herself had no money, no education and only erratic employment, most recently and implausibly in a bookshop.

'How can that be?' Diana had once said to her husband. 'She doesn't know how to read.' George's silence was his habitual response to Diana's sharpness.

When she was not failing to find books for customers in Mayfair, Fanny spent her time moving from one weekend party to another, hunting in winter, sailing, playing tennis in the summer. If she could manage to make her money run to train fares and tips for the servants, she was fed and housed from Friday to Monday or Tuesday in the greater or lesser country houses of the south of England. She had quarrelled with her parents who could not understand why her débutante year had not produced a husband, a house, an estate, babies, which should fill a young woman's life. Fanny, too, could not understand why these things had not happened; her response was to keep moving rather than shut herself up in Wiltshire with parents whose world had never been the same since her brother had been killed on 15th March 1918 on the Marne. She did not really regret the way things used to be and had adapted very well to the life of a not-so-young, unmarried woman in London. Men were her natural prey.

In the old days one man was captured by you or your parents to maintain you as best he could for the rest of his days. Today you had more variety. Men still had to provide, but it was now more a question of captivating than capturing, and there was no longer the necessity to stick to a particular man for worse or for poorer. In fact, to have several men on the go was the answer. The fear that they might find out about one another was nerve-racking and the scenes they provoked when they did discover one another were tiresome. Nevertheless, several men could be tapped for streams of cash which, put together, were more than could be expected from any one by himself.

Fanny lit a cigarette and put both legs over the arm of the chair she was sitting in. Would she ever decide, like Diana, to get married, to concentrate, mostly and ostensibly at any rate, on one man? Only if he were rich enough. And George was. Fanny herself had only realised too late that George might have supported her very well. But then, she would have had to support him. She would have said of herself that she was someone entirely unmercenary. She was not interested in money, though she had found by experience that a lot of it was necessary to live and it was with living that she was really concerned. It was true that Fanny had no time for money itself, adding it up, amassing it, manipulating it. Had she had a fortune she would have paid no attention to its care and conservation and would have expended it, as she expected others to do, for her pleasure. The discovery of her life was that she herself didn't actually need money, apart from a little cash for those relationships with taxi drivers and officials of the Great Western Railway which can only be expressed financially. The very little liquidity needed for this could be obtained by borrowing, or working in bookshops or art galleries. Otherwise, charm and sex paid for everything and the only essential was to know the right people and be included in the right parties.

So she had no hard feelings against Diana; indeed, she thought Diana had done George well. After being tied

35

to George for five or six years and producing an heir, she herself would have found a friend or two. She wondered if Diana had done so with a discretion that had evaded even her knowing scrutiny and decided that she had probably not. Fanny's mind drifted away from George and Diana, for she had little interest in human relations for their own sake, and turned to the more absorbing topic of her diary.

Edith was almost late for dinner, reaching the drawing-room just before the party passed into the dining-room in the pre-war fashion, in pairs, Diana on Jono's arm. She slipped into her position, alone, at the tail of the little procession. George, she was sure, would have put a black mark against her name, never to be erased, for a failure to reach the dinner-table at the proper time. That fate of arousing George's undying enmity was destined for some-one else, she observed, as she opened the stiff folds of her napkin. Her neighbour's seat was empty: the Frenchman had not yet arrived.

With the removal of the first course Pollexfen wound down his conversation with Pia, a lively one at least on her part, and turned to Edith. He asked after her parents, recalling her father, 'a grand old man of Cambridge science,' recounting an incident which he must have known she already knew, and which was certainly apocryphal, flattering to her father in its amiable eccentricity. She watched his neat, well-manicured fingers which handled his knife and fork with unexpected clumsiness, spattering the white cloth with specks of sauce.

'. . . Then he picked up his wine glass and emptied his red wine over the salt that the Bishop had spilt.'

He must have a fund of stories, Edith was thinking, for all purposes, to bring out for his constituents. No matter whom you're talking to, you must maintain the flow of words.

There was a disturbance at the other end of the table. The door had opened; Diana had risen to greet the belated guest, who was bending over her hand. Edith was never to forget her first sight of the Frenchman. She saw a figure almost caricaturally gallic. He was puny, well below average height, with a thin, narrow body. His head, in contrast, was disproportionately large with thick, springy black hair, below which his long, humorous face was marked by the horizontal bands of his eyebrows and moustache. When he spoke, his English was fluent but so heavily accented that he might have been an Englishman pretending to be French.

There were cries of greeting as Diana led him to his place, saying, 'No, no, I shall not permit you to be French and shake hands with everyone. You must sit down and they will bring you food at once. You know everyone, of course. Here is Gaëtan whom we have awaited impatiently.'

The Frenchman was now standing beside his chair. George Pollexfen had risen. 'My dear Diana, you are returning to your roots, I see. No colonial roughness here. Let us not lose the chance to be introduced to your guest correctly, in spite of his quite natural desire to appease his appetite.'

Pia regarded Pollexfen with undisguised dismay. Diana, who was no doubt more used to him, Edith thought, showed no sign of either chagrin at the reproof or contrition for her earlier informality. She did not look at her husband.

'Fanny,' she said, 'let me present M. du Breuilh de Cantegnac; my husband's cousin, Fanny Pollexfen.' The Frenchman circled the table and dutifully raised Fanny's hand to within a centimetre of his lips. He turned back to his host, stretching out his hand.

'You imply we have never been presented, but I recall meeting you somewhere, long ago.'

'I don't know where it could have been.'

Edith, seated between them, saw the blankness of George's eyes, a vacancy she remembered from the war, of a mind refusing to recall. Gaëtan sat down; conversation resumed. Edith was invisible between the two men whose concentration on one another had not relaxed for a second.

'Before the war, perhaps. I used to hunt near here, with the Belvoir.'

'I'm a shooting man.'

'You don't ride at all?'

'I prefer motors. What is the point of riding from A to B on horseback when you can do it quicker by car?'

'The train overtook the horse half a century ago but we still go on racing.'

'A pointless exercise in my view.'

'I think the thing was never for its utility; only for pleasure. And pleasure is never pointless, wouldn't you agree?' This was addressed to Edith who had not been able to prevent herself from laughing at the mention of pleasure.

'You mustn't,' she said, 'mention pleasure as a motive here. You are in England after all. We do things for duty and for respectability and because other people do them, not for pleasure.'

'Do you never act for pleasure?'

'Of course. I am here for my pleasure. Yet in order to come I had to say that it was my duty to be present at my friend's birthday.'

'Duty. The call of duty: that's what you say. Well, we all

have our national hypocrisies; duty is simply the Anglo-Saxon version. Is it not?' He suddenly abandoned his amused tone and looked challengingly at George Pollexfen. Their glances locked; Pollexfen looked abruptly away.

2

Saturday 20th June

Diana's birthday was as beautiful a June day as city dwellers could imagine for their ideal weekend in the country. The early mist rising from the river, swathing the lawns and the trunks of all the trees in the garden, was only seen by the sleepless and the early riser, George Pollexfen and Jonothon Pybus, each looking out of his south-facing window just after dawn. By the time the rest of the household was awake all traces of mist had dispersed and the sky, without a cloud even the size of a man's hand, presented a clear, shimmering blue that promised real heat in the afternoon.

Pia recalled that morning as innocent, without anything to prefigure what was to come. Diana took Jono out riding straight after breakfast and when they had gone, Fanny organised Arkadi and Gaëtan for tennis. Pia saw in Edith a willingness to play that seemed more than her usual wish to sacrifice herself to the desires of others and claimed that she would rather spend the morning with her godson, which was not altogether untrue. Though she enjoyed tennis, she did not enjoy playing either with or against Arkadi whose languid demeanour changed once a racquet was in his hand. He played all games with a fierce, even rancorous, competitiveness which Pia preferred not to face.

She took Peter from his nurse and the two of them set off for a walk in the garden. The child had recently been given a butterfly net and this was placed in his hand with the suggestion that he might like to use it on their expedition. Once on the woodland path leading to the park, however, he ceased to wave it in the air like the banner of one of Edith's troubadors, but reversed it, plunging the handle into clumps of grasses, swishing it to and fro under bushes. He was a silent and serious child, with his father's sturdy frame and fine, blond hair. He responded politely to Pia's questions, initiating no conversation of his own until they had paused for some minutes for him to scoop his net in and out of a large sea of silvery grey catmint.

'Can you keep a secret?' he asked, halting in his self-imposed task.

'Of course. If I am told not to tell I never shall. Can you?'

'Well, I can. Nurse said I wasn't to tell. But she meant Mother; so I can tell you.' He paused for dramatic effect. 'I saw a snake. In the garden.'

Pia was not sure of what reaction would be most satisfying to the story-teller, a cry of horror, astonishment, an expression of nonchalance. As she had no fear of snakes, she settled for her natural response, of serious interest. 'What kind was it?'

'Nurse says a grass snake, but it could have been a viper.'

'If it had been a viper, it would have had a V on the back of its neck. Did you see that?'

'No,' reluctantly. 'But that was because it ran away very fast into the grass. It was on the terrace in the sun.'

'And you're looking for it again?'

'Yes, I want to see what kind it was. "On thy belly shalt

41

thou go and dust shall thou eat all the days of thy life," ' he added unexpectedly. 'Nurse says.'

Their walk and viper hunt lead them down to the stream below the spinney, then across the expanse of lawn which gave the drawing-room and terrace their fine open view to the ha-ha and the park beyond. Finally they reached the tennis courts where they found that Arkadi and Fanny had soundly beaten Gaëtan and Edith, which was the right way round, Pia knew, for a happy day. Arkadi, though affecting indifference, sulked if he did not win, while Edith and the Frenchman showed no vexation at their lack of success.

The sunlight, pink and gold, filled the air of the dining-room at lunch, filtering through the lowered blinds, lightened still more by George Pollexfen's absence on estate business which might take all day, he had warned them, as he left after breakfast. Without him the formality of the previous evening's dinner evaporated. The table seemed, perhaps was, smaller, the guests seated closer together. Conversation flowed without restraint, and Fanny, to Pia's astonishment, punctuated all Arkadi's remarks with uproarious laughter.

'And what about the photographs?' Pia asked as lunch was coming to an end. 'You said you would make portraits of us all while we were here. It's going to be too hot this afternoon to go outside: it's the perfect opportunity.'

'Shall we make a tableau? Kings and queens of England or the Nine Muses?'

Diana had learned to curb what would formerly have been her reply to suggestions such as Fanny's, Pia observed, for she ignored the idea of the tableau and replied to her friend, 'If you'll submit.'

'It would mark your new decade, and mine, of course. On my twentieth birthday in 1915 you took photographs, do you remember?'

And not just of Pia. Charles on his last leave, Jono, Francis and Arthur, Mrs Yaldwyn. The photograph of Charles, his crinkly dark hair in a military crop, his mobile face arrested in the glare of love and coming death, now stood beside her mother's bed. Pia glanced round the faces, laughing, reluctantly flattered, turned towards Diana. Which of them would die in the coming ten years? Who would be left to appear next time? Ten years ago, the idea of substitution, a photograph for a life, had been clear. Now, for the survivors, there was no risk, no war; they were still young, they would live for ever.

'I'll have to prepare the studio. Come over later, in an hour or so. Pia, do you want to come to sort the costumes? You will all have to agree to put on what I choose.'

'As long as we don't have to take anything off.' Fanny was squealing with laughter as Pia and Diana left the room for the studio over the stables.

They began by kneeling together on the floor, sorting through the racks of clothes, Pia chattering and exclaiming, holding garments up against herself, as she had the previous day, Diana absorbedly contemplating, extracting, organising what she needed. She moved the lights, a screen covered with a thick camel-hair rug; hung up a sheet that had been dyed a deep shade of indigo; positioned a stool. There were sounds from below.

'May we come up, Diana?' Edith called. 'We are all here.'

'Yes, yes.' Pia opened the door and spoke to the upturned faces in the tack room. Diana was frowning slightly.

'How can I concentrate with everyone here? I want to do you one at a time.'

'Diana, you have become just too grand.' Pia continued to hold open the door to permit the entrance of the

43

remainder of the party. 'I remember your taking photographs of Edith – Sitwell, not you, Edith – in your bedroom in Iverna Gardens with someone – who could it have been? – holding up a blanket from behind as there was no method of hanging it. Here you have everything imaginable and you complain about a few of us to watch.'

'Have you glasses, Diana? Every studio in Paris has at least glasses.' Gaëtan had a bottle of champagne in one hand, a bottle of whisky in the other.

'Of course there are no glasses. We are not in Paris.'

'I shall find some.' Pia was already on her way down the stairs. She returned some time later with a basket, reporting that the kitchens were empty, the servants off and that she had only been able to find 'These'. She held up water tumblers. 'Not really the kind you require, Gaëtan.'

'No matter. One can drink from tumblers, more space for the champagne, or whisky, if you prefer it, Jono. Diana, we shall toast your birthday now in your studio before we do so at your table.'

Pia never saw the photographs that Diana took that afternoon. She wondered years later whether they had ever been developed or whether they had been destroyed, as she would have destroyed them in an attempt to cancel the past, as indeed she did with photographs of Arkadi. She suspected that Diana, whose art was mediated by a mechanical lens, was much more detached from her own work than she, Pia, was. Diana, probably, had developed them later and examined each one of them dispassionately, like butterflies pinned to a board.

Her memory of the afternoon was all of movement, culminating in George's devastating entrance. No moment seemed to hold for long enough for Diana to have taken her photographs which in the past had demanded achingly long poses and silences.

Edith had been the first victim, 'because she's the easiest,' Diana said, not elucidating whether she meant the most submissive or the clearest character. Pia, under Diana's direction, was wardrobe mistress and dresser-in-chief, efficiently thrusting Edith's straggling bob into the damask toque to reveal a sharpness of profile which was normally concealed by her gentle manner. Gaëtan, she recalled, came next. He demanded a great deal of time and attention, showing a wholly unEnglish seriousness in the project, and in obtaining exactly the right light and angle for his profile. Jono, in contrast, though he obviously liked the idea of a portrait, felt it beneath his dignity to treat the matter other than carelessly, having to be cajoled into different poses until a satisfactory one was found. Pia herself was the penultimate subject, left almost to last as Diana wanted Peter to be photographed with her and Arkadi had to be despatched to find the boy and to obtain his release from Nurse. Diana had produced not the embroidered silk in which she had swathed Pia the previous day, but a night-gown of enormous proportions made out of thick country-woven linen.

'Who could have worn this? Only a giant.'

'A stout farmer or his huge wife perhaps.'

'Pantagruel, certainly.'

'You must wear it because I want you to stand on the stool. We can take in the extra width with pins.'

Pia always remembered the rough texture like a supple canvas in her hands and the uneven creamy flecked colour in her eye, for she was wrestling the garment off with the hindering assistance of her godson when George entered.

Arkadi was the last of Diana's victims. He sat, isolated, in front of the screen over which a white sheet had been stretched. Diana had persuaded him, though he had been very amenable, hardly needing persuasion, to remove his

45

jacket and tie and put on the kaftan, which proved too narrow for him. Diana had improvised a false front from a piece of quilted silk of a glowing pinkish-red which she had attached around his neck like a bib.

None of them heard George's step on the stairs, nor his opening of the door. He was suddenly there among them, amid their noise, glasses, champagne bottles, discarded clothes. In the silence that fell Pia recalled that George's entrances always had that effect on Diana's friends, as if they had been caught *in flagrante*, and they always tried to assert their innocence of anything by beginning to talk again hastily, guiltily, so that it sounded as if they had previously been discussing something else: George's behaviour, for example, which of course they had not, for he was a subject of no interest to them. The embarrassment this time was greatest for Arkadi and Pia both eccentrically dressed, looking tawdry and theatrical beside George's linen suit and highly polished brogues. The pins pierced Pia's back as she tried to remove the night-gown.

Fanny and Peter, closest to George, reacted most naturally. The little boy cried, 'Papa, Papa,' in welcome and Fanny, excited by the champagne, Gaëtan, by the photography, began to speak and explain. Her voice died away as it became obvious that George saw no one save Diana who, originally standing with her back to the door, turned to face him, her hands dropping defencelessly to her sides, without moving. Rage transfigured him. Pia, crouching beside and below him, observed the individual hairs of his blond moustache like trembling gold wires. Spittle gathered, white as pus, in the corners of his mouth, and sprayed out in a fine shower, the minuscule droplets caught for a second in the light. His fair skin, already ruddy on the cheeks, became suffused with colour. Pia's observant eye caught the tide of blood that rose from his collar over his neck, jaw, face to his forehead. A pulse beat on his temple; his hands, like Diana's, were at his sides; they clenched and unclenched like the muscles of a pumping heart.

All this time his voice was shouting, though Pia, caught by the fascination of appearances, heard nothing of what he said. Only when Peter beside her began to whimper in terror was she released from her own eye and, seizing the child's hand, gathering up the surplus cloth of her still encumbering gown, she stumbled out of the door and down into the stableyard.

Edith stayed to the end. Her father was given to appalling bursts of temper if his breakfast eggs were not to his liking. The production of a solidified white and liquid yolk with no transparency in the former nor coagulation in the latter was not an easy matter on a range as temperamental and antiquated as that of the Duxford kitchen, as his daughter had frequently and patiently explained to him. This was a fact that the Professor would not retain and the morning rages were a motif in the normal pattern of her existence. She, therefore, did not flee in terror, like Fanny and Pia, nor sidle out in embarrassment, like Jono and Arkadi. Why the Frenchman did not leave she was not sure. Whether it was an abstract curiosity or a warmer wish to help Diana that motivated him, he remained, his hands clasped loosely behind his back, unmoving.

George, whose unceasing flow of words suggested that he had well chosen his profession of politics, was now pacing the length of the studio. Diana stood motionless between her camera tripod and the trestle table on which photographs had been laid out by Jono and Arkadi at an earlier stage. She did not look at her husband, waiting for the wave to roll over her and pass on. She offered no defence to George's fluent accusations of constructing the studio without his permission. It was not a technique used by Edith who always tried to counter her parents' tantrums with reason, calmly stating and restating the explanation for the situation that had so enraged them.

Diana did not react at all until George, swivelling on his heel, turned back in his march and seized a couple of enlargements from the table, tearing at them with both hands. He struggled for a moment with the thickness of the mounts, gained momentum, ripping through them, pulling his arms apart as if wrestling with a dangerous opponent. Diana's shriek, 'George,' coincided with her husband's order, 'There is to be an end to all this. I will have no more photography, do you hear?' He stopped, both his speaking and pacing, and faced her.

'George, if you ever do that again . . .'

He threw the pieces contemptuously on the floor and left the studio. As his footsteps receded Edith caught the Frenchman's eye and found it impossible to interpret his expression.

Rather wearily Diana stooped to pick up the scattered fragments of her photographs when she noticed, as if only then, Edith and Gaëtan. 'I'll arrange things here and see you at dinner,' was all she said.

Diana's presents were piled on the round table in the centre of the drawing-room and Peter, already in pyjamas and dressing-gown, was once again included in the party for the grand opening. He was put in charge of carrying each parcel from the table to his mother who was seated on a sofa to receive her gifts. Peter was employed, too, in the unwrapping, a service which he performed with a joyous tearing off of ribbons and ripping of paper. His own present, a picture he had painted himself, once it had been opened and admired by his mother, he reappropriated to give to Pia.

'You can have it,' he remarked, 'because we looked for it together.' He protested so furiously when Pia tried to return it to the growing pile beside Diana that his mother handed it back to her friend saying, 'We'll share. You must keep it now.'

If there had been some constraint among his guests when they met again that evening, George Pollexfen appeared to feel none. He was once again playing the benign host, without betraying a moment's consciousness of the circumstances of their last meeting. Diana, too, Pia noticed, was looking her most beautiful, opening, admiring and thanking as if nothing had happened. Arkadi's book was received with a pleasure that seemed genuine; Pia resolved to get him a replacement to reward him for his sacrifice. Gaëtan's present was the most magnificent, a Degas sketch of horses galloping. Diana said no more than, 'It's wonderful, Gaëtan,' and let Arkadi carry it off to admire.

George's present, Pia thought, could hardly have been more bizarre. It was about the same size, when wrapped, as Gaëtan's, and when unveiled was revealed as a photograph of himself. The frame was admittedly exceptionally fine: an Asprey's affair of brass and tortoiseshell. Pia wondered whether it was a joke or a threat or a signal for another explosion. Nothing occurred. Diana's eyes and hands acknowledged what she was holding without manifesting any surprise. George, bending to allow a grateful kiss on his cheek, seemed proud of his idea. Nurse arrived with the butler for the announcement of dinner and Peter was led off, protesting vigorously.

At dinner Pia found herself next to George again, who began to tell her ('You're an artist, you'll be interested in this sort of thing') about some work being done in a nearby church where a wall painting had been discovered when rotting plaster had fallen off the wall of the end of the nave, uncovering a Last Judgement.

'A very interesting place. I'll take you over there tomorrow.' Pia accepted the offer which would account for a few hours. Only one more full day to go, then she could leave and take Arkadi with her. But Diana was here for life.

She glanced round the table. Everyone was eating duck with green peas and new potatoes and mint with some enthusiasm, more in Jono's and Gaëtan's case or less in Diana's or Arkadi's. The tiny peas jostled together in a thick sea of cream. Their pattern of green and ivory was reversed in the ivory and green of the flecks of mint on the potatoes. Mouths opened and closed on food and words. None of us, thought Pia, has said or done anything about what we saw this afternoon. If he had taken Diana by the throat rather than just shouting at her, would we still have just left and pretended it had not happened? I must speak to Diana and I must make her talk to me. It's her own fault, she thought. She chose this; she chose him. She had to admit, however, that Diana was not complaining, at least directly. She remembered the remarks Diana had made yesterday about married life. No wonder.

3

Sunday 21st June

Edith woke the next morning with a luxurious and spacious feeling of not being obliged to sit down with Bertrand de Borne to try to fit in two hours' work before her parents' rising. She dressed and went out into the garden. Above the grass hovered a thick sea of mist through which she walked as if through water.

George Pollexfen was certainly ill; she had seen enough cases of shell-shock and its aftermath to recognise his behaviour. She wondered if he had been like this since the end of the war and managed to conceal it or whether it had only recently emerged. His wife, though she made no protest at his irrational behaviour and did not appear to complain to others, was clearly no help to him at all. There was something in Diana deeply unsympathetic to all weakness and illness. She had made her life by a series of acts of will and she had no understanding of those whose existence had been harder or who did not make choices, allowing events to take their course and to act upon them. Though Edith had little to link her with George Pollexfen but an old friendship with Diana, her sympathy, as she watched them together, went out to George. The common ground between Edith and George lay in the terrible no man's land of the war and the Front. It was something they could never speak about and, for his part, he might well be unaware of her time as an ambulance driver. The extraordinary horror of that period cast a benediction on those who had survived it. Her compassion embraced the wounded, the unemployed, the unemployable, the disaffected, the mad, all the jetsam of the war, who seven years afterwards were unwanted reminders of what everyone was doing their best to forget.

She looked back at the house which, on its grey terrace surrounded by the silver mist, seemed to hang in the air. To see the owner of all this in such pitiable terms might appear to more unfortunate war cripples to spread her compassion too thinly; she had no doubt that he was an injured man.

Sunday breakfast was a more magnificent affair than usual and Edith, freed from the almost daily wrangles that normally prevented her from doing more than snatching a mouthful of cold tea, intended to enjoy it. Her host, looking as little like a wreck of the war as could be imagined, was helping himself liberally at the sideboard as she entered the dining-room. He hospitably insisted on showing her all that was concealed under the silver domes of the chafing dishes and urging as much as possible of the contents on her. She served herself with kedgeree which she could see had been properly made and was not just the hotchpotch of leftovers which Mrs Dawson at Duxford perpetrated for suppers. Perhaps poor Papa had cause for his incessant complaints about their food. Jono had followed her into the room and was already consuming eggs and bacon as he talked to George about politics. Edith felt a moment's revulsion at his open mouth taking in a piece of toast wrapped with a shining strand of yolk and issuing forth a surge of political speculation. Pia and Arkadi entered with Fanny who chattered with great vivacity. Edith doubted whether Arkadi had risen at such an hour for years.

The last to arrive, even after Gaëtan had installed himself at the table, was Diana. As she came in, smiling and greeting all her guests, with messages to Pia from Peter to explain her lateness, Edith felt her habitual little movement of, she was not sure what it was, jealousy, admiration, indignation. Diana somehow altered the rules of the game, cheated, defied the conventions. She was always more beautiful, more elegant, better dressed than was necessary for any occasion, just as she had always in the past been more reckless and more outspoken; and she always got away with it. Her excess was successful. Edith, who had always lived by the rules and felt she would never have the courage to be other than correct, felt diminished. It was not even that in her dowdiness she could pride herself on her intellectual output. Diana's capacity for work was phenomenal and the range of her photographic style made a scholarly study of a poet who wrote in a now dead language as peripheral and meaningless as a life caring for angry and selfish old people.

She glanced at George Pollexfen as Diana leaned over the back of his chair to kiss his cheek. In his expression she thought she read a reflection of her own self-comparison with Diana. She immediately reproached herself for her disloyal and unfriendly thoughts, and when George addressed the whole table with an invitation to church, she said, too quickly, that she would join him.

Jono, now eating toast and honey, said, 'George, since I go to chapel every evening of my life, in term of course, I think I shall skip Mattins today.'

Gaëtan refused on his own and Arkadi's behalf. 'As representatives of older and rival churches,' he said, 'we shall have to rely on your prayers for our salvation.'

'I don't, George, I'm afraid,' Pia said, as if refusing a cigarette or cocaine.

Fanny said, 'I'm coming, of course, George.'

George waited, but no further response came. 'Diana?'

She said with a carelessness that was not quite convincing, 'No, I think not today, George. I'll be in my studio. When you get back, we could walk over to the farm before lunch. Peter has been asking if he could see the goats. He is going to be in the hall at half-past eleven if anyone else wants to come.'

Edith returned to her room to prepare herself for church. She put on her hat, picked up her gloves and bag and stood in front of the mirror, chin jutting forward critically. She was thirty-one, too thin, badly dressed. She had done nothing with her life except study Bertrand de Borne and who cared about him? She smiled at herself, crammed her hat farther over her forehead and left her room.

As she began to descend the stairs she saw below her that the front door was open, filling the hall with light. On the central table was a great bowl of white roses and she imagined she could smell their scent from where she stood. Framed in the open doorway were Diana and Gaëtan in close conversation. There was something comic in the two figures, the small Frenchman with his narrow, dapper person and huge head and the elongated, stork-like Diana with her small, dark skull looking down at him. They were laughing; Gaëtan took Diana's right hand and raised it to his lips, holding it there for a moment and looking at her.

The library door opened and George emerged, prayer book in hand. Edith had now ceased any pretence of descent. She remained on the half-landing, one hand on the banisters, looking down the curve of the stairs into the chequered hall. Gaëtan lowered Diana's hand; she slowly withdrew, smiling, walking out into the garden, paying no attention to her husband. He, too, seemed oblivious of her, taking up her position beside Gaëtan, a position which had been quite natural for a woman but was somehow too close for a man. He started speaking at once and though she had not caught what Diana and Gaëtan had said to one another, Edith heard clearly George's words and Gaëtan's reply.

'You've recalled where we met.' George's remark was a statement, not a question.

'Yes, I remember. Late July 1916, I think was the time. If I studied the question more I would arrive at the date and the hour. We were at the English Battalion Head-quarters, I recall.'

There was a pause before George spoke again. It was as if he were relieved. 'On the edge of the Butte at Vic,' he said in confirmation. 'Hill 245 in front, the church of Thouaiville to the right.'

'Shells and mortar bombs had been falling at twenty a minute since dawn on the French line. At midday precisely, silence. Then German movement out of the wood.'

'No fire from the Chasseurs on the right. They should have mown them down.'

'But they were, unfortunately, already dead.'

Edith began to run down the stairs. 'George,' she called, 'I hope I'm not late.'

At the same moment the housekeeper approached the two men. 'Miss Fanny's gloves,' she was saying. 'She was looking for them.'

George and Gaëtan turned towards the women. Pollexfen's face was a rictus of fury; he had visibly to adjust his thoughts to understand what they were saying. Gaëtan turned to Edith and bowed slightly. '*Bonne promenade, et bon office,*' he said and strolled out of the front door.

Edith took the proffered gloves in an instinctive effort to conceal the minute oddities of the meeting which would be only too obvious to the servant.

'Thank you so much, Mrs Everett. She'll be down in a minute. I'll give them to her.' She spoke in the gentle, placatory voice that she always used with domestics. The lower lids of Mrs Everett's protuberant eyes were puckered, giving her an air of suspicion and knowingness. The muscles relaxed as she focused on Edith who was momentarily reassured by her successful disarming of hostility.

Relationships with servants were one of the unceasing trials of Edith's life. Servants were necessary; how could you run a house without them? If you were not as rich and grand as Diana, much of your time at home was spent in the company of servants. The conspiratorial friendship and unity of purpose between herself and Mrs Dawson, cook for twenty-five years at Duxford, could only have grown out of their common exploitation; because of it, Edith always looked for the human being behind the servant's uniform. Diana, she noticed, saw her servants as people with jobs to do and did not trouble herself beyond that.

In church, seated between Fanny and George, Edith closed her eyes in a semblance of prayer. Bertrand de Borne was irrelevant to the modern world and to everyday existence, and therein lay his solace. A weekend away from her parents, with Jono, had seemed, in anticipation, a respite of peace and pleasure. In reality, the troubled weekend confirmed Bertrand de Borne as the only refuge. As she listened to the orotund tones of the Vicar reading the Collect for the day, the form of the Frenchman appeared behind her eyelids, lifting Diana's hand.

Though every moment of that Friday to Monday was to be scrutinised for meaning and for signs, no period was to be subjected to greater questioning than Sunday afternoon and evening. Was there a purpose behind the actions and activities of each individual and group, and, if so, who had been the prime mover in the arrangements? The splintering of the party after lunch had seemed to Edith quite random, though she remembered very well, for her own reasons, how she had made her choice which turned out to be so momentous, that afternoon.

Lunch finished, George reminded Pia of the church with the newly discovered frescos. 'It's about a mile across the park. Pretty little place, stands by itself in the fields. Just a farmhouse beside it. There used to be a village, hundreds of years ago, but my ancestors wanted the land for sheep so they upped all the villagers and moved them over here to Ingthorpe, knocked down the houses and ran sheep there. Made themselves a fortune. Then they lost it all again in the Civil War.'

Pia and, inevitably, Fanny agreed to go and Edith was about to volunteer when Jono signalled that he would be of the party. The agony of watching Jono struggle two miles over rough ground was too painful for Edith. She could say nothing to discourage him and she was aware that he had, in fact, decided to go because he knew of the effect it would have on her. She hesitated, said nothing.

'I shall not walk,' Gaëtan announced. 'I shall take advantage of your hospitality to have a brief ride around your park. I should not be too heavy for Diana's horses.'

George Pollexfen did not respond; Diana with her quick enthusiasm said, 'Oh you must, you can take The Elder, you will like him enormously. I . . .' It seemed as if she were about to propose to accompany him when Gaëtan broke in on her, 'And if Miss Scrafton is not walking, she would perhaps care to ride too?'

Edith had been watching Jono. Gaëtan's plan had made

him hesitate. She could see the movements of his mind so clearly; the pleasure of irritating her was not great compared with that of a ride with Gaëtan. However, the second part of the latter's proposal decided the matter; he would not share with her. With a little disappointment at the thought of having handled the arrangements for the afternoon badly, he settled back on his first plan. He had no intention, Edith knew, of actually walking as far as the church. She wondered how it was possible to know, to love and to understand someone so well and still be so wholly divided from him.

Diana, in the meantime, had completed the planning. 'Edith, you must take my breeches and boots. I'll tell them to get The Elder and Makalu ready for you. And that just leaves you, Arkadi. Will you ride too?' The Frenchman turned a frowning gaze on the Russian.

'Oh no thank you,' Arkadi replied. 'You know quite well that I am with George on this. I never trust myself to the beasts. I shan't walk either.'

'Then you can stay here with me and Peter.'

And thus they had grouped themselves. Edith, later, never had any doubt that the planning mind had been Gaëtan's which had wanted and achieved a particular end. Pia always refused to see anything but chance in the pattern of the afternoon, because she feared that there had been purpose and she could not bring herself to decide whose.

At the time it looked as if George were in charge, for he had successfully marshalled half the party under his command, once Jono had returned from the studio where he had left his walking stick the previous afternoon. However, even this degree of unity of purpose did not last long for they had hardly progressed beyond the ha-ha before Jono mutinied. The path led alongside the lake and when he and

Fanny, already lagging behind George and Pia, reached a small folly, a ruinous Greek temple in the form of a circle of columns capped with a shallow dome on the water's edge, he said, 'You've seen these paintings before, haven't you?'

'Oh yes, they're very fine. They say.'

'In that case, there is no need for you to see them again. Instead you will stay here and amuse me until they return. We shall sit here,' he stepped skilfully over a muddy bank that separated the path from the temple, 'and watch the swans. What an excellent thing that I remembered some bread. I thought it might be useful as a sort of danegeld to the cows, and I can see it will serve a similar purpose for swans.'

George and Pia were almost at Charlton church before they realised that Jono and Fanny were no longer with them.

'They must have turned back without telling us.' George's voice was irritable at a world in which nothing could be relied upon.

'Jono's leg must have made it difficult for him,' Pia said consolingly. Then, 'Look, they're waiting for us by the lake. We'll go back to them when we've seen the frescos.'

The fact that he had not been completely deserted cheered George up. He led Pia first to the farmhouse, a square Queen Anne house, built with pretensions to dignity which had been gradually lost over the ages until it now had all the ramshackle, piecemeal appearance of a working farm. Its face had been turned around. The fine front door with its baroque pediment clearly was never opened and the row of windows above were blank and uncurtained; at the back, in the farmyard one little building after another had accrued. Doors stood open giving glimpses of hay bales, implements, hens scratching softly under cart axles. In the warm afternoon air a chained dog declined to bark, merely padding towards them with a vague curiosity. George opened the door of the back porch and Pia smelled long-cooked cabbage. A similarly stagnant odour seeped out as George opened the door of the church, this time accompanied by penetratingly cold air.

The darkness within was split by poles of sunlight which leaned from the upper row of windows across the nave.

'Bit difficult to see,' George was saying. 'Probably there for years but no one looked in that direction. What happened was that the plaster and whitewash began to fall off and there was a head peering out at you. That one, do you see, Christ at the top.'

Standing with her back at an angle to the sunlight Pia looked up at the wall above the west entrance where, her eyes becoming accustomed to the contrasting light and dark, she could pick out the shape of a full Last Judgement. Though the tones had faded the artist had used a technique of outlining the figures in black so the shapes, only faintly coloured, stood out clearly. If George was right and the Christ's head had been the first to emerge, it must have been an impressive, even fearsome, sight with its black-rimmed eyes and narrow mouth. Below, the Archangel Michael held up the scales and the dragon's looping body, down which the sinners were sliding into hell, divided the saved from the damned. White-clad winners were being led off, weeping with shock, relief and happiness to heaven.

George had perched himself on the book rest in one of the pews. 'I like to bring people here. Nice walk, nice church and Mrs Watts sometimes gives us tea with bread and honey. I like the idea of judgement too. Good picture. I believe, you see, that we have to pay for what we've done. I've no time for these people who argue that we should let the Germans off their reparations, for example.'

Pia put her hand on the back of her neck as she continued to gaze upwards, her eyes moving from scene to scene, amazed at both the liveliness and the authority of the orchestration of the whole.

George's stream of consciousness continued in the background. 'They started the war; they should pay for it. And the punishment should fit the crime, I say. Look at those little fellows in hell: boiling alive, roasting in the flames, eyes being pulled out. You can see that it's not just a fiery furnace for everyone. Each one gets his own or her own punishment.'

It was true. Pia looked more closely. Devils with furred legs and forked tails were dispassionately organising a variety of tortures in the bottom right-hand corner of the fresco. One pair manipulated a brazier and pincers in a businesslike fashion; another was carelessly tossing an infant into a cauldron. The calm and organised air, the lack of frenzy, was horrific. On the other hand, the saints and the saved, arrayed in white, were equally passionless, standing in patient queues for the start of bliss.

'I always like to be even,' George was saying. 'I won't allow anyone to take advantage of me and I think they respect that. That way we all know where we are. The only person who does is Diana. She isn't fair, Pia, and I wish you would tell her so.'

Pia, who had been allowing her eye to spiral up the snake's tail from the zombies on the human plane to the balance of souls, brought her attention sharply to what George was saying.

'A wife's duty is to support her husband, not to carry off the limelight herself, don't you agree? She should be made to see . . .'

'Ouf, my neck. Let's go outside, I'm getting cold in here.'

She strode out and leaned against the sun-warmed stone to rid herself of the chill that had entered her bones. She let George walk back to the farm alone, rehearsing what she would tell Arkadi about the spirit and intelligence of the painting, harnessed to the horror of the subject. That great, gloating god above it all, supported by bending, sycophantic saints; the mechanical horror of hell, the faceless, unindividualised hordes in heaven. The only figure with any feeling was the powerful archangel, sword in one hand and scales in the other. And George likes it . . .

What, she wondered idly, was Arkadi doing. At least she had saved him from an afternoon with George. She shuddered at the thought of Arkadi's having been there. She would be able to tell him about the revulsion that the fresco had engendered in her, not about what George had said, for Arkadi would use it in a short story. For Pia, any weakness or shame, such as that George had inadvertently revealed, filled her with a desire to protect and shelter, to hide the exposed place. George had shown a crack to the base of his soul. He saw himself as a failure. He had married Diana to use her beauty and talent to shore up the gaping fissures in his personality and found that they could not be so used. Pia saw all this without framing the words to express what she knew and pushed it immediately to one side. She wished she had not seen; only by forgetting could she be sure of not taking advantage of such knowledge.

Fanny and Jono were both in excellent humour when Pia and George reached them in their folly. Fanny's extensive acquaintance and her energetic social life provided her with information of an amusing, tangential kind that Jono appreciated. Their mutual knowledge had been much increased by their exchange of rumour and speculation to the satisfaction and enjoyment of each, and their gaiety was sufficient to give the impression of cheerfulness to the whole party.

There was no immediate sign of the others on the terrace as they returned and Pia went immediately in search of Arkadi. She judged the studio a place to which he might have retreated and walked rapidly through the house and round by the stableyard. All was quiet when she entered the tack room, and the studio, the blinds drawn against the sun, was empty. She made her way back through the shrubbery and heard before she could see them that Diana and Arkadi with Peter had rejoined the group.

She examined Arkadi anxiously, assessing his mood to estimate his level of boredom or distraction. In repose, leaning against the back of his chair, he had an emptied, spent look; as he saw her he rose energetically and his greeting was almost effusive. Jono was now talking of returning to Cambridge; George was encouraging him to stay until next morning. Jono was determined; a physicist from Austria was visiting the Laboratory and Jono, who took his social life seriously, took even more care of his professional contacts. Nothing would persuade him to change his mind.

Tea had already been brought to the drawing-room when Gaëtan and Edith entered, still in their riding clothes, full of praise for Diana's horses, the breeze and the views to be seen from the Ingthorpe ridge. Diana handed them cups of tea and said, 'Edith, Jono is very keen to get back tonight. Is that going to be all right with you? Won't you stay a little longer?'

Pia interpreted the faint distress that appeared on Edith's face as pain at having even momentarily delayed or thwarted Jono.

Edith set down her full cup. 'No, no, thank you. I must change. In any case, I told my parents I would be back tonight; they'll be expecting me.'

'At least drink your tea. Jono can't be in that much of a hurry.'

'Jono.' Gaëtan was standing over him, a moment of superiority over a seated man. 'I thought I might come back with you, if that would not be inconvenient. I have to see someone tomorrow at Newmarket. If you are not taken by your Schrödinger, perhaps we could dine together in the evening.'

The fidgety donnishness, which had become more marked in Jono during the last hour, lessened. This diversion pleased and flattered him; Edith correspondingly was eased. Gaëtan had an ability, Pia noticed, to make himself liked by everyone, except, of course, George, who had maintained an air of suspicion and hostility towards him the whole time.

'And perhaps you would care to come with me to Newmarket tomorrow?' Gaëtan was now addressing his charm to Edith. Pia waited for her flustered excuses. The idea of taking Edith from her frowsty bedroom full of books and papers filed on the floor so that she could barely reach the bed or open a cupboard door and introducing her into the world of horse traders was wonderfully incongruous.

Edith, however, merely said, 'I should love to.'

The day petered out after that. George announced that he had business to attend to and that he would make his farewells at once. He shook hands with Edith and Jono, bowed to Gaëtan and included those to depart the next day in a general tracking of the eye round the room. He then took himself off, saying to his wife, 'I must speak to you later, Diana.' The Cambridge party left to change their clothes and organise their departure. Nurse came in to collect Peter and carry him upstairs to prepare for bed. Arkadi and Pia, after waiting for a desultory twenty minutes or so with Diana and Fanny in order to say goodbye to Edith, Jono and Gaëtan, who were still not ready, decided that they would wait no longer but go out to walk by the lake.

'Say goodbye for us,' Pia begged. 'Do you think Gaëtan will be terribly offended if we *file à l'anglaise* like this? The French are always so correct.'

'You go,' Diana encouraged them. 'You can wave to the car from the path. You might wait for ever here. You know what Jono's like. Go through the rose garden. It's heavenly at the moment.'

The long shadows of the trees already stretched over the open lawns and the rose garden was shaded by the tall yew hedges that surrounded it, so that it was like a house with the roof removed for the sky above was still a lucid blue. They walked under a pergola which seemed to drip perfume.

Pia put up her hand to cup one of the flowers which disintegrated into a flutter of petals around her. 'Heavenly weather,' she said. 'Heavenly place, at least.'

Arkadi understood very well the exculpatory intention of this and for once acknowledged it. 'Yes,' he agreed. 'A perfect English weekend; a perfect English country weekend in a perfect English country house.'

'Oh darling one, has it been terrible for you? Jono has grown so fat and pompous, hasn't he? And George . . . George is really very peculiar indeed. And what has happened to Diana? I would feel so sorry for her if she didn't seem, well, to like it, at least to accept it. What's happened to us all?'

'They are growing older, that's all. We are just slower

than everyone else in doing so.'

Pia slipped her arm through her husband's and fitted her palm to the inside of his wrist; his hand was jammed into his pocket. 'I'm sorry I made you come. We'd have had a much more amusing time in London.'

'You didn't make me and I'm not sorry. It's interesting to see the unreflective classes at play.'

'Arkadi! Jono and Edith, unreflective? And Diana and Gaëtan?'

'They're not reflective. Jono and Edith are hewers of learning, toilers at the coalface of physics and poetry. Jono, I am sure, is advancing into areas entirely uncharted, yet he does not think about the meaning of what he is doing. He only thinks of where to get the money for the next piece of research, where to publish the next little item. And Edith, she works in order not to think. At home it would be impossible to spend a few days among such people without any discussion of ideas. I mean in Russia, of course.'

Pia tried to imagine the estate somewhere in Tver province where Arkadi had spent every summer of his childhood, a house filled with Chekhovian talkers, where instead of the elegiac fainéance of Russian aristocrats there would have been the energy and optimism of Moscow millionaires; artists, writers, potters, sculptors and their patrons, entrepreneurs only two generations from serfdom and already Maecenas to Matisse. The sense of loss and waste that had derouted Arkadi swept over her.

'What did you do this afternoon with Diana?'

'While you went to the church? She finished the photograph that George interrupted yesterday. Never one to give up, your Diana. George won't get the better of her, however much he shouts.'

'Do you think he is mad?' Pia asked seriously.

66

Arkadi laughed. 'You don't know men, Pia. That is the proper way to behave. I am sure George thinks that if I shouted at you, beat you a bit, you would come and live in London and look after me.'

'Do you think he beats her?'

'Of course not. Can you imagine Diana permitting that?'

'Could you have imagined Diana being abused like that? Perhaps she will one day run away, taking Peter with her.'

Arkadi considered this seriously. 'No,' he said eventually, sadly. 'She won't run away. She'll find some other way to deal with him.'

In the drawing-room Fanny and Diana remained to amuse one another, a situation that had arisen before and which they had learned to accept.

'Are you going back tomorrow, Fanny? Or are you staying the week?' Diana asked. She had long ago abandoned subtlety with her cousin-in-law.

'I'm going up to London tomorrow with George. Did he say what time he would leave?'

'Not to me.'

'Well, I'm sure he is going. He told me he is seeing someone for dinner. Anyway he said we could travel together.'

Fanny wandered around the drawing-room picking up bibelots, turning them over and examining the undersides. Finally Diana rose.

'Let's do George's jigsaw. It's been out for weeks now.' She pulled up two chairs at the table behind one of the sofas. On it lay the scattered pieces of a jigsaw of which edges and part of the top left corner had already been put in place.

'Dare we?'

'Of course. He can always break it up again if he minds. That's what jigsaws are for.'

Feigning timidity at touching George's pastime Fanny came to seat herself beside Diana. They worked in silence for a time, shuffling and turning the pieces, testing them against the part completed.

'Why isn't there a picture?' Fanny said eventually. 'What's it supposed to be of?'

'Oh, you've got to guess. George thinks that to have the picture in front of you is cheating. Even Peter isn't allowed that. Usually I cheat, of course, and look, but he has hidden the box of this one.'

'George has always liked puzzles.' Fanny was taking a piece of sky and testing it against every available opening. 'I remember he used to make them for me when I was a child. Some were too difficult so I never bothered to solve them; some were very good. Treasure hunts with clues all over the house and garden. Does he do that for Peter?'

'Well, not yet. Peter can't read very well so clues would be no good. George did try having a puzzle of wooden blocks made by the carpenter for him but somehow the poor little thing wasn't interested in it. It didn't amuse him. Try this over there; there's a bit of cloud that might do. Peter's like me, he hates puzzles.'

'But you're doing this one.'

'Yes, to fill in time, to amuse you and possibly to enrage George, all of which are good enough reasons in themselves. I don't need to like doing it.'

Fanny found this motivation worrying. She got up, a movement that was explained after the event by the appearance of the Cambridge party to say goodbye. They were all in good spirits, made their thanks and farewells with what seemed like genuine conviction and warmth and installed themselves in the car. Diana and Fanny waved them off and returned to the drawing-room. Diana once again applied herself to the jigsaw while Fanny chattered in a lazy, inconsequential monologue.

Barely an hour later Edith reappeared in the doorway. Jono had forgotten some papers and had insisted on returning to find them. Edith went to telephone her parents and forestall the simulated anxiety which would greet her angrily on her arrival, early or late. It took some time for all of them to reassemble, and Diana urged them to stay to eat dinner. The two men would probably have done so, but Edith's anxiety to return home made it impossible for them, with politeness, to agree. Diana called for Mrs Everett who was instructed to wrap up a picnic to be eaten in the car.

'I adore picnics in cars or on trains, eating on the move,' said Pia, who had arrived from her walk with Arkadi. 'I imagine myself in a sleigh, a troika, in Russia a hundred years ago, drinking champagne, under a bearskin rug and eating . . . what would one eat?' She concentrated for a moment as if on a film visible only to her. 'Slivers of smoked sturgeon with a grain like wood, silvery greyish on black, black bread. I don't suppose I could have caviar: it would be so difficult to balance.'

'Not at all,' Diana joined in with verve. 'The caviar would be in a sort of pot, lacquered red and gold, and you would eat it with a gold spoon, heaps of it, passing it backward and forward to your companion . . .'

'One would have to have some meat in reserve because of the wolves. They wouldn't be pacified with a few spoonfuls of caviar.'

'. . . who would be wearing a Cossack hat of grey astrakhan and huge moustaches . . .'

Mrs Everett entered to say that the picnic was ready.

'Is it too much to hope that it consists of smoked

sturgeon and caviar and champagne?' Diana asked.

Edith noticed the slight clenching of Mrs Everett's brows; in her failure to understand, the housekeeper saw mockery in Diana's words.

'No, madam. I have had Cook put up some cold chicken, a galantine, some fruit . . .'

'Yes, yes, that sounds perfect. Thank you so much.'

They all rose and moved out into the hall to the open front door. The gravel sweep in front was in shadow; a band of sunlight still ran along the border facing the house.

'No sign of George. Mrs Everett, I don't suppose you know where Mr Pollexfen might be? I shouldn't wait. Edith wants to get back. Don't let them be too horrid to you. I think I shall ring them up myself. Will that do any good or will it make matters worse? Jono, goodbye. Have you got everything now? I take it that all this forgetting things here is because you don't want to leave us. Gaëtan, *on se téléphone avant votre départ et on se revoit à Londres fin de la semaine prochaine. D'accord?* Thank you for coming, dear Gaëtan. I have seen what has happened – good luck.'

They watched the great car engage its engine and gently draw itself down the yew tunnel towards the gates and the road, before they turned inside.

'And now we can have whatever greedy old Jono has left for us.'

They ate together, the four of them at a little round table in the window of the dining-room.

Fanny said tentatively, 'Where's George, do you think?' to which Diana replied firmly, 'He could be anywhere. We won't disturb him. He's said his goodbyes.'

Pia went over and over the events of that evening, not only, not even primarily, because of the insistent, sceptical questioning of James and Starling, the two policemen; she was searching for a sign, an explanation of what she saw later. Nothing of any significance occurred; nothing came to her mind's eye. After dinner, Diana went up to the second floor to see that Peter was asleep. Arkadi disappeared at the same time. Fanny could be heard making telephone calls for half an hour or so before she returned to the drawing-room. There was a dying cadence in the air, breath expended.

Pia went up to her room early, followed immediately by Fanny. She undressed slowly, listened to faint noises of the water pipes that indicated that the bathroom they shared with Fanny was free, bathed. She lay in bed for a long time awake, not reading, looking round the room from within the frame of the four-poster. It was comfortable, luxurious. Arkadi never slept before one or two in the morning and Pia did not expect him to join her before she had fallen asleep. She had drowsed off and had been sleeping deeply when she awoke with a start. Arkadi was still not there; her watch had stopped. Without knowing why, half asleep, she slipped out of bed and out of the room.

Lights still burned on the landing; no sound or movement could be heard. Drawn by the only sound she could hear, the faint and regular tick of the grandfather clock in the hall, she moved barefooted to the top of the stairs. The staircase snaked down, coiling round the central table. The hall was empty. She was about to descend far enough to see the clock's face when Arkadi and Diana entered the hall from opposite sides, Arkadi from the library, Diana from the drawing-room, with a timing so pat as to be theatrical.

'I'm going up now. You'll be reading or working for hours yet.'

'Yes.'

'George is still up, too, somewhere.'

'Good night, Diana.'

'Good night, dear Arkadi.'

They had moved towards one another as they spoke. Arkadi halted for a moment in front of the table and put out his hand; Diana's movement towards the stairs was unbroken. Pia turned before Diana looked up and ran rapidly back along the corridor to her room.

4

The following day formed a terrible pendative to the weekend, and the events after ten o'clock that followed so swiftly one upon the other and hung so heavily made it difficult to recall the last moments of normality which preceded them.

There was no George at breakfast hospitably to urge kidneys and bacon on his guests. No one commented on his absence. The table was quieter than previous mornings, not solely for lack of the host. Fanny appeared sleepy, Diana preoccupied and Pia was debating internally what to say and whether to say it and to whom, to which of them, the revolution of her thoughts on what she had witnessed last night distracting her from all else. The car to take Pia and Arkadi to the station was called for half-past ten. Diana issued various instructions for the arrangement of the day as she sat at breakfast; Pia noticed, as Edith had done the previous day, Mrs Everett's closed face as she listened.

Diana was waiting for her in the hall when Pia once again descended the stairs, ready to leave, with half an hour to leaf through the papers and walk restlessly on the terrace before the car would stop with silent punctuality in front of the pagoda-roofed porch.

Diana took her friend's arm and said, 'Just time for a

walk in the garden before you leave. I want to know when I shall see you again. Can you come and see me here some time in the middle of the week without Arkadi, or does that cut into your work? You could always bring it with you and set up your easel in the corner of my studio. We could work together as we used to at the Slade.'

She led them out of the house and into the garden, taking the path through the spinney that Peter had chosen on Saturday morning. Diana talked and Pia responded with half her mind on what she wanted to say. She never reached the decision to speak, or she thought afterwards, perhaps she had decided to say nothing, for with dreamlike speed they had circled the lawn and reached the shrubbery on the east side.

James and Starling, the policemen, asked repeatedly who had chosen their course. Why had they circumambulated the house, finishing by passing through the shrubbery to the north front which had surely been their destination, rather than taking the steps up to the terrace and walking through the open doors of the morning-room? Had her companion led her on or resisted the passage towards the shrubbery? Pia, by then distanced from Diana, felt nevertheless that whatever she said would have gone to erect evidence against the accused woman, because either case assumed there had been foreknowledge of what they would find at the end of the apple walk. Pia in her heart accused Diana, but she could only answer truthfully, to the policemen's evident exasperation, that neither one had led the other.

They had walked with linked arms and their footsteps had followed their words in a natural course. She had not planned their route; she had barely been conscious of which paths they were taking; neither had she had any sense of a weight bearing her left or right, drawing her on.

According to her firm testimony which she could see discounted in the investigators' eyes, it was pure chance that they had walked that way and chance, too, that they had lifted their eyes in the sun that came blindingly over the kitchen garden wall and glanced to their right along the gravel path instead of pacing, eyes to the ground, as they had walked for much of the time.

For that glance took in everything. Pia realised with what terrifying speed the eye sees everything, relevant and irrelevant, and understands everything, before the body can act or the voice cry out. The roses arching on the pergola were of the thick ruffled kind, of the very palest pink. There was a breeze, for they moved faintly. The stone was patched with crinkled lichen which sprouted a stiff, reddish fuzz.

George's suit, the same as yesterday, was a greenish grey, not dissimilar to the lichen-encrusted stone and the texture, clearly visible, had the same slight roughness to the imagination. One hand was flung out towards them, as he lay face down in the gravel and Pia thought of the grinding of the tiny pebbles into the faintly rasping flesh of his jaw.

What had been their first reaction, James had wanted to know. To call the servants, the doctor, Pia had replied.

'No, no.' He suspected obstruction. 'The very first thing you did, you and Mrs Pollexfen.'

'She cried out and began to run; I ran too, in the opposite direction, towards the yard and the house.'

The words conveyed nothing of the extraordinary shriek emitted by Diana, nor her lurching dash over the thick shifting gravel. She, Pia, had the same sliding sensation underfoot, as if running over sand, as she raced towards the house to find Arkadi. What good he could do she had no conception, for she knew, and had known from first sight, that George was dead.

Part Three

A DEATH

1

A Friday evening in central London in June; it was nine o'clock as Helena turned the key in the latch and stepped into her silent house. Behind her was a low hum, like a refrigerator, of the distant west-bound traffic. Even that sound ceased as the door swung behind her; the evening light hung softly in the room. It was the eve of her thirtieth birthday which it now seemed she would spend here alone. Those zeros. Not at twenty perhaps, but at thirty it begins, the casting of accounts, the recalling of doors not opened and roads not taken. Only in noise and distraction, companionship and conversation becoming progressively more sentimental, could it be avoided. In the stillness and light of her own house nothing could prevent it.

She had not planned it this way. This moment was to have been spent – she looked at her watch to estimate precisely – in the air. Somewhere over the Alps at this moment flew strangers, blessing their luck at the last-minute cancellation of two seats on the plane to Venice. It would be they who would wake with the light coming through the louvres of the shutters of the hotel whose tall windows looked out over the canal, who tomorrow would sail out to Torcello to stand under the beneficent gaze of the Madonna and afterwards eat lunch at Cipriani's, choosing the liquid sweetness of melon with the salty pink ham flesh rimmed with white that she always had. In Venice would have been distraction enough for every sense to save her from brooding on the passing of time and of choices to make before it was too late.

It was not rare for him to phone before a long-planned meeting to cancel or postpone. He never did so wilfully, always for some pressing reason whose priority she too recognised. The call would come in the middle of the afternoon, the brief, level-voiced explanation, the careful rearrangement of their diaries and then her mind, in reverting to the demands of the moment, would already have placed the new date and time on her horizon: dinner on Thursday of next week, Saturday night in the first week of next month. The alarm was reset and the clock began again to turn towards the expected moment, the second hand sweeping comfortingly and inexorably around the enamelled rim hidden in the leather case. It had stood beside her bed since he had given it to her five years ago. It measured out their time together, its almost timid ring at five thirty in the morning announcing the approaching car to the airport, to the office and their time apart. The beloved clock gave a certainty and regularity to a world filled with contingency: crises abroad and constituents at home, debates, votes, wife. This time it had been his wife; she had been going to Tuscany for a week, but the last-minute offer of tickets to Glyndebourne had decided her to delay her departure for three days, their three days in Venice.

When Robert cancelled their arrangements at short notice she often worked instead. She knew that this had been one of the elements in the distrust of her among her male colleagues. While they grumbled about other female employees who were married and who occasionally cancelled meetings because of the sickness of their children or other domestic mishaps, in Helena's case, she knew, they made the opposite complaint. She had no family obligations as her male contemporaries had, was subject to no demands from spouse and children for companionship at weekends in buying curtains or visiting theme parks, and so gained an unfair advantage. Now, as the only female among the four partners in a small City law firm specialising in patents and intellectual property, her Stakhanovite capacity for work could only be applauded. The peace of her office on a wet Saturday afternoon with the switchboard silent, her files and books piled beside her under the cone of the lamplight, had proved a solace on many occasions, effectively deadening the pain of absence and disappointment. But in the golden light of that Friday evening the thought of returning to her desk on her birthday lacked its usual consolation.

In the yellow and white kitchen, its order usually only disturbed by a growing line of breakfast coffee mugs for the cleaning man to wash up on his twice-weekly visit, she examined the contents of her fridge: a lettuce slipping into compost, tomatoes under a roof of cellophane marked with a sell-by date two weeks earlier, a very dry loaf, some butter, long-life milk, a jar of home-made marmalade given to her by Mary, her great-aunt's housekeeper, when? Soon after Christmas it must have been. Surely there had been an opportunity to eat marmalade since then. But not now.

The bread in the tomb of the refrigerator had grown a grey-green bloom of mould. As she reached in to remove the carcasses of meals not eaten, she paused for a moment, allowing the chill air to flow around her. Friday? Was João coming on Fridays now? Something was minutely different from when she had opened the door that morning hoping for yoghurt. The bread was on the top shelf; she always kept bread on the right, in the middle. Someone had been in, moving things around. Alerted to the presence which had manifested itself in her absence, she now saw other signs: the chairs slightly realigned, two of them no longer standing parallel to the table, as if João had sat down in one and turned the other towards him; perhaps he literally put his feet up.

She took the loaf out and pushed it into the rubbish bin with the rest of the perished perishables, not even bothering to feel annoyance that João had changed his day without warning. She sniffed the milk and poured it into the sink. She took out the Bollinger, kept for those rare occasions when Robert arrived unexpectedly, looked at it and put it back. From a collection of tins she picked one at random, crabmeat, opened it and tipped it on to a plate. She sat down at the kitchen table with a glass of water, a cracker and the newspaper.

After this uninspired meal which she barely tasted and would only have been able to describe after rereading the label on the can, she went upstairs and, seating herself by the phone, she dialled the number of her oldest friend. Isobel had married Helena's cousin, a feckless and charming man whose consultancies demanded much travelling and socialising but produced little income to support his lavish tastes. They lived with much keeping up of appearances in Surrey, a style and place Helena found hard to bear. The edifice of house, marriage and family was supported by Isobel with an ever more successful business whose core was the production of face creams, attractively and variously packaged, for women, younger and older, for men, for babies, all essentially derived from the same receipt handed down to her by her pharmacological grandmother. To this original emulsion had been added innumerable other products for what Isobel called Beautifying the Person. She controlled her factories, her shops, her contracts to supply other outlets at home and abroad with the same formidable energy that she dedicated to organising her husband, two children, au pair, nanny, dogs and enormous house and garden.

Isobel, like Helena's other friends, was used to her calls at weekends suggesting a concert, dinner, an outing with the children, that very day. Her work was her excuse for these spontaneous eruptions into their lives. And if Isobel asked herself why the life of a City solicitor should be so ill regulated as to be unable to plan a few days or weeks in advance, she did not extend the question to Helena herself who had found incuriosity about the details of others' lives both widespread and convenient. Only those in love anxiously follow the beloved *in absentia*: the mother with the child's timetable pinned to the kitchen board, the lover tracing the stages of the beloved's day. Helena, leaving a meeting, routinely glanced at her watch to place Robert, she was almost certain incorrectly, in the House, at his office, in his car.

The trouble with the equally busy and more predictable lives of others was that they were already filled up when Helena found she was free. The phone rang twenty times before Helena acknowledged that Isobel could not be at the end of the garden enjoying the evening air and that the whole family was away for the weekend. She pressed the CD player and Pavarotti began to sing. Helena listened with pleasure; she had forgotten that she had a disc of *Lucia*. She turned him down a little in order to dial again. If Isobel, who now had Simon and her children to take priority over their old friendship, failed her, Great-aunt Fox, who shared her birthday, could always be found.

2

Great-aunt Fox lived in Rutland in a Regency house, surrounded by a large garden which she had spent all her life tending and, although she was now well over ninety, she still walked in it every day, supervising its management. The routine of her life had hardly varied during the thirty years of Helena's existence. She almost never left home, once a year joining a small group of friends in what she called a charabanc for a week of visits to other gardens, private ones rarely open to the public, where she and her fellow enthusiasts would pass the days wandering with the characteristic gardener's stoop, head jutting forward, eyes on the earth. She never went to London. Though the house had a room known as the library, which was indeed well stocked with books, none, from Helena's cursory examinations, had been placed there later than fifty years ago. The Great-aunt did read: new gardening books and old poetry satisfied her and volumes on these subjects were stacked on a round table in the hall and in her dressing-room according to the poets and plants that were of current interest. She took the local newspaper and the *Guardian*, which Helena saw as one of the last signs of the family's Liberal, nonconformist origins. However, she suspected the paper was only ever used to light the evening fire.

A long time ago when the first months of Robert (Helena could never say 'with Robert', they were never together enough for that) had lengthened into the first year of Robert, Helena had begun to look around at those women, her contemporaries and her elders, whose lives had not fallen into the pattern of marriage, motherhood, divorce, remarriage into which most of her friends were gradually merging their existences. She tried to judge who among the dowdy and androgynous dons, the glamorous honorary men, the young and fierce feminists, had achieved a good life, or was simply happy. She looked with dismay at the dry dedication of some, to learning, to the job, to the cause, to the cat, and with distaste at the energetic promiscuity of others.

The Great-aunt, who had taken Helena in after the deaths of her parents, was someone who had come through. Her house radiated calm and contentment and she never lacked a detached and benevolent interest in her fellow human beings. Helena had to remind herself that she was contemplating someone of an age who could have lived for years amid passion and unhappiness before reaching the tranquillity of the present. However, there was no evidence of a tumultuous past: indeed, the chief characteristic of the Great-aunt was that she resisted change. She always wore the same clothes, renewed periodically and marginally modified by what fashion made available; from year to year she was to be found in the garden in black corduroy trousers and a grey polo-necked cashmere sweater, in the evening beside the morning-room fire in a cream skirt and silk blouse.

Helena, at that time suffering more from the irregularities of her relationship with Robert, more, because of its newness over which the protective skin of habit had not yet grown, had looked at the halcyon detachment and passionless benevolence of the Great-aunt and envied them. Though she recognised they were qualities attainable by her, at least, like St Augustine, not yet.

The phone rang for a long time before it was answered and Helena heard Mary's cold-muffled voice, taking fractionally too long to reply to her greeting, long enough for Helena to register that something was wrong, to wonder if Mary, a sober and responsible employee for seven years now, had been drinking, but not to expect what should have appeared much more likely.

'Helena?'

'Mary, what's the matter? Are you all right?'

'I'm all right.' Helena now realised that she was not drunk but crying.

'What's the matter?'

'I was just going to ring you. It must be . . . you know . . . fate, telepathy. I was just going to tell you. I was making the tea for the doctor.'

Helena's mind had reached the point of understanding at last.

'Great-aunt?'

'She's gone. She went out for a walk this afternoon and as she came into the hall she said to me, Mary, she said, I'm cold. She said, I'll go and lie down on my bed; you can bring me something hot later. Cold? I said, on a day like this, you can't be cold. I should've called the doctor then but she went up by herself and I let her be. And then when I took her up a cup of soup and some bread, for she never ate much of an evening, she was just lying there not moving at all. I ran to call the doctor. He's here now. Do you want to speak to him, Helena?'

'She's dead.' Helena had a lawyer's need to confirm, to express unequivocally what had happened and Mary was one of those women for whom repetition was not unnecessary, time-wasting, but had a comforting, lulling quality. She did not find the statement as ridiculous as Helena herself did, as soon as she had spoken.

'She's dead,' Mary said. She was snuffling again. 'It was a nice way to go, a nice, easy death, one of the best, just coming like that out of the blue and her in such spirits today. She just felt cold and lay down on her bed without suffering or worry.' Mary seemed set to talk about death in general and the Great-aunt's manner of dying in particular for some minutes.

Helena interrupted her, her voice still brisk. 'Mary, look, is the doctor still there? Are you going to be all right?'

'Oh, yes, I don't need anything. I'll just have a nice pot of tea. He's writing out the certificate.'

'I'll be up in the morning early, by ten at the latest and I'll let Richard and Simon know, so don't you worry about that.'

'All right, dear. I'll see you then. She looks lovely, you know, such a good lady. And now I'll have to leave here.'

Helena replaced the phone with Mary's last sentence on her mind. She was already reaching forward to the practical things to be done. Grief she did not yet feel and when it came, much later that night as she lay in bed, her unselfish sadness for the old woman's death mingled, like Mary's, with her own troubles, with Robert's absence and her dawning birthday.

3

Soon after seven Helena was on the A1 on her way to Ingthorpe. She had succeeded in reaching both her cousins the previous evening and telling them of their relative's death.

Richard Fox, who had followed family tradition into the law, was, with Helena, the Great-aunt's executor. He had abandoned the Bar for Parliament and was a Labour Member for a central London constituency where he lived. He and Marta, his Swedish wife, also owned what they called a country cottage, in fact a rather large house, in Cambridgeshire, where Marta and the children spent summer weekends and holidays in a Bergmanesque atmosphere, absorbing through every pore what little sunshine filtered through the Fenland clouds. It was there that Helena had phoned him. Richard had immediately volunteered to cancel his weekend arrangements and to come over to Ingthorpe on Saturday morning to help with whatever needed to be done, adding that he would have to come alone as Marta had not only the children on her hands, but Isobel and Simon and their lot. Helena declined the assistance, suggesting instead that Richard should come in the evening.

'In fact,' she had added, 'why not bring Marta and Isobel and Simon as well? It would be nice for me to see them. Don't expect much, Mary will make us an omelette and a salad.'

Richard had hesitated. 'You don't think it looks a bit . . . frivolous, meeting for dinner in her house when she's lying dead?'

'Why are MPs so convention-ridden? If it upsets you, don't come. Mary and I shall be there and we've got to eat something. Anyway, the body will have been removed by then, I shall see to it.'

So it had been agreed and Helena could see even though it was also a wake, she would have a party of sorts on her birthday.

She arrived at Ingthorpe at nine, driving through the tunnel of the yew hedge, past the herbaceous border that had been the Great-aunt's especial pride, ignoring the pagoda-roofed porch of the main entrance, to park in the stableyard. The back door was open and in the flagged corridor leading to the kitchen Helena could hear the indistinct chatter of the wireless from the kitchen. As she opened the door her eyes went immediately to the familiar box-like shape on the dresser with its central speaker and two control knobs below. Though it fitted perfectly with the old-fashioned kitchen, the noise emanated from a small Japanese radio standing on top of it. For the most part the kitchen was in accord with the old wireless rather than the working radio. The Aga which still ran on solid fuel was now extinct for the summer months, leaving Mary to cook on an immaculate gas stove dating from the 1950s. Only the programmes issuing from the Japanese interloper incongruously brought the late twentieth century into the room.

Mary was sitting at the pine table nursing a mug in her hands, a cardigan slung around her shoulders. Helena recognised these signs of loss and sat down with her to drink tea and hear again, in greater detail, of the Great-aunt's last hours. Only much later was she able to push back her chair and say, 'I must go and start work. I'll stay tonight, Mary, if that's all right with you. Richard and Marta will come over to supper with Simon and Isobel.'

Mary roused herself at the idea of producing food, glad to be distracted. Helena left her in the larder examining the contents of her cupboards and went through to the library to begin the chores involved in closing down someone's life.

She had been composing the notice for the newspapers in her head as she drove and it had been in doing this that it had occurred to her how little she knew about her great-aunt, who was not even a blood relation but a great-aunt by marriage only. She doubted whether Richard or Simon would be any better informed.

Family tradition told her that the Great-aunt had married her grandfather's brother, a marriage that had been a family joke as Benjamin Fox had been a pedantically selfish bachelor until, at well over fifty, he had announced his engagement. Curiosity and some lewdness about his bride had changed into astonishment when his family met her. The question was no longer who had managed to entice old Ben into matrimony, but how had Ben met and managed to win so extraordinary a creature, not only elegant and charming and, if not young, at least, to all appearances, rich. Attitudes changed again, with more ribaldry underlying shock and a little grief, when Ben died of a heart attack after five years of marriage.

This close but fleeting connection might have been the end of the Fox family's acquaintance with the Great-aunt, if she herself had not maintained the link, partly through friendship with her dead husband's nephews, the parents of Simon, Richard and Helena, and even more through her devotion to the next generation. Her interest in them as children, the visits, treats, expeditions that she arranged for every school holiday, were repaid by their affection, by their bringing their friends to her house as they grew older, filling it at weekends with their contemporaries from university, using it as a second home in the country when they began their careers in London, bringing their wives and eventually their own children to Ingthorpe. For Helena in particular, whose parents had died in a car accident while she was in her teens, the Great-aunt had provided a home, affection and interest which had sustained her ever since.

Ingthorpe had belonged to Diana Fox before her marriage to Great-uncle Ben and had been one of the elements that had surprised and impressed his family when he had been installed there by his bride. It was a small house with pretensions, built by an unknown architect for a war profiteer of the Napoleonic period who had grown rich on supplying boots to Wellington's army.

From the kitchen corridor Helena emerged into the hall where the staircase, with its white wrought-iron balustrade, circled round in a snail-shell curve towards the lantern crowning the shallow dome which lit the hall from above. When and how the Great-aunt had acquired the house Helena had never known, accepting without question what had been there since her earliest childhood. It had occurred to her some years ago, when the Great-aunt had asked her to be her executor, that Diana Fox's resources must, at least once, have been considerable. She had lived for the whole of Helena's lifetime, not lavishly, but in a style that had showed no erosion by the years of inflation. She had never worked as far as Helena knew and her self-taught ability as a gardener was her only skill.

The hall that she crossed to reach the library was as it had always been: a grandfather clock, its pediment tipped with a little brass spire, the marquetry table with the poetry and gardening books arranged as spokes to the hub of the bowl of roses.

Helena remembered years ago she had once asked, 'Was the garden always like this?' They had been working in the herbaceous border in the late autumn, pruning, cutting back, dividing. Before going in for tea they had walked through the spinney, where autumn crocuses and cyclamen were scattered on the bare earth, towards the water garden which had been much damaged by the previous year's drought. It must have been in 1977, just after her parents' death. It was a daily walk taken by the Great-aunt, visiting the sick to see what had survived or might renew itself next spring. 'Or did you lay it out yourself?'

The Great-aunt's sharpness of attention which could recall the planting of an *Acer negundo* forty years earlier gave way to a misty vagueness. 'Well, not always like this; fashions change. I put in the water garden myself. A hundred years ago it would have been magnificent with dozens, but dozens, of gardeners to look after it, if you liked that sort of thing: bedding out, I mean. And even when I first came there was a huge kitchen garden to feed the house. If you think of that, you can see how much one has had to simplify.'

They had turned back to admire the view of the house lifted up on its terrace and backed by the pale blue of the evening sky. Helena had learned no more of the history of the house, garden or Great-aunt Fox.

The library was a dark, masculine room facing north with mahogany bookshelves lining the walls and others placed at right angles to them to form bays. At the far end two leather sofas with hard surfaces of fine craquelure faced one another in front of the fireplace. It had not been a room favoured by the Great-aunt and it seemed as if from lack of use a faint trace of Edwardian cigars still hung in the air. In the central aisle between the bookcases was a desk and here Helena installed herself and began her tasks by phoning the doctor, the undertaker, the solicitor. Stringer Plews, the last of the triumvirate who presided over the affairs of death, lived in the village of Ingthorpe and had been a friend as well as lawyer to the Great-aunt. He had already heard about her death.

'Do you know how she has left things?' he asked.

'No, except that Richard and I are the executors.'

'I've a copy of the will in the office which I can pick up for you. You may have trouble tracking down hers in that house. I drew it up for her about eight years ago and it hasn't been touched since, oh, except to put in a little something for Mary a year or so back. Quite straightforward. But odd.'

Helena asked if he would come to have dinner that evening when Richard was there. 'And perhaps you would bring your copy of the will with you. I'm not optimistic about finding anything here.'

The desk, though its surface was clear, only adorned with a fine tortoiseshell inkwell and a pair of writing candelabra, soon revealed a crammed interior, suggesting that the Great-aunt was not very orderly in her business affairs. Each drawer was filled with loose piles of old envelopes, certificates, advertisements, prospectuses, bank statements, annual reports, accountants' letters, so that it could barely be opened.

'Terrible old mess there.' Mary had padded in unheard, as Helena replaced the receiver for the twentieth time. Calls to the Great-aunt's gardening friends were very exhausting; they were all so old and so deaf. Death was no surprise to them. They all expected a telephone call to bring news of another loss and for some there was even a tinge of grim satisfaction as they rehearsed their condolences to the bereaved great-niece; they had outlived another one.

'Yes, frightful; I can't find a thing.'

'She was a great one for order, but it was only on the surface; inside the cupboards there's always a terrible pickle. I thought we should take your things to your room and then I'll give you some lunch.'

'Oh, right; I don't need much.'

'You need something to keep you going through that lot. I've got your room ready. She won't like it,' she remarked as Helena picked up her overnight bag which Mary had brought through from the kitchen, and followed her up the stairs.

'Who won't like what?'

'Marta, eating here with your aunt.'

'She'll be gone before they come. Two o'clock this afternoon.'

'Then you'd better come and see her.'

Helena felt a moment's reluctance to visit the dead. She had not seen her dead parents and thought she might prefer to remember the Great-aunt as she had been, alive. Mary, however, took it for granted that it would somehow be a failure of good manners not to see the Great-aunt while she was still here in her own house.

Mary opened the door into Diana Fox's bedroom. She had pulled down the blinds at the long windows, shutting out the view over the terrace and the lawns to the park beyond, and the room was filled with a diffused golden light. The figure on the bed seemed doll-like, vulnerable. Helena had expected death to mark the Great-aunt in some way but she looked as she always had. The loose flesh of her face draped the bones like cloth, silk jersey Helena thought, or cashmere, something with the faintest down, like the powder-bloomed cheek that the Great-aunt always presented for her kiss. The nose looked sharper than ever; around the mouth the skin was ribbed but the grooves running from nose to chin were eased and the pads of her cheeks thus renewed looked childlike, guiltless.

'Sleeping like a baby,' Mary commented, ironing the counterpane with her knobbed, liver-spotted hand. 'Innocent as a child.' Helena looked at the Great-aunt for a moment longer and turned away. She made no attempt to touch her, to give any sign of farewell. She had come to fulfil Mary's expectations and that would have to be enough.

As she opened the door to the room that had always been Helena's, Mary said, 'You'll have more luck in her dressing-room than down in the library. She never put anything there except bits and pieces she wasn't interested in. Anything important she kept upstairs.'

It was not until mid-afternoon that the Great-aunt left her house for the last time. Mary had disappeared to her rooms after lunch where she always spent the afternoons, listening to the chatter of Radio 4 and knitting. The house was quiet; the muffled noises of its internal workings, the water heater, the refrigerator, the dishwasher, did not penetrate into the central hall. Even the grandfather clock whose beat regulated the centre of the house could no longer be heard when Helena closed the Great-aunt's bedroom door and passed through to the dressing-room.

She had hardly ever been in this inner place; the night when the Great-aunt had collected her from her boarding school with the news of her parents' death, she had spent there. The obsessive quiet of the room had contributed to her own heavy, deathlike sleep. It was painted and furnished in white with a day bed and a wing chair on which lay ancient tasselled cushions of petit-point. On the walls framed photographs, once black and white, were now faded to so pale a beige that their subjects had disappeared into the past and it was simply the pattern of the black rectangles of their frames on the white walls that served the purpose of decoration. She peered at them hoping for family likenesses and holiday scenes. She saw that they were art photographs. One, a woman behind bars, stirred a memory; it was the sort of image you saw in colour supplements, familiar yet unknown. Another was a profile of a man. They meant nothing; Helena turned away.

She seated herself at the little secretaire which stood at right angles to one of the windows and opened its flap. Mary was correct in saying that anything the Great-aunt had been interested in had been taken to her dressing-room. Helena found letters and cards that she had sent dating back to her school-days; more recent were home-made birthday cards from Richard's and Simon's children, correspondence about the garden; no sign of a will. She took a long time over the secretaire, consigning more of the papers to a dustbin bag, scanning each note before she discarded it, wondering whether it had been sentiment or idleness that had preserved these scraps.

Normally Helena enjoyed throwing out: the purging away of the past always made her feel cleansed and renewed. In this case the throwing away was irrevocable; there would be no fresh untidiness made by the Great-aunt; the cycle of acquisition had ended for her. The weight and volume of the papers and objects to be disposed of began to oppress Helena. What was to become of this house full of a long lifetime's accumulations? Presumably it would be sold, its contents packed up, redistributed, thrown away. Perhaps it had all been left to a cats' home: that might have been what Stringer Plews meant when he said 'straightforward but odd'. Where would the French ormolu clock on the mantelshelf find a home, the books piled beside the day bed where the Great-aunt had taken her afternoon nap, the papers stacked on the bookshelves? They at least could be burned on one of the bonfires that had given the Great-aunt such pleasure every autumn.

Helena idly scanned the shelves which in their upper reaches were filled with books, covered in the soft dust jackets like blotting paper of pre-war publishing. She picked out a copy of *Mrs Dalloway*; its paper cover was friable and tore gently under her fingers as she opened it. A first edition? She turned the fly-leaves to check. '*To Diana – with love – Pia and Arkadi, 20.vi.25.*' On the lower shelves were stacks of ledgers, arranged on their sides and occupying the shelves up to waist height. They looked like a lifetime of accounts. Helena bent down, picked one at random out of the middle of a pile and opened it; the foolscap cover was red, the spine stiffened with black cloth. The pages within had coffee-coloured edges fading to cream; they displayed not the figures and underlinings of the estate accounts she had expected but bold writing in a broad-nibbed pen, instantly recognisable as a woman's hand. From the ledger she was holding two sheets detached themselves and fluttered to the floor. She bent to retrieve them.

Today at half-past two in the afternoon I was acquitted of the murder of my husband . . .

Crouching on the floor, Helena read through the two loose sheets without stopping. The woman's voice rang clearly but not truthfully. This woman, Helena thought, is lying. She killed her husband. Then, this is Great-aunt Fox. She sat down again at the secretaire beside the window looking over the south lawn and began to reread more slowly.

Friday 4th December 1925
Today at half-past two in the afternoon I was acquitted of
the murder . . .

This time her mind rejected her first recognition of the
writer. The handwriting was not the Great-aunt's; the
dates were wrong. The Great-aunt had married Benjamin Fox in 1948 or 1949; in 1925 she would have been
a child; no, she would have been thirty. Thirty? The
decades of the century covered by the Great-aunt's life
stretched, buckled, elided. How old was she? Ninety-
six? No, the party for her ninety-fifth birthday had been
two years ago when Robert had just finished in Northern
Ireland. She was very old, so old that Helena had hardly
bothered to differentiate between eighty or ninety. She
had been born in 1895; she had been an adult during the
First World War, she had been over fifty when she
married Uncle Benjamin.

With her incorrigible neatness Helena began to turn the
pages of the ledger looking for the proper place in which to
insert the loose leaves. It was evidently a journal, for the
pages were dated, though it had not been kept daily. Some
dates were followed by short entries, others by much
longer ones and there were often gaps of several days or
even weeks between dates. Helena skimmed the pages,
stopping to read a gobbet or two.

As I am on remand I do not wear the uniform of a
convicted prisoner. Stanley chose the clothes she thought
suitable for the occasion: some dark skirts and white
blouses. I saw that they were all garments that I had in
London before I was married, as if she wanted to dissociate
me from my married life. They are all, of course, old-
fashioned now, very long and drab. They make me déclas-
sée, a maid, like my mother. I have never been sure what
Stanley thought of me. Is her choice her way of making me

look respectable and innocent or her statement of what she thinks of me?

Oh, why do I spend my time examining the trivial surfaces like this? Stanley has no thoughts; her choice is instinctive. But I cannot stop dissecting every glance, every gesture. What twelve ordinary people think will decide whether I die. I have too much time. There is so little time left.

Helena chose another volume from a different shelf much farther along, allowing it to fall open. The same handwriting, but this time the journal was in the form of a list under each date.

14th April 1947

Rain during the night, mist in the early morning.
Narcissus on south lawn cream and lemon at their best.
Temperature forty at eight a.m. rose to forty-nine in the afternoon.
Worked in kitchen garden a.m.
Sprayed apple and pear trees.

The handwriting was Diana Fox's. Although for the last ten years her Great-aunt's gnarled hand had had difficulty holding a pen, Helena now recognised the writing as a younger, fiercer version of that which she had received on hundreds of envelopes during her teens, at school, university, in her first years in London. She felt like someone in a dream walking on a familiar road who finds that without warning, without sound, the path has given way and where there had been a route trodden hundreds of times before there was suddenly a pit of darkness.

What did she know of Diana Fox after all? She had married her great-uncle before Helena was born and had been a presence in her life and in the family for all the time she could remember. She had always been the same, always lived here, always tended her garden; she never changed. It was only by looking at photographs or old letters Helena recognised that behind the unchanging façade of the Great-aunt there was a half century about which she knew nothing. She did not know where she had been born, what her maiden name had been, how she had acquired this house. She did not know that she had been tried for murder.

She glanced at her watch; Robert would be settling into his seat for the second act at Glyndebourne; Richard's party would soon be arriving from Cambridge, Stringer Plews from the village.

Helena picked up the first ledger she had opened and carried it off with her to her room. As she washed and changed, the first sentence she had read rang in her head. She must discover whether Richard and Simon, perhaps through their parents, had always known what she had not. She must discover what it was all about.

It was like, she thought, finding out that the man you were married to had been having an affair for years and years. This would be what Sara Occam would feel if she ever, God forbid, found out about her. She felt no lessening of love for her great-aunt; simply that her perspective had changed sharply and she was seeing something familiar from a totally unexpected position. Characteristically, she knew that she must hide what she had discovered; she would not mention it, but try obliquely to find out what the others knew.

4

The first guest over the threshold was Isobel, her arms full of presents which she toppled on to the marquetry table, over the poetry books, in order to embrace Helena in the first acknowledgement of her anniversary.

'What a way to celebrate being thirty; a real reminder of mortality. It must be like losing your mother all over again.'

Helena felt such a sudden and painful surge of tears that she turned away abruptly to greet her cousin Richard. He was one of the tall Foxes and towered over his companions. Heavier now he was middle-aged, he carried his weight well. He had become rather ponderous in manner, too, in a disengaged way. He had once been full of energy and enthusiasm, if not exactly for changing, at least for marginally improving the world, one of the youngest and most promising MPs in the House. Born into such a family as his, in the year of the great Labour victory, arriving at adulthood in the mid-Sixties, Richard could have chosen no other than the Labour party, but it had been the wrong choice for a man who wished for power. Years of fighting his colleagues, of staving off reselection and outmanoeuvring Militant and the Social Democrats, had burned him out. He had never held office save for a spell as PPS to a junior minister in the mid-Seventies. Another general election just past and just lost, the future of action and results was still to arrive. He now gave the impression of one striving to overcome his origins and upbringing and live for pleasure. With some notable success, Helena thought; he had the appearance of a bonhomous Tory squire.

Marta, thin and incandescently pale, still lived in a perpetual rage against the injustices of life. She had worked for many years as a social worker in London; at last, despairing not of human nature but of local bureaucracy, she had conceived two children rather late in life and was now interested in acid rain, hedgerows and the ozone layer. She and Isobel and Helena had met in Switzerland when the English girls had been on an exchange and Marta had been working as an au pair to perfect yet another of her languages. Much later, through Helena, Marta had met and married Richard. Helena often thought it rather unjust that Marta, who believed in social rather than personal responsibility, held her to blame for the downs if not the ups of the marriage.

The last to enter, to embrace and felicitate Helena, was Cousin Simon, Isobel's feckless husband, plump, smiling, dressed in a pink shirt and yellow tie, sunny, childlike colours to disarm and placate.

Bearing Helena's presents to be unwrapped, the party passed through the drawing-room towards the terrace where Mary had placed champagne and glasses.

'Don't worry about it,' Marta was reassuring Helena. 'I have passed forty even. For weeks beforehand I worried about the date approaching. Then when it came, I decided to have a new start, I felt fresh, reborn. The forties are my best decade yet.'

'Well, you certainly look very good on it, Marta.'

'Thank you, darling. You will find your life improves too, if you have the right attitude. You will change many things: work less, enjoy more.'

'Find a man,' said Simon.

'No, no,' said Marta, 'that's going too far. The pleasure in that is not guaranteed.'

'Stringer, how nice to see you again.'

'Stringer.'

'Richard, Simon.'

Stringer Plews had arrived directly on to the terrace, walking through the park from his cottage in the village. He shook hands with the men, relishingly embraced the women. A widower for many years, a man of indulgent habits, he had made the numbers even at the Great-aunt's dinners and cultivated his garden under her direction. Neat and dapper, useful with champagne corks and advice on where to go to save a few pounds on almost anything, he was a familiar figure at Ingthorpe to all the Great-aunt's family.

'The garden is looking wonderful. Who do you think will be able to keep it up now that the Great-aunt's gone?'

'What's going to happen to the house, do you know, Helena?'

'I have no idea. I'm relying on Stringer to tell Richard and me this evening what we are to do about clearing things up; in fact I am relying on Stringer to do everything for us.'

'How are we going to manage this executor business together, do you think?' Richard asked.

As a child Helena had regarded Richard, seventeen years her senior, with awe. Only when he married Marta had the generation gap suddenly been diminished and Richard become a friend and a regular opponent in discussions which Helena undertook with passion and Richard with detachment. Simon, though he was over ten years older than her, had always been a childhood friend and ally.

103

Although Helena had instructed Mary to go to no great trouble over dinner, she had not been obeyed. Mary was a perfectionist as a cook and in this had suited the Great-aunt admirably. Diana Fox had found it hard to bear the dependence of her last decade and even harder to share her house with the women employed to look after her. Mary had had several predecessors whose irritating mannerisms or conversation had made their companionship intolerable. With Mary a *modus vivendi* had been reached: the Great-aunt had sat through but not listened to Mary's verbatim accounts of plays on Radio 4 and telephone conversations with her nieces in Dundee. Mary had not taken offence at receiving no response to her conversation because of the appreciation given to her skilled and delicious cooking.

Tonight two soufflés, their elevated crusts brown and trembling over the almost molten golden interiors, were placed on the table. As Marta broke through the roof of the one at her end of the table, Richard leaned forward to look at Stringer Plews on her other side.

'Stringer, I hope you're going to be able to tell us what sort of mess Helena and I have to sort out here. We know nothing about the Great-aunt's affairs. She isn't really even any relation of ours. I wouldn't be surprised to find it all belonged to some distant cousin whom she quarrelled with fifty years ago.'

The solicitor, enjoying the power of his knowledge over their ignorance, took the serving spoon from Marta and poked the soufflé, lifting a generous brown-flecked heap to his plate. 'Mushroom, I think,' he said.

'This one's cheese.' Isobel was placing a golden pile on her own plate. 'If you prefer.'

'I might try a little of both. Mary's soufflés are famous. Much appreciated by dear Diana.'

Simon greedily began to serve himself. Then, seeing Helena's empty plate, he diverted the spoonful to her. 'Sorry. Here, Helena, have some of this one.'

Eventually everyone was served with one or both of the soufflés and Stringer could no longer delay answering Richard's question.

'If you really know nothing about your great-aunt's affairs, then you will perhaps be surprised to hear that she is, sorry, was, a very wealthy woman indeed.' There was intense concentration round the table. 'You may also be surprised to hear that Diana had other great-nephews and nieces in Australia.'

There was a relaxation of tension; if there had been a momentary glimpse of riches, it had gone. Simon helped himself to more soufflé. 'They, too, have been remembered in the will.'

'As well as us?' That was Simon.

'As well as some of you. Diana's will has certain oddities, as I mentioned to Helena on the phone this morning.'

Simon's impatience at last became too much for him. 'Stringer, you're not charging by the minute for this conversation. There's no need to draw it out. How has she left her money?'

Stringer was not to be thwarted of his pleasure. 'First, her collection of photographs and negatives have been left to the Victoria and Albert Museum, together with a fund to pay for the fitting out of an appropriate display area.'

There was a moment's silence.

'Her collection of photographs?' Richard asked.

'Yes, a very fine and very valuable one, apparently. I am not an expert on these things and I have never actually seen them. But they have already been offered to the

Museum and accepted. A curator came down to examine them some years ago, I recall.'

'But, where is it, this collection?'

'Ah, there I can help you. She used the upper floors in the stable block for them. There was some extension work done there about fifteen years ago to increase the space available and ensure that the storage conditions were optimal.'

'Did you know she was interested in photography, Helena?' asked Marta.

'No, no idea at all.'

'Right, the photographic collection. What other surprises have you got for us, Stringer? What about Chinese porcelain or Victorian pornographic books?'

'The next oddity is that, and this is explicitly stated in the text, she only willed her possessions to women.'

Simon began to laugh. 'Bad luck for us, Richard.'

'No, not at all,' Stringer interrupted himself. 'In her will (I looked it up this afternoon) she says, "Women need money of their own for mental independence." Quite what she means by this is not clear, but it matters not. However, you, Simon and Richard are not forgotten; you benefit indirectly, through your wives. Diana owned two houses in Rutland Gate in London. They are currently let as an hotel, I believe; one goes to Isobel and the other to Marta. They are to be theirs absolutely; there are no clauses to keep them within the family in the event of divorce, for example.'

'Since we are not related to her by blood we could hardly argue against her rather eccentric disposition of her goods on the grounds of family interest,' Richard commented to Simon. Marta was silent, sorting out the ideological implications of this unexpected legacy. Isobel was more businesslike.

'An hotel? Is it a long lease?'

'The lease is relatively short, I think. Of course, it is the freehold that Diana owned.'

'And what other women are beneficiaries? Helena, of course.'

'Yes, Helena is straightforward. She gets Ingthorpe and its contents and is the residuary legatee. The others to benefit are your children, Simon and Richard. I don't know what she would have done if you had had sons, either of you. As you have only produced girls, they all get some money, £10,000 each I think. And then the same for the great-nieces in Australia, four of them, if I remember rightly. Something for Mary and for Jim's wife. What he'll make of that I don't know.' Jim was a village boy, not quite simple, who had started to work for the Great-aunt some twenty-five years earlier to do the heavier tasks in the garden. 'And that's about it.'

Certainly that was it for the soufflé. The two dishes had been scraped clean by Richard and Simon of as much of the crusted coils as could be prised off their sides. Mary, coming in to remove the plates, listened with pleasure to their praises of her creation. Isobel rose to carry out the soufflé plates; Marta followed Mary to bring in the next course. Mary, her hands full, indicated with a lift of her elbow the platter of duck, the lacquered skin decorated with wheels of apple.

'Mary, you've produced a feast, it's too much.'

'You can't starve because she's gone. And the truth is it kept me busy. I was glad to do it.'

At the table the food was consumed with enthusiasm by all except Helena. Death sharpens the taste, she thought, reminds you that you are still alive even if you are thirty. But somehow it didn't work for her. She watched her cousins leaning forward, mouths gaping to receive a forkful of duck flesh and apple.

Richard, wiping a gloss of duck fat from his lip, said to Stringer, 'Do you know where this money and property came from? Did she inherit it? I presume she must have done; women of her generation didn't make money.'

Marta, who saw her role in the world as a living contradiction of her husband, said, 'They made money by marrying it, or sleeping with it. I suppose there must have been a few of the *grandes horizontales* who made their fortunes.'

Stringer looked around at them. 'You really don't know anything of your great-aunt's life, do you? I should think I am one of the few people left who does and I only know at second hand; my uncle was Diana's solicitor for years before I was. She inherited the money, yes; not from her own family but from her husband or, to be absolutely correct, much of it from her son.'

'She'd been married before?'

'She had a son?'

'Yes, she had been married long ago, before Ben Fox came on the scene, and had a son, Peter, who worked for SOE and died in France during the war.'

'Helena, you're not eating anything.'

'What happened to the husband?'

'Ah, him. It is altogether a very tragic story. You Foxes are really Diana's second attempt at a family. She had more success with you, even though poor Ben died so soon.'

Today at half-past two in the afternoon . . .

The picnic at Glyndebourne would be coming to an end; the bell ringing for the last act. Helena looked round at her cousins and friends. What secret lives went on behind the accepted fictions of their existences? Or were she and

Diana the only ones with second lives, past or concurrent?

'Strawberry tarts. Mary, you are a genius; will you marry me?'

'Get away with you.'

'From the garden?'

'I'll tell you the whole story after dinner. I was never vowed to silence and now Diana's gone I can't see any reason why you shouldn't hear it.'

'We'll sit on the terrace with some of Diana's brandy. I suppose it's yours now, Helena, if we may.'

'And what's all this about women? The Great-aunt never appeared to me to be a red-hot feminist, did she, Marta?'

Dinner over, Helena carried the coffee tray on to the terrace where the light was fading. The sky ran from a grainy navy in the east to a strange citrus-green behind the spinney where the trees were already a compact black mass. Beyond the stone balustrade the lawns, their finely shorn texture becoming indistinct, stretched towards the blurred hollow of the water garden. Marta brought out a candle and placed it on the table. Richard poured out brandy, Simon lit a cigar.

'Do you remember,' Stringer began, 'did you ever know, Diana's name before she married Ben Fox?'

'She was a Diana Codrington. I am sure Uncle Ben married Miss Diana Codrington.'

'She may have even become a Miss by then. Formerly she had been Mrs Codrington; she had to be because of Peter, of course. So, until 1949 when she became Mrs Benjamin Fox, she had been known for almost a quarter of a century as Codrington, but that wasn't her name, it was her mother's and she adopted it for herself and her son in 1926. And she didn't just change their surname but the house's name too. This place is called Ingthorpe House today, but until the Twenties it was called Laughton Hall. She changed the lot.'

Simon made as if to speak and then stopped himself. Stringer continued, 'She was born Diana Millard in Australia in – when would it have been? – 1895 and she used her maiden name as her *nom de guerre*, if I can call it that, for her professional life.'

'And what was her profession? You're not saying she was one of Marta's *grandes horizontales*?'

'Good lord, no. Her profession, you should have guessed, was photographer. Some of the photographs which the Museum is so pleased to accept are her own. She was known as A.D. Millard.'

'And what was her married name?'

Simon suddenly sat forward, seizing Stringer's denouement from him. 'I know, good God, I know. Laughton Hall and Mrs Pollexfen. She must have been Mrs Pollexfen.'

'And who was Mrs Pollexfen?'

'Sorry, Stringer, you go on.'

'No, no, you obviously know the story.'

'No, I don't. I just know that Laughton Hall was the scene of a famous murder of which Mrs Pollexfen was accused and got off.'

Stringer, his thunder stolen, sat silent; he sipped his brandy rather sulkily. Isobel in her matter-of-fact voice said, 'This is almost too much for one evening. First a fortune and then a murder. Can we believe it all?'

'How do you know this story, Simon?'

'I have somewhere at home an old book called something like *Passionate Crimes*, or *Great Crimes of Passion*, written by a sour and prurient American lawyer called Buckherd about famous murderesses, like Lizzie Borden and Mrs Pollexfen. According to him, she was as guilty as

110

hell but her lawyer got her off; always a satisfying story for a barrister, eh, Richard?'

'Stringer, do go on.'

'There's not much more to tell. Simon has it all. It was a very celebrated case. Laughton Hall belonged to Diana's first husband who was an MP for a local constituency, a Tory, as I recall. You must have heard of the house under its old name: it was mentioned over and over again in diaries and letters of the Edwardian and post-war period. Before the war it was George Pollexfen's aunt who brought people here; afterwards it was Diana. Everyone came, artists, writers, politicians. Then in the mid-Twenties George Pollexfen was found murdered. Diana was arrested and tried; in the end she was found not guilty. She became more or less a recluse, changed her name and her son's, changed the name of the house, never went out, never invited anyone, cut herself off from local society, let alone that of London.'

'I thought A.D. Millard was a man,' Isobel remarked.

'You've heard of A.D. Millard?'

'A.D. Millard was a fashion photographer in the Twenties. There's a very famous image that's often reproduced: a woman and sunlight falling through a window on to her so that she looks as though she is behind bars. In black and white, of course. That's by A.D. Millard. I thought he was dead.'

'I think she actively encouraged the idea. You could say she exaggerated stories of her death, at least her death as A.D. Millard and as Mrs George Pollexfen. She became Diana Codrington, a gardener, and then Diana Fox, your great-aunt.'

There was a long pause. The light had almost entirely gone by now. Helena could see Isobel leaning forward to talk to Stringer, her fair hair turning reddish in the candle-light. Marta had one leg curled beneath her and was holding her ankle prisoner.

'How one takes the old for granted and assumes that because their lives are uneventful now they were always so.'

'It feels rather strange,' said Marta, 'to think that all the time one knew someone who might have been a murderess.'

'Would knowing have made any difference?'

'I don't know. I feel differently now, about her. A bit afraid. She seems more . . . more powerful than I had thought.'

'That could be the money,' Isobel said drily. 'She was richer than you thought.'

'No,' Marta objected, 'it's the idea of a secret kept all those years. The way she remade herself, using the Foxes as background and incidental detail.'

'That's not fair, Marta. The Foxes didn't come into it until, what? twenty-five years later. Perhaps we should have been more perceptive, or just more interested in her past.'

'Was anybody convicted of the murder?' Simon asked.

'No, it is one of those unsolved crimes beloved of popular writers on forensic matters. Unlimited speculation permitted.'

'Perhaps she did it after all.'

'Richard!'

'Only a lawyer could suggest that and about his own great-aunt.'

'Why would she have done it? Apart from the general assumption that all wives want to get rid of their husbands?'

'There would have been a lover in the case; there always is,' said Simon.

'Money,' said Isobel.

'It's true that her inheritance was enormous,' Stringer agreed. 'The Pollexfens were a local family, small gentry, yeoman farmers, not wealthy, settled round here for generations. Then in the middle of that last century one of the younger sons was packed off to the colonies, South Africa, to farm. It turned out he had a talent for marketing, as we would say now. He made a fortune supplying provisions to mining settlements, a sort of general trading company, buying and selling anything, then another in gold and diamonds. His son continued to develop the business, though he never went out to Africa to live. He was childless, collected art in a big way. He adopted a nephew who was George Pollexfen, Diana's husband, though he was never involved in the business. That's what Peter Pollexfen, and subsequently Diana, inherited.'

'But', objected Helena, 'she had the money anyway. She married it. Why did she kill for it?'

'Helena,' Isobel put in, 'you must realise there is a difference between money allowed you by your husband and what you control yourself, whether you make it or inherit it.'

'Love rather than money is the more powerful motivator in life,' Simon stated. 'In my experience.'

Helena got up abruptly. 'You are all speaking as if she was guilty. She was innocent.'

When she had first read the page of the journal she had thought, this woman is lying. Now she resisted the idea.

'Richard, we must be going. Up, stir yourself.'

'We'll see you again at the funeral; Wednesday, did you say, Helena?'

'Well, see you there.'

'Thank you for my presents.'

'Goodbye.'

113

'Thank Mary again for us.'

'Goodbye.'

'Oh, Simon, would you lend me that book you mentioned?'

'Goodbye.'

As they had talked on the terrace, Helena had said nothing about the journals she had found in the cupboard in the Great-aunt's dressing-room. This was due in the main to her habitual caution and habits of secrecy. The journals might contain the answers to many questions, not least to the most important one of all: did Diana Fox really murder her husband? Helena preferred to discover more by herself and decide later whether she wanted the rest of her family to know.

Before going to bed, she chose another ledger from the shelves, carefully marking its position in the pile with a slip of paper. In bed, before she opened it, she glanced at the little clock. In an opening below the dial beat a tiny pendulum. A moment's attention to its quiet rhythm was a necessary part of her composing herself to sleep, when she gathered the scattered threads of the day into the central strand. Twelve thirty. Robert would be . . . She knew that the life she made for him was unlikely to bear any relation to how he really passed his time and she never tried any form of verification. She simply needed to place him so that he did not become an abstract figure or even a creation of her imagination as he sometimes seemed after too long a separation.

Helena read on, turning back and forth in the ledger, tasting a day here and there. Her thirtieth birthday had passed and she had cast no accounts, nor Janus glances backwards and forwards. She did not even congratulate herself on her success in finding distraction, for she had too long schooled herself not to ask why she lived as she did, with so important an area of her life hidden from her friends and family, blocking marriage and children. Steadfastly refusing to contemplate her own life over the last eight years, she was captured by the self-revelation, or self-concealment, of the journals, the daily turning over of pleasures and discontents.

5

Helena returned to Ingthorpe four days later for the funeral under sympathetically grey skies. The Great-aunt had left instructions that she was to be cremated and her ashes scattered in her garden. A small plaque was to be placed beside the one to her son inside the church in the village; both her husbands, Helena now realised, were buried outside in the sloping graveyard.

The funeral was attended by the family, local friends and acquaintances, one or two elderly gardeners. The Vicar, whose sermon was mercifully brief, spoke of gardens, Eden and Arcadia. 'A literary bloke, evidently,' Simon remarked afterwards.

'Diana Fox, whom we mourn today, was a great gardener, a creator of life and beauty. She will be remembered by all of us who knew her so well for the Arcadia she created and which she so generously shared with others.'

Helena, sitting in the front pew with Mary, opposite her cousins and their children, allowed her mind to wander to the gravestone which she had searched for before the service. Laid flush to the turf, it was curiously lacking in the usual anecdotal detail of memorials, stating simply: GEORGE POLLEXFEN 1884–1925.

The metaphor of the garden, the beauties and serpents within it, took up the Vicar's allotted five minutes, leaving little time for comment on Diana Fox's life or personality.

He, like most of his congregation, seemed to know nothing of her past.

Mary had insisted that there must be tea and sherry, and what she called a collation, afterwards for those who attended the service. Many of them came, to see the inside of the house, to ask what was to become of it. To this Helena had as yet no answer. What she was to inherit had made no impact on her. She felt that she already made more money than she had time to spend, so the financial aspect was of little interest. On the other hand, she found that she was becoming obsessed by the revelation of Diana Fox's past, of a whole life, or series of past lives which had been lived by the peaceful, elderly woman she had loved. Her own compartmented life made her feel an even closer sympathy, and she wondered whether the Great-aunt had guessed or sensed something about Robert. Underlying that was an unease, an unassuageable doubt, to which she constantly reverted.

One evening a week after the funeral she slotted her car into a space which had appeared outside her house as she arrived. This was something that happened so rarely, once in three weeks on average, not counting Sundays, she reckoned, that she felt a small lift of spirits which were bowed under thirteen hours in her office and a particularly troublesome case of intellectual property which she thought had been settled months ago and which had revived itself with lazarine vigour. She observed her own small triumph and thought sourly that it was a sign of age and singleness that she now counted the space outside her front door as hers and jealously noted when she obtained her non-existent rights. Five years ago she would not have been so petty nor so possessive. These thoughts brought her, fumbling in her bag for her keys, to her front door.

She unlocked, with a moment's hesitation before she

pushed with her shoulder on the tightness of the door. These days she often had the sense of being watched in her own house, the feeling, not so much of a presence, but rather of an absence, of someone who had been there but was no longer, someone who had familiarly touched her possessions, examined them, moved them slightly and then lost interest in them. The sensation was so absurd that she felt embarrassed that she could have conceived the idea; none the less, it persisted. She was afraid that the presence would next reveal itself, moving furniture and banging doors, when she was in the house. Her fear lay not in the supernatural itself, rather that she would believe she had experienced it. She remembered the first time she had been aware of the presence, the absence; the evening of the Great-aunt's death, and the association which she tried to avoid had been inextricably made.

She performed the rituals of the solitary homecoming, looking at the writing on the envelopes of the mail, pressing the playback of the answerphone, after dropping her keys and briefcase into their habitual places.

'Helena,' Isobel's firm tones spoke from the machine. 'Please ring me if you're free tomorrow evening. I've got to come to London to see my accountants and Simon wants to give you some book he's going to lend you.'

Helena hooked the receiver between ear and shoulder, waiting for Isobel's number to connect and looking at the row of cookery books on the shelf beside her. She frowned at the sight of a misplaced volume. She always put books by the same author together and in descending height order. How could it have been moved? Perhaps João had taken to reading recipes? Perhaps the presence . . . Perhaps she was going mad. She left a message with the nanny about the following night and then pulled down the kitchen blind against the twilight. She needed a treat: baked beans.

She emptied them into a pan and, as they were being heated, she sorted out a few uncrushed raspberries from the bowl which Mary had sent back with her from Ingthorpe.

She was haunted. The idea of the Great-aunt being a murderess was ludicrous. She could accept that Diana Fox had been an admired and adventurous photographer sixty years ago, yet she rejected the idea that she had killed her husband. There was no logic here. Helena herself knew very well how it was possible to live a life that was full and open and only concealed the central fact of her existence. She lived it daily; Diana Fox could have done it for sixty-five years.

As Helena's mind swung between the Great-aunt's guilt and innocence, the balance continuing to tip back and forth. With every factor considered, she would resort, like a lapsed Catholic returning to the authority of the Church, to the Law. Diana Pollexfen had been found Not Guilty by a jury of her peers, she was therefore innocent. But Helena was not a fervent believer, even in her own profession. Naturally sceptical, she saw every day how Justice's scales, let alone those of St Michael, could be tipped by some extraneous leaf that had blown on to one side or another. In talking over her cases with colleagues, in instructing barristers, she spoke as if the Law were a game and one in which chance, the personality of the judge, the make-up of the jury, the appearance of the accused, had at least as great a stake as skill or truth. Diana Fox might have been Not Guilty, but the question of whether she was innocent remained open.

As she ate her baked beans it came to Helena that if she was going to keep Ingthorpe she would have to convince herself that Diana Pollexfen (in some way a different being from Diana Fox, the Great-aunt) had not murdered her husband. Once formulated, the idea seemed obvious. She would assemble the evidence anew and come to her own decision. If at the end she had proved to herself that Diana had killed her husband, or if there was still a doubt in her mind, she would sell the house, dispose of its contents. And the money? Give that away too.

She felt more content than she had since the day on which the Great-aunt's past had been revealed. Action would exorcise the haunting presence. She would read the book Simon had promised her, the diaries, anything else that she could find.

The diaries were an astonishing piece of luck. She had not yet had time to look at them thoroughly; now she would go through them systematically, beginning in the years of the marriage to George Pollexfen. Their value as evidence was far from clear. The bias that was bound to exist would not be easy to determine. Had Diana written from the heart? If she had censored what she wrote, what motive had directed her selection of material? The unconscious pressure of guilt to reveal itself; the conscious desire of guilt to conceal itself; innocence, easily misinterpreted; even the desire to protect someone else whom she knew to be guilty?

All these questions, which would be resolved by the exercise of logic and intelligence, soothed rather than unsettled Helena. What had disturbed her was the conflict between her affections and her reason; her emotions rejected the Great-aunt's guilt on grounds that her reason knew to be unsound. Now her course was decided and reason had taken charge again.

The following evening Isobel and Simon arrived separately, Simon arriving so promptly on Helena's own return that she suspected that he had been waiting and watching for her. He brought with him what he called his *Boys' Best*

Book of Murderesses, a thick 1955 edition of a work called *Passionate Crimes* by Lewis J. Buckherd. Helena carried the book into the kitchen, longing to make a start on it.

'Stringer enjoyed unveiling the secrets in his care,' Simon commented as he turned the corkscrew in the bottle of wine Helena had given him. 'You felt that he must have so often enjoyed sitting at Diana's table with people who knew nothing when he knew so much.'

'He's very discreet. Much better, if you are a family solicitor, to enjoy keeping secrets than to be gossiping about them all the time.'

'And his power over an audience; he enjoyed that too, holding us all spellbound.'

'He was as effective as a story-teller, with his surprises and cliff-hanging moments. He did it rather well. A pity you spoiled his denouement.'

'I resist displays of power like that. I have a lot of practice at home.'

Helena went on unpacking her carrier bag of pasta and salad. She had learned to evade all talk of her friends' marriages because it usually led on to her own apparently celibate life. So she said, as if he had not spoken, riffling the pages of the book with one hand, 'It was clever of you to recognise Stringer's story. Did you look at the chapter on the poor Great-aunt again?'

'It will make you see the old girl in a new light. Not just as a murderess, but as a self-publicist and social climber.'

'I find it amazing that such things should have been published; it's clearly libellous.'

'He obviously thought she was dead. In fact, I think he says as much somewhere. The publishers didn't do their research properly: she could have taken them to the cleaners. But if she ever knew about it, I don't suppose she was interested in taking any action. If you change your name and the name of your son and your home, you are hardly going to stand up in court to proclaim who you were, even if it is to insist on your innocence.'

'Lewis J. Buckherd, whoever he was, seems very prejudiced against her. Will he convince me?'

Simon laughed. 'No chance. The writer's a chauvinistic old sod. You'll come out battling for the rights of abused wives to rid themselves of their unpleasant husbands any way they wish. I predict it. When you've read it, give me a ring. We'll compare notes.'

At that moment the doorbell rang and Helena sent Simon to let his wife in. A few moments later Isobel entered, accompanied by Richard and Marta whom she had met on the doorstep.

Isobel, without waiting to be asked, began to put knives and forks on the table, while Helena threw tagliatelle into a pan of bubbling water. Simon poured more wine for himself and for Richard and Marta. Richard propped his back against the fridge door.

'What about Mary?' he asked Helena. 'Have you given her notice? What are you going to do about her?'

Helena knew that sooner or later she would have to explain her plans. What had seemed a sensible course of action to defend herself against the presence seemed less so when she was about to tell her cousins.

'Mary will stay for the moment, unless she wants to go, of course. Until I've made up my mind what I'm going to do.'

'And what are you going to do?'

She began to recount her idea of proving the Greataunt's innocence to herself. It was difficult to do, as she did not want to go into all her motives. She was ashamed to admit to her awareness of a presence in her own house and she was afraid to acknowledge the fascination that the

Great-aunt's secret life had for her. In the end she just had to say rather lamely, 'I have to know. I feel so uncomfortable, so undecided. How could the Great-aunt, whom we were so fond of, be someone who first of all killed her husband (I mean, lots of people do that and she might have been provoked) and then went on living in his house and on his money afterwards? There's something horrible in the whole idea.'

By now the bowl of pasta was in the centre of the table and Isobel was helping herself. 'You are extraordinary, Helena,' she said. 'Obviously you would murder for some high-minded reason and pride yourself on refusing to profit from the action. The benefits, the house and the money, are usually the whole reason for a murder, if it isn't passion.'

'If she didn't do it, who did?' Simon asked practically.

'That's probably your best hope: to convince yourself that someone else did it.'

'But how are you going to prove this, Helena? You realise that the evidence is old, stale, second-hand and you will simply select what seems to be most convincing because it is what you want to hear. It will be interesting for us to see on which side you come down.'

'I know it's absurd, I know, I know. I know I can't prove it as for a court of law, though look at what you can get away with there. But I think I am a bit more dispassionate than you give me credit for.'

'I think it is an excellent thing for a lawyer to do this. It will show up all the uncertainties, implausibilities, vaguenesses, shades of meaning, different points of view, in a way which will mean something to you personally. You're in a profession that aims to discover and maintain the truth, as though it were a single identifiable thing.'

'You're rather unfair, Isobel,' Richard came to his

cousin's defence. 'I don't think we set ourselves up as arbiters of truth in such a totalitarian fashion. In any case, objectively, whether we know who it was, someone murdered George Pollexfen. His death is an unalterable fact.'

'Helena will find it more complicated than she thinks and it will do her good. She relies too much on reason providing her with the answer.' Isobel was now vigorously turning the salad in its huge ceramic bowl.

'This is far too abstract,' said Simon, putting down his glass and helping himself copiously to cheese. 'Helena needs to feel that she hasn't benefited from a crime. The first thing to do is to find newspaper or legal reports of the case, read those over, weigh it up, see what you think.'

'I wonder if anybody else involved is still alive.'

'It's really not possible. The Great-aunt was incredibly old, ninety-seven almost. It's unlikely anybody else made it to such an age.'

'Don't you ever read the Deaths columns? There's never anyone younger than ninety; people live for ever nowadays. I'll see what I can find out for you.'

Richard was frankly scathing about the idea. 'You're mad,' he remarked. 'Why set conditions on that lovely place? It all happened a long time ago and is nothing to do with you. She wasn't even our aunt anyway.'

Marta, who had up till then made no intervention, gave a final form to the quest. 'What you need Helena, is a judge, no, a jury,' she said. 'You cannot be prosecuting counsel and defence lawyer and judge all by yourself. You need a detached observer to pronounce on your findings. You will have to reveal your findings to me, to us all; you should convince us that your great-aunt was guilty before you give away your inheritance.'

'Can you be called detached?'

'It means nothing to me whether you keep or sell

Ingthorpe. Of course, I'm not detached about Diana, but I'm not as disturbed as you are. We can include Simon and Richard and Isobel in the jury, if you like. We accept her innocence; you have to prove her guilt, so you will have to make concrete your unease. If you can't do so, she is innocent. And if in the end you're not convinced, you will sell whatever we say.'

So it was agreed, as they ate strawberries and cream in Helena's book-lined dining-room, that they would be the Great-aunt's jury. Helena would gather her evidence and present her case. Her cousins were laughing, making suggestions about where to find evidence. A murder sixty years old has lost its horror; it is a fact of history, a bleached bone on the shore above the tideline; it is only interesting as an intellectual puzzle. Helena smiled and noted their ideas of what she should do and where she should look; she could not treat the subject with their light-heartedness. Some resonance in the air, some echo of the presence, told her that her search was serious.

Part Four

THE TRIAL

1

from *Passionate Crimes* by Lewis J. Buckherd

The murder of the Member of Parliament for South Rutland, George Pollexfen, remains as mysterious today as when *The Times* of 23rd June 1925 announced the fact in its sober headline, MEMBER OF PARLIAMENT FOUND DEAD. Six weeks later the same newspaper reported WIFE OF MP ARRESTED FOR MURDER. Mrs George Pollexfen was arraigned for the crime and tried at Bedford Assizes. The jury was out considering their verdict for three hours and she was finally acquitted: the Law had declared her innocent. No one else was ever indicted for the killing and the murder remains one of the unsolved mysteries of English crime. Today we can reconstruct the story and attempt to reach the just conclusion, as the jury failed to do. Though it is too late now for retribution to reach the guilty, at least history will record the truth.

Mrs Pollexfen was a well-known, indeed notorious, photographer, a sparkling hostess, a beautiful woman, and these factors dominated her trial and fascinated the popular press of the day, which was not as restrained as *The Times* in either its headlines or its comment. Events were followed avidly by a mass readership and speculation about whether or not she had poisoned her husband focused less upon the facts of the case and rather more on the physical appearance of the accused woman and on her character as it was deduced from her performance in the witness box. The questions posed were not, did she do this terrible crime? Did she have the opportunity and the motive? But: would someone so beautiful, so apparently gentle and artistic have been capable of planning and carrying out such a crime? The prosecution painted her as a passionate and calculating creature. It is no injustice to her brilliant defending barrister, Hector Wallace, KC, at the start of his rise to eminence which was to end in the House of Lords, to say that he was ably assisted by the public prejudice that no woman who looked as Mrs Pollexfen did could possibly have done what she was accused of doing.

Mrs George Pollexfen was born Athene Diana Millard in Sydney, Australia in 1895. Her origins were not distinguished and she always concealed her colonial birth as far as possible, turning herself into the English lady she desired to be. Her father began life as a clerk in a shipping office, soon setting up his own shipping agency and making his fortune. He was then able to establish himself in a house in one of the wealthy suburbs and to allow his wife, a former ladies' maid, to live in a style to which she had not previously been accustomed. However, Nathanial Millard's interests for his family were not simply material and were certainly not social. The elegance and brilliance of his daughter's life had not been among his ambitions for her. Nathanial was a strict chapel-going, Sabbath-observing, teetotalling Methodist and his family life centred on the new chapel that he had helped to found and to which he was a large subscriber. Nor was religious observance the limit of his interests. He was an autodidact and self-improver of the widest scope and most energetic kind. As a young man he had taught himself Latin and Classical Greek and read the Greek philosophers for pleasure. Mathematics, astronomy, geology, biology, in particular Darwinism, absorbed him and, with an ability to compartmentalise his interests, he never allowed a clash between his religious beliefs and his scientific studies or his business affairs to trouble him. His deepest love was for the Greek Classics, as his daughter's name suggests.

Athene Diana was his eldest child, and subsequent offspring, all girls, had similarly antique names which must have set them apart from the Lizzies and Mabels who were their playmates. After the birth of six daughters (two of whom died of diphtheria in early childhood) Nathanial Millard abandoned hope of a son and began to educate his girls as if they had been boys, in a fashion highly unusual for that time and place. They went, naturally enough, to the best and most fashionable girls' school in the colony and the correct education they received there was supplemented by an extensive programme of home learning. The masters who trooped one after the other, on the hour, into the Millard residence in the evenings, on Saturdays, in the school holidays, were not teachers of accomplishments, such as drawing, singing or dancing, but of Latin, Greek, French, German and Mathematics, subjects covered, in Nathanial's opinion, insufficiently or not at all by the curriculum of the girls' school.

When his eldest daughter was in her eighteenth year in 1912 Nathanial Millard embarked with his wife and two eldest girls on an extended visit to Europe. During the winter of 1912–13 the family visited the classical sites of Turkey, Greece and Italy. As Nathanial prided himself on being a tough Australian, his expedition was not limited to admiration of the Parthenon or the Colosseum. He took his family by local train and donkey cart to see the more remote ruins of Antiquity and this journey was the starting point of his eldest daughter's surprising and brief career.

It is not recorded whether Diana Millard purchased her first camera in Australia or in Europe. Though no photographs of Sydney or of her family in Australia were ever published, it is more likely it was at a date anterior to her first arrival in Europe that she acquired an apparatus, for the photographs of Troy, Delphi, Ephesus, published as *Classical Beauty* eight years later, were already of a high technical standard.

As the summer of 1913 approached, the Millards progressed northwards to cooler climes, visiting Paris and London, as much for the classical marbles of the Louvre and the British Museum as for any more modern wonders to be found in these capitals, and in the autumn Nathanial prepared to return his family to the Antipodes. At this moment the eldest Miss Millard announced that she would not go with them; here for the first time we notice her strong will, her determination to have her own way and at no cost to herself. She wanted to stay in Europe and to study, an ambition worthy in itself and if it had been to pursue the Classics at one of the women's halls of Oxford or Cambridge, her success in convincing her God-fearing, family-minded father that this was a suitable course of action for his carefully educated daughter would have been less surprising.

However, what she wanted to study was Art, and not the art in the classical period but the practice of painting in the modern style, and in Paris, a city synonymous with immoral life in the Anglo-Saxon mind. Yet this is what she eventually achieved. The scenes of persuasion and refusal can be imagined, but it is hard to visualise how her triumph was won. Her parents installed her on a generous allowance as a paying guest in the home of a respectable widow in the Sixth Arrondissement from where she could walk to the Ecole des Beaux-Arts and her lessons in painting and drawing. The apartments set aside for her were evidently spacious enough for her to be provided with a small atelier where she spent more and more time on her photographic activities, taking pictures of the city itself and making a start on those portraits which were to make her famous.

In 1914 war broke out in Europe and panic in the Millard household in Australia. Telegrams and letters ordered Diana, pleaded with her, to come home. In the end it appears that only threats of cutting off her allowance forced the reluctant daughter to abandon Paris. The compromise she accepted was to retire to London; return to Australia she would not. In London she enrolled at the Slade School of Art and continued with her drawing classes, while spending more and more time on her photographic hobby.

At the Slade she met Pia Yaldwyn, the daughter of one of those huge upper-middle-class English families whose ramifications spread into every area of English professional life. Pia's father, an eminent scholar and man of letters, was dead and she lived with her Italian mother and brothers in a large house in Kensington. She was later to marry the Russian *émigré* writer Arkadi Novikoff and both were to be present on the tragic weekend of George Pollexfen's murder. The Yaldwyn family was unconventional enough to welcome the little colonial and accept her for what she was without concern about her family origins.

Photographs of the Yaldwyns and their friends were the starting point of A.D. Millard's fame in England. She posed them, fantastically dressed, standing on tables, crouched on steps, drifting in unsuitably light clothing in Kensington Gardens, draped in velvet, silk and brocade. Through the Yaldwyns she met many of the writers, artists and intellectuals of the period and it was on the back of their fame, or notoriety, that she rose to prominence. Her life in London can be traced in a number of the memoirs that have subsequently been published about the luminaries of the so-called Modern Movement in the capital in these years. Her first encounter, for example, with the Slade teacher, Henry Tonks, famous for his caustic criticisms of his students' efforts, which left the master for once in his life speechless, is recorded in at least two accounts by artists whose careers began at the School. She was a friend of the American poet Ezra Pound, like her a consummate self-publicist, later disgraced as a Fascist sympathiser. Many of the images of the young poet with his stiff brush of ginger hair and of his friend the sculptor Gautier-Brzeska are known to us through photographs by A.D. Millard.

In 1915, at Gordon Square in Bloomsbury, she met Lady Ottoline Morrell, the sister of the Duke of Portland, whose professed purpose in life was to advance the cause of art and beauty. The Morrells' country house at Garsington in Oxfordshire became her regular weekend home for several years during the war. There she photographed Stanley Spencer and his brother, Lytton Strachey, Dora Carrington, Bertrand Russell, the striking Lady Ottoline herself, as well as her daughter and local country people. A.D. Millard was evidently at this stage in her life an artistic lion hunter and she succeeded in introducing herself to, and ingratiating herself with, rival literary packs so that she was permitted to photograph the Bells and the Woolfs in their unconventional ménages, as well as the writer D.H. Lawrence and Frieda, the German aristocrat who ran away from her husband and children to live with him. The American poets, H.D. and T.S. Eliot, were also grist to her photographic mill.

Although men such as Pound took her up, and she found

a willing group to clamour about her work in little reviews, it was not among such people that her social ascent was to be made. It is impossible to trace how Diana Millard engineered her introduction to political circles. Probably at some dinner in 1916 or 1917 at which the aristocratic, political and artistic worlds overlapped, she met the notoriously susceptible prime minister, Henry Asquith. Thereafter, though she by no means abandoned her artistic friends whose life and morals were most congenial to her, she began to appear at socially smarter parties and weekend gatherings.

Thus during the war in which thousands of her compatriots were being slaughtered at Gallipoli, in which the young men of England were dying in the trenches, among them the three Yaldwyn brothers, Diana Millard ruthlessly pursued her social advance. She proclaimed herself a pacifist, but not very loudly, for it is hard to imagine that she would have been welcomed into those many households whose sons lay dead on the fields of Flanders if she had expressed her views honestly. It was through her political friends that she received permission to return, semi-officially, to France and Belgium in 1919, where she took a series of photographs of the aftermath of the war which were published to much acclaim in 1931. By then A.D. Millard had ceased to work, the connection with Mrs Pollexfen was forgotten, and they were to be the last appearance of her work as a photographer, work for which she was willing to go to the last extreme.

Nineteen nineteen was the year in which she met George Pollexfen and she married him six months later in 1920. A greater contrast between the families, education and interests of the spouses can hardly be imagined; it is easy to see why they married and still easier to understand why they fell out afterwards. George Pollexfen came of a wealthy country family. He had been brought up in a way traditional for an English gentleman: after Harrow he had entered the Army, resigning his commission in 1912 to travel and to develop his growing interest in politics. He rejoined his regiment in 1915 and was one of the lucky few who survived three years of the Great War. He fought gallantly and was twice wounded, mentioned in despatches and decorated for bravery. On the face of it a good war; but the experience marked him deeply, unsettled him in some respects and left him with shattered nerves. In this state of mind, he met Diana Millard and was much struck by her charm and beauty, her energy and vivacity, which seemed what he needed after the horrors he had undergone. For her part, what did she, used to the company and conversation of foreign intellectuals, see in this solid Englishman? Tradition, security, wealth and position. It is not an unusual marital bargain, beauty traded for status, and in many cases where the two parties honour their contract, it works well enough.

The new Mrs Pollexfen, however, had no intention of altering herself for her new role. During the years of her marriage, defying the expressed wish of her husband, she continued to work. She published books of her photographs of landscapes and people, and her very striking, strangely posed portraits continued to fill the pages of society journals. This unusual insistence on her own career was only partly hidden by the use of her maiden name for her professional life. This point is pressed, as it became an important element in the trial. Mr Pollexfen was not happy about his wife's working and the notoriety to which it exposed her.

Just before her wedding her first volumes of pictures, *Classical Beauty*, appeared in which the sites of Antiquity and the statues of classical Greece and Rome were seen from strange angles and from a very unclassical point of view. The many nudes in the volume caused one reviewer to declare that it was unfit for young people 'or those of an emotional or easily roused nature', which added considerably to its sales. However, illustrious sitters continued to give her their time. Such publicity might have been shaken off or even welcomed by a photographer. It was anathema to a Member of Parliament. As a society photographer she was little better than a tradeswoman, while as an art photographer she was a source of scandal; neither was a happy role for an MP's wife. However, it has to be admitted that in other respects Mrs Pollexfen was an ideal political consort. She was charming, a good conversationalist, an even better listener. She was an excellent hostess, attracting to their houses in Mayfair and in the country a wide cross-section of people, from prominent politicians and businessmen to artists, writers and men and women of the theatre.

In 1925, at the time of George Pollexfen's death, the couple had been married for five years and had a four-year-old son, Peter. On the surface the marriage appeared solid enough. The Pollexfens travelled and entertained, yet their time was often spent apart and, as witnesses at the trial were to affirm, there were frequent, subtle signs of friction between them, which burst forth into a major confrontation on Mrs Pollexfen's birthday, Saturday 20th June, the day before Mr Pollexfen's murder.

The fatal day was a Sunday, and Mr and Mrs Pollexfen were in the country at Laughton Hall where they were entertaining a small party of guests consisting of a number of Mrs Pollexfen's oldest friends, gathered to celebrate her thirtieth birthday: Mr and Mrs Arkadi Novikoff; Dr Jonothon Pybus, a cousin of Mrs Novikoff and a Fellow of King's College, Cambridge; Miss Edith

Scrafton, the daughter of Professor Scrafton of the Cavendish Laboratory and author of *Bertrand de Borne and the French Poetic Tradition*; Miss Fanny Pollexfen, the host's cousin, and Mr Gaëtan du Breuilh de Cantegnac, a Frenchman noted for his fine stud at Chantilly, his prowess as an Alpine climber and his charm for women.

The events of the weekend can be reconstructed from the various accounts given at the trial by both house guests and domestic servants. The first event of significance, the quarrel between Mr and Mrs Pollexfen, was witnessed by all the guests. The humiliation of this exposure was, it may be conjectured, the precipitating factor in deciding Mrs Pollexfen to murder her husband there and then, carrying out an action which it seems from the smoothness of its execution she had probably been planning for some time. The quarrel took place in a new photographic studio which Mrs Pollexfen had had constructed in the stables of their country house, a change of use of which she had not informed her husband. When the latter discovered her in the midst of a photographic session with her guests, he heartily reproached her for her deceit as well as for pursuing her photography. His expression, by all accounts, was extreme and violent, giving vent to the rage and disappointment of a man whose wife has taken all he had to offer, which was much, and refused to give in return what he required of her.

The following day, Sunday, everything seemed restored to normality. Mr Pollexfen was all charm and hospitality to his guests and Mrs Pollexfen hid her rancour under smiles. The entertainment of the sabbath consisted of the service of Mattins in the village church, attended by Mr Pollexfen but not his wife, a visit to the farm to admire Mr Pollexfen's rare breed of goats, and then luncheon. Various activities, more or less strenuous, occupied the afternoon and after tea three of the guests departed, driven back to Cambridge by the Pollexfens' chauffeur.

After their departure George Pollexfen retired to his library. In the early evening he was seen walking, slowly and ruminatively, in the grounds. The last sighting was by a strapper who saw him in the tack room at about seven in the evening, his master having apparently made a brief visit of inspection to his horses. The strapper, his evening tasks completed, left before Pollexfen. The scene of this meeting was important, for above the tack room was the newly made photographic studio. Here, Mrs Pollexfen kept a variety of toxic substances employed in her photographic work, including calomel and hydrochloric acid which she used to make mercuric chloride for the purpose of intensification of the images she had achieved. It was this poison, soluble in water and alcohol, that, administered in a glass of whisky and water, killed George Pollexfen.

A question which much concerned Chief Inspector Starling of the local police force and Chief Inspector James of Scotland Yard, who were charged with the investigations, was what brought Mr Pollexfen to the stableyard, a place he rarely frequented, and the studio. It was assumed that he went there by appointment and the obvious person to suggest such a rendezvous was his wife. The housekeeper, Mrs Everett, testified that Pollexfen had said to his wife after the departure of the guests, 'Diana, we must have a word this evening,' and her reply had been, hastily and dismissively, 'Later, George.' The clear implication was that the two had met in the studio during the evening and that Mrs Pollexfen had taken the opportunity to lace her husband's drink with a lethal cocktail of chemicals. This was countered by the defence that Mrs Pollexfen's movements for the whole evening were accounted for, and that at no time had she disappeared from view even for the twenty minutes or half an hour necessary to carry out the murder. Mrs Pollexfen had left the drawing-room in the course of the evening, according to Miss Pollexfen, only to go up to the nursery to see her son. Her presence on the second floor was vouched for by one of the nursery maids who was on duty with the child.

For some unaccountable reason Sir Crispin Angell, KC, prosecuting, only half-heartedly put forward an alternative and more plausible theory: that Mrs Pollexfen had made an appointment with her husband, selecting the studio as a quiet place, suitable for her purpose, where his angry remonstrances would not, this time, be heard by guests and servants; that she prepared the poison and left it ready for him and simply failed to come to the meeting. She was thus able to poison her husband without her hand appearing anywhere in the business.

Hector Wallace, for the defence, had anticipated this line of attack, for he was able to show that there was no physical evidence in the way of fingerprints to connect Mrs Pollexfen with the whisky or the chemicals, and that a number of other people had briefly visited the studio on the Sunday and would have had the opportunity to put the poisoned glass in place. Why they should have done so was not explained: Wallace's purpose was not to accuse others but to throw doubt on the case against Mrs Pollexfen. Among those who had entered the studio were Mrs Everett, the housekeeper, to find a pair of Miss Pollexfen's gloves; Violet, one of the maids, to clean; Dr Pybus, in search of his stick; and Mrs Novikoff, looking for her husband. Miss Pollexfen claimed to have seen Mr de Cantegnac emerging from the tack room door into the stableyard, implying that he too had been up to the studio.

This suggestion was endorsed by Miss Scrafton, a most meticulous witness, who agreed that, after her afternoon ride with Mr de Cantegnac, she had spent some time with the horses in their loose boxes, and her companion had left her for some ten minutes before rejoining her to return to the house.

The question of who had had access to the fatal studio on the Sunday afternoon and evening was clearly crucial, and the fact that several people had entered for various purposes greatly helped Hector Wallace in his defence of Mrs Pollexfen. His tactics of casting mists, shadows and doubts on the events of the Sunday evening were brilliantly skilful and successful. When it came to his account of the horrible discovery of the Monday morning, his speeches spun a halo of heroism over the widow, leaving the pedestrian and practical questions of the prosecution unanswered.

Although after the departure of the car to Cambridge Mr Pollexfen did not appear again at his own house party, his absence did not arouse any concern. The strange fact that he had not eaten his dinner, changed his clothes or slept in his bed, though it had been commented on by the servants and mentioned to his wife in case she did not know, had caused no alarm nor outcry. When confronted with these points at the trial, Mrs Pollexfen denied that there was anything odd in her behaviour, saying that she had put them down to her husband's sometimes irrational or impulsive behaviour. She assumed that he had either slept in his library and gone for an early morning walk, or that he had departed (on foot and without baggage!) for London without telling her. Their relations were such that her husband did not keep her informed of all his plans or movements. Even this highly implausible tale was used by Hector Wallace to enhance Mrs Pollexfen's claims of innocence. Would she have left her husband's last hours unaccounted for and then discovered the body herself if she were really the cunning criminal the prosecution alleged?

It is indisputable that the lady behaved with great calm (her defenders said courage) when the death of her husband was revealed. Mrs Pollexfen and her friend, Mrs Novikoff, were strolling in the grounds of Laughton Hall after breakfast, using their last opportunity for gossip before the guests' departure. They left the garden and plunged into a shrubbery which blocks the view of the stables and tennis courts from the house. There, in one of the secluded walks, face down in his own vomit, lay the late George Pollexfen.

The subsequent autopsy showed that he had been poisoned by a lethal dose of mercuric chloride mixed with a considerable quantity of whisky and water. The time of death was estimated by the police surgeon as approximately nine o'clock on Sunday evening. The researches of the local constabulary quickly established that the poisoned cup had been administered, or at any rate prepared, in the photographic studio. There was found the cut-glass decanter which had originally held whisky and into which the deathly cocktail of photographic chemicals had been introduced.

There was some doubt about a final, melodramatic detail of the discovery of the body. Mrs Everett, the housekeeper, who came hurrying from the kitchen on hearing the cries of Mrs Pollexfen and Mrs Novikoff, stated that the dead man's hand, outflung, had inscribed in the gravel the initial D. This was denied by both her employer and Mrs Novikoff, and certainly later arrivals at the scene saw no significance in the scuffing of the gravel around the corpse.

The local police were immediately summoned and, after the first day during which the household at Laughton Hall was questioned, a statement was issued to the press which ended, 'The Police are satisfied that it is a clear case of murder and the help of Scotland Yard has been called for.' The local authorities never particularly liked appealing to the Metropolitan Police, but in a case which involved such nationally known names they clearly felt they had little choice. An inquest was held three days later in Oakham Town Hall by the local coroner. Mrs Pollexfen appeared as a witness to answer questions both as to the identity and the discovery of the body. She appeared composed, visibly grief-stricken, and was praised by the local papers for her 'heart-rending courage'. The inquest was adjourned for two weeks to permit the court to hear the full report of the post-mortem. When it was resumed the jury had no difficulty in passing a verdict of Wilful Murder by Person or Persons Unknown.

The police spent some six weeks assembling sufficient evidence to enable them to feel confident enough of a conviction to arrest Mrs Pollexfen. They were all along aware that the evidence against the widow was only circumstantial, and the arrangements she had made for the execution of her enterprise were well concealed, but they put together as good a file of evidence as they could.

Mrs Pollexfen had the knowledge and skill to carry out the poisoning and she had ample motive, both in her disagreements with her husband and in the existence of her French lover. This most important question for the prosecution was not properly stressed at the trial as Mr de Cantegnac, a foreign national, refused to appear to bear witness.

It is here that we reach the heart of the case which marks it as a true crime of passion. For the disagreements between Mr and Mrs Pollexfen, including the fundamental one about her work, might not have been sufficient to precipitate her to murder if she had not been deeply in love with the Frenchman whom she had known since her time in Paris, as an art student before the war. No doubt his presence on that fatal weekend played its part in deciding her to act. Certain facts were brought forth during the trial, such as the friendship, or something warmer, which had subsisted between the accused woman and Mr de Cantegnac since the period pre-dating her marriage, something she had effectively concealed until the trial. There was some drama in court when Sir Crispin challenged her on her long acquaintance with Mr de Cantegnac. Mrs Pollexfen, with a sangfroid indicating her powers of concealment, claimed that it was not a secret, and there had been no covert relationship with Mr de Cantegnac either before or after her marriage. More tellingly, however, it was conceded by a number of witnesses that there was antagonism between Mr de Cantegnac and Mr Pollexfen and that, though no incident of open hostility occurred between the two of them that weekend, it was evident that they heartily disliked one another.

The prosecution case had certain weaknesses, partly because of the refusal of Mr de Cantegnac to come to England to take part in the trial. None the less, under normal circumstances, that is with a stout, plain, crude woman of the people charged with murdering her husband, it would have been sufficient to hang her. As Sir Crispin summed it up, the accused had long been on bad terms with her husband, who wished to prevent her from exercising what she called her profession. This chivalrous care for his wife was bizarrely construed by her as an infringement of her rightful freedom. The death of her husband, she calculated, would enable her to live independently, to continue her photography, and to meet her lover. The easier alternative of separation or divorce would not do. Pollexfen would never agree to what would be the ruin of his political career; nor would he permit his son to be removed from under his roof and Mrs Pollexfen was recognised by all sides to be much attached to her child. Only her husband's death would fulfil the conditions of the good life, according to Mrs Pollexfen's ideas. The accused had the motive, the knowledge, the means and the opportunity to kill her husband.

The trial opened on Monday 30th November 1925 at Bedford Crown Court, Mr Justice Wyllie presiding. The prosecuting counsel, Sir Crispin Angell, was a worthy and conscientious barrister, unfortunately never renowned for his brilliance or quickness of response. Mrs Pollexfen had retained the comparatively young counsel Hector Wallace, who, though already known in the legal profession as a sharp mind and skilled pleader, had not previously performed at a trial which had excited similar popular interest. It was on this occasion that he discovered his talents for creating and manipulating an atmosphere in the courtroom, a psychological sensitivity which was entirely lacking in the dry delivery of Angell. It was principally in accentuating the element of uncertainty in the prosecution's case that Wallace performed so brilliantly. Whereas circumstantial evidence very often can be built up cumulatively to produce a conviction, in this case Wallace succeeded in converting every likelihood which the prosecution put forward which amounted in reality to something near a certainty, into more than a doubt, into an improbability. However, he never pressed his position so far as to be considered unreasonable or to antagonise the judge.

Mr Justice Wyllie was, in 1925, in his seventy-third year,

a Red Judge of long experience and bearing a reputation for toughness. He had hitherto been known as a hanging judge for his simple view that wrongdoing should be punished and there was no excuse for murder, not even incompatibility within marriage. He must have been bewitched, it was said afterwards, for only a spell could account for the leniency to the accused in his summing-up in which he laid heavy stress on the uncertainties of the case. His melting at the trial of Mrs Pollexfen may have been the first signs of the onset of senility for he retired the following year giving 'ill health' as his reason. He was famed for his impassivity and his lack of interference with either counsel or witnesses. He sat at the trial as he always did, showing few signs of life, though his summing-up as usual bore witness to his sharp attention to every significant detail of the trial.

It was afterwards discussed in legal circles whether it was Mr Wallace's eloquence or Mrs Pollexfen's gaze that affected the tone of his speech on this occasion. It was as acute and clear as usual, yet the brisk rejection of doubt, the blowing away of the mists of unlikelihood with the sharp blast of reason, which was expected by those laying odds in the courtroom, did not come. Instead, each doubt brought out by Wallace was honed and laid in the scale of Mrs Pollexfen's innocence against the contrary accusation made by Sir Crispin Angell. There was nothing unfair about the judge's summing-up; it was simply out of character. Mrs Pollexfen's comportment in the dock and still more her response to cross-questioning had enchanted him. She had sat in court like 'Patience on her monument, smiling at grief', every day in a new dress, chosen for its elegance and simplicity, always innocently white or cream. The spell of her beauty did its work.

Another interesting factor in the case was the reaction of

the popular press. It is a commonplace that women, the gentler, more humane sex, are correspondingly more fiercely vilified when their actions deny their life-nurturing nature. In the case of Mrs Maybrick, for example, also accused of the murder of her husband, the entrance to the court and prison were frequently crowded with women jeering and booing her as a traitor to her femininity. It has been observed that the more beautiful the accused, the more rigorous is the sisterhood in its denigration. This indeed occurred in the case of Mrs Pollexfen and her daily entrances and exits to and from the court must have been exceedingly painful to her, showing with what horror other, less fortunate women regarded her actions.

However, inside the courtroom, journalists were captivated by her beauty, and by the cunning simplicity of her quiet responses when she took advantage of the accused person's right to give evidence on her own behalf. The idiocy of the popular press, which is only moved by what will stir emotion and sell newspapers, was never more clearly on display. For the question of the necessary relationship between appearance and action was never posed. Such beauty, such tenderness, such suffering touched the hearts and pockets of newspaper readers. And there was an anticipatory outcry even before the verdict about whether the death penalty was appropriate for women. It is to be hoped that, had Mrs Pollexfen been declared guilty, such claims would have had less success in England than they were to have in the case of Miss Elizabeth Borden in America, and that the Secretary of State would have rejected any plea for clemency on the spurious grounds of her sex.

However, that particular point was not to be tested; Mrs Pollexfen was acquitted and though the press maintained its interest in the subject for several weeks afterwards she herself disappeared from view. In the years that followed she changed her character, became a recluse, and shunned all publicity. She continued to work as a photographer, though she found commissions from the socially and artistically celebrated hard to obtain. Her last book was published in 1931 and she herself died at an early age in 1941. Spurned by her French lover, she never remarried.

So it seems there was a justice of sorts. She did not receive her true deserts by the legal system but her subsequent life, denied the work, notoriety and society on which she had thrived, was perhaps a sort of living death.

2

Photographic Evidence

(i)

A week after he and Isobel had had supper with her, Simon rang Helena at work. 'Let's have lunch. I have a huge gap between meetings from twelve to three thirty.'

'You may have holes in your day to spend eating; I certainly haven't.'

'Have you read the *Boys' Best Book of Beautiful Murderesses* yet?'

'I have.'

'And what do you think?'

'It is so appallingly biased that it must be false. I must let you have it back.'

'No, keep it for reference. It should have given you some lines of attack at any rate. Now, I have some information for you.'

'Not now, Simon. We'll have to meet. What about Thursday evening?'

Lewis J. Buckherd had infuriated her; all her loyalty to the Great-aunt rose up to contradict him. She tried to convince herself that the grounds for her rejection of his account were reasonable and logical ones but she knew that the true foundation was emotional. Buckherd was at bottom a misogynist who saw the world stalked by fierce, predatory women devouring honest simple men. Gaëtan de Cantegnac was, in the American's view, a stage Frenchman whose role as womaniser and lover was fixed by his nationality. Arkadi Novikoff was seen hardly at all.

George Pollexfen as victim was the most interesting portrait and its validity would only become evident as she read Diana's own writing, from which an alternative view of her husband would presumably appear. He seemed, according to Buckherd, a solid Englishman, brave with the courage of the unimaginative, conscientious because lacking the initiative to strike out on his own, devoted to his family with a love that, not unreasonably, challenged his wife's interest in her former profession which he found incompatible with his own. There was a hint of some instability or barely controlled violence in him in the description of his anger at his wife's misdeeds. It was as if his rage were fuelled by more than the immediate incident, drawing on a reserve of what? – jealousy, perhaps, which he had not been able to express.

Glancing at her watch, Helena simultaneously registered that she had ten minutes before her next meeting and placed Robert, in Rome this morning, one hour ahead. She began to pick out the necessary files from the tray beside her desk; the phone rang.

Sophie, her secretary, said, 'It's Richard Fox's secretary. She won't put him on until you're on the line. Who is the man?'

'Sophie, it's my cousin. I'll deal with it quickly.'

When she had been passed through to Richard she said, 'You have most devoted assistants, Richard, who think everybody's time is less precious than yours. So let's be quick.'

Richard was embarrassed. 'Are you pressed? Well, it's a

bit difficult on the phone. Can you meet me for a drink this evening? Say about eight, there should be a lull then. Come here and we'll be on the Terrace.'

There was a concert in Smith Square; Helena could see lights, faintly hear the organ, as she parked in Lord North Street. She wondered why she had agreed to come. Richard wanted to tell her something, or propose something, and yet obliged her to come to him, she thought crossly. She was too accommodating. Her irritation was synthetic and she knew it herself; so too was her self-accusation. If it had not been Richard and he had not suggested the Commons Terrace, she would have insisted on other arrangements; in this case, there was pleasure in being in that place and anticipation, that she knew could not be fulfilled, of seeing a sleek grey head or pin-striped back instantly recognisable amid all the other middle-aged heads and conventional suits. So she smiled at Richard who had afforded her this treat and met his conciliation with a welcome that he evidently had not wholly expected and that encouraged him to embark straight away on what was concerning him.

'Marta,' he said. 'Marta was much struck by the story of Great-aunt Fox's life. She could see you were too. Now, Marta wants, well, she's decided she wants to do something about it, to follow your research and write it up. But obviously you've got to agree. No, that's not well put, but you'll understand, Helena. Marta wanted to rush into this: it's a new enthusiasm. I explained to her it was your thing; she couldn't just muscle in like that, and I said perhaps you could co-operate. You can't have much time after all and Marta has.'

Helena looked across at St Thomas's Hospital. The river was at slack water, flat and grey as stainless steel, darkening to an opaque green where the opposite embankment was reflected. The water swung tentatively, on the turn, running neither up nor downstream. From the other end of the Terrace amid the torrent of conversation she suddenly distinguished a voice, the voice.

'What does she want to write?'

'I'm not sure about the details, I don't think she is yet. She just saw it as a fascinating subject.'

Helena's ear continued to sort through the background babble as she gazed upstream refusing to let herself look.

'I can't say that I would be delighted if she came to the conclusion that the Great-aunt did poison her husband and wrote a rip-roaring bestseller to that effect. And after inheriting half an hotel from her, wouldn't it look a bit ungrateful? But I can't stop her.'

'Ah, well, I've put it to you badly. I don't think you need worry that Marta would make an exploitative use of what you jointly discover. She would be more interested in vindication than vilification. She said all this to Isobel who, I must say, was a bit nervous that the press would get hold of it. Has Simon been in touch?'

'Yes, I'm seeing him on Thursday.' She had lived for years with what the press might get hold of. The Great-aunt would have to take her chance, along with Helena herself.

The voice came again, this time quite unmistakable. Helena said, 'Look, Richard, tell Marta to call me and we'll talk about what she wants to do. I don't mind, much, if we decide the Great-aunt was innocent. We must decide what she will do if Diana Pollexfen really was the poisoner.'

She permitted herself to turn her head sufficiently to glance along the Terrace to a knot of men at the far end by the screen.

'Helena, the last thing I want is a family row with you on

this. That's why I said I would sound you out. Marta depends on you. You hold the papers, in any case, and stuff she needs. She can't go ahead if you are hostile.'

'Well, I'm not. In principle tell Marta OK. In fact I'll give her Simon's book. She can start there. And now I must run. I've just remembered . . .' She put down her glass and rose precipitately. Richard watched, bemused as she placed a kiss on his cheek and disappeared inside with all speed.

Helena had started to expect a manifestation of what she called the presence every time she re-entered her house. Most often her gaze, sharpened by suspicion, found nothing, no change at all. The book on the floor by her bed lay, as it should, parallel to the bedside table; the cosmetic jars on the glass shelves of her bathroom remained ranged in the order that she always applied them; the dishevelled piles of papers on her desk, domestic administration which awaited a weekend without work or Robert, lay in their proper chaos. Other nights when she came in, her wariness saw fractionally displaced books, rearranged fruit in the bowl on the dining-room table, even, once, extra yoghurts in the fridge; she, surely, could never have bought pina colada fromage frais and low-fat toffee yoghurt? By turning on the television news rather too loudly, by refusing to dwell on these minute adjustments of matter within the house, she could convince herself that not only had she not noticed them, they had not even occurred.

For it was the thinking that they had happened, the debating if there had been a change, that was the worst. Or almost the worst. When a change was palpable, undeniable, she felt close to breaking down and telling someone. On one such occasion she found the *Times Atlas*, which, too large for her bookshelves, lived under the sofa, lying on one of the chairs in the drawing-room. Without touching the book, she had seized the telephone and called João, staring at the uninformative cover, as she listened on the line to the television tuned to a game show and the children quarrelling over the top of it. João's wife went to call him from the bedroom. He sounded plaintive. His days were Tuesdays and Thursdays. He hadn't changed and come today, today was Wednesday; nor could he. He had his other clients to think of. Helena had put down the phone, after apologising too profusely for even thinking of disturbing his routine. She smoothed her hair and replaced the atlas under the sofa.

At least she was not imagining this; that was a consolation of sorts, a reassurance that her mind was not playing tricks. Straightening up, she remembered that just as she fell asleep last night the phone had rung: Robert to tell her that he was going unexpectedly to Potsdam on Thursday and Friday. They had talked for ten minutes or so and when he had gone she had thought, Potsdam, where is Potsdam? It had a fine eighteenth-century ring to it; it was in Prussia perhaps, or was it a little south German princely capital with a superb baroque organ inside a church soaring with pastel-coloured putti? She had even visualised the atlas, a frequent source of reference for placing Robert. Had she come in here this morning and looked up Potsdam without being conscious of having done so? If she had, she was still none the wiser about where Potsdam was.

The fear of finding another displacement, or of suspecting one, made returning home, alone, unpleasant. An evening on Thursday with Simon was a welcome distraction. The activities of giving him something to drink, of going to the loo, brushing her hair, re-applying lipstick, leaving the house in haste, prevented her from observing too sharply. She slammed the door behind them with relief.

At the Italian restaurant around the corner in Radnor Walk she admired the simple greed with which Simon abruptly ceased talking and concentrated on the menu as soon as it was given to him, closing it a few minutes later with an air of satisfaction, his decision made. She held hers open, talking and glancing at it, hesitating until the last moment.

Simon took out an elegant, leather-bound pad. 'I've found out quite a bit about your characters; I'm afraid they're mostly dead as far as I can see. I'll have fettucine all'Alfredo followed by seppie al nero, please.' Helena added her order, and, after some polite but unconvincing argument about who was in charge of the wine and the bill, she chose a red for Simon and mineral water for herself. She then changed her main course, and might well have returned to debate her first course if the waiter, knowing her vacillation over food, had not left. The decision made for her, she fixed her attention on what Simon was reading from his notes.

'George Pollexfen, MP, et cetera, born 1884, died 1925, blah, blah, you know all this from the Buckherd book. Ah, yes, his will shows he left two million to his son with generous provision for his widow during her lifetime. She got it completely when Peter was killed in the war. An enormous sum in 1925. Interesting to know what it has turned into now.' He looked up enquiringly.

'You mean what the Great-aunt left? I don't know exactly. You can add up the ten thousands to the nieces and so on. I'm not sure what I get.'

'Helena, you're priceless. You're left a fortune and you don't yet know what it's worth. Stringer should have worked it out by now. Anyway, the point is that she could hardly have been murdering him for his money since the bulk went to her son.'

'So that's good news, I suppose.'

'Now, the others. Arkadi Novikoff published two volumes of short stories in 1928 and 1931. Ever come across them?'

'No, I can't say I have.'

'I don't suppose they ever went into paperback.'

'I might go to the British Library to read them.'

'What on earth for? They're fiction, they won't tell you anything.'

'I'm not so sure. In any case, we may be scraping round for information to such a degree that a fictional account of a murder may be the nearest we'll reach to the truth.'

'He was editor of some kind of review which failed about 1933 and he went off to live in Paris. Don't know what he did in France, until he was carried off to Dachau in 1942. He was caught in the round-up of foreign Jews in Paris when they were herded into a sports stadium called the Vél' d'Hiver. Died in the camp, of course.'

'And what about his wife?'

'I've not found much on her. She was a painter, you know, Pia Novikoff, and she only died last year. Think what a witness she'd have been . . . Just too late.' Simon leaned back to allow his fettucine to be placed in front of him. Helena looked at her plate. Risotto always looked in reality less tempting than it sounded on the menu. She picked up her fork and prodded the pile of rice dubiously. Simon had already begun to eat with a joyous and vigorous mastication.

'Now who else?' he said.

'What about the cousin, Fanny Pollexfen?'

'Yes, I wondered whether we could make her the murderess, as a neglected lover or something on those lines.'

'George Pollexfen does not seem that kind of man, according to Buckherd at any rate.'

'I shouldn't let that stand in the way of my theory. In my experience plenty of men who appear to be the most respectable citizens have quiet sidelines. Worse than us playboys. She doesn't have to have been Pollexfen's lover, she could have been Diana's. But it was more a speculation than a real hypothesis.'

'Not very useful, that sort of hypothesis,' Helena said ungratefully. 'So what about her?'

'Not much, I'm afraid. I found her in Debrett. She married late and often; for the first time when she was about thirty, then twice more in the next fifteen years. Dead, now. I didn't look further at this stage as I was really trying to see if we had any living witnesses.'

'The other woman is the bluestocking, Edith Scrafton of Cambridge.'

'I've nothing on her. I don't even know if she's alive or dead, though presumably she's dead. I tried tracing her through her famous father. He died in 1926 and his wife went just before him. His obituary says he was survived by his only daughter and that's about it. There's quite a lot about the heroic days of Cambridge science with Scrafton, Thomson and Rutherford, but nothing about their family lives that I could find. She published a book, the one that's mentioned in Buckherd; after that, nothing.'

'And the other men: Dr Pybus and the Frenchman?'

The plates for the first course were being removed, Simon's bearing only the tracks of his bread which had swept up the last of the sauce.

'I have nothing on Cantegnac; I don't know where to begin. On Pybus I found a lot. He was a physicist, a theoretician and he went to Germany in the mid-Twenties to work at Göttingen and later to Nils Bohr's institute in

Copenhagen. Ah good.' This referred to the pile of cuttlefish swimming in its black ink that had just been put down in front of him. He swirled the dark-red wine in his glass in anticipation. 'He was one of the gays of that generation who found liberation in Weimar. He came back to Cambridge in the Thirties and was very involved in getting Jewish scientists out of Germany before the war. In 1943 he went off to Los Alamos and helped build the bomb. He committed suicide in the States in 1952. He was sometimes mentioned as a significant friend of Burgess and Maclean and he seems to have been a fellow-traveller during the Thirties and Forties. Pretty good, eh? I got the whole lot from a book on the making of the atom bomb, just looked up Pybus on spec in the index and there he was. Now, with all those millions on his conscience, I don't suppose it would do him any harm if we off-loaded a minor poisoning on to his account.'

'I don't know how the recording angel rates these things. I'm not so hopeful; Dr Pybus sounds as if he would have been a most honourable and upright person. A Communist, a theoretical physicist, he was obviously an idealist. He might have been able to make a weapon of mass destruction to wipe out the persecutors of the Jews; I am sure he would never have cheated on his bus fare, let alone killed someone he knew, even an enemy.'

'He might have done it to help a friend in that case, to murder altruistically.'

'So that leaves the Frenchman.'

Simon was reading the dessert menu. 'I'm not sure.'

'You must. Look, tiramisu. I know you adore it.'

'I shall. Isobel's not here to act as my superego, reminding me of my weight and my cholesterol. I shall blame you if she finds out. The woman tempted me and I did eat.'

Helena noticed that it was Isobel's discovery of his

misdeeds and not their ill effects that he pretended to fear.

'Objectively, I suppose the Frenchman is the best bet,' she said. 'Though I'm reluctant to credit anything that Buckherd says, he may be right when he says there was bad feeling between George Pollexfen and Cantegnac. The case is somewhat weakened by not knowing why.'

'He was the Great-aunt's lover, Helena, that's reason enough for both bad feeling and murder. That's how Buckherd squeezed the case in under crimes of passion.'

'But Cantegnac had left by the evening Pollexfen was murdered. He was part of the group that went back to Cambridge early on the Sunday evening, according to Buckherd.'

'Oh, he could have slipped a few grains of mercuric acid into his drink before leaving, no problem.'

'Simon, you've been very kind finding out all these details, but you're not taking this seriously. I don't want just to put the blame for the crime on to another character in the story.'

Simon straightened his face, wiping out his habitual smile. 'Of course I take it seriously. It's all great fun. Now what next? No living witnesses, apparently, to interrogate.'

'Next comes the Great-aunt's diaries. Who knows what we may find there.'

After dinner Helena firmly put Simon in a taxi for Victoria, ignoring his murmurs of brandy, before returning home. She rarely saw him alone, regarding him nowadays as an appendage of Isobel, a view she realised he resented sharply.

At home, she picked up the mail from the hall table and, switching on a light, began to shuffle it, tearing open the envelopes and strewing them on the floor along with invitations to visit department stores for special make-up sessions; bills on another pile. Thinking of Isobel made her feel tired: the organisation of the twins and Simon, of nannies, cleaners, food, laundry, all on top of her gruelling work. Helena could not imagine how she would cope with three other people's lives: her own took all her energy. And, she realised, she did not want her life merged with another's. If Robert did not exist she would have to invent him; he fulfilled all her needs and made no demands apart from patience. Whereas a man like Simon . . . It was true he had many personal attractions, but he was domestically incompetent, had to be looked after like an old-fashioned husband and at the same time resented his wife's mastery.

She left the waste paper on the floor and, picking up the bills, began to make her way upstairs. On the half-landing she halted. Something was not right. She had the overwhelming feeling that there was someone in the house and experienced a sudden surge of adrenalin making her heart race. She slipped off her shoes and descended the stairs rapidly and silently. In the dimness of the dining-room where she had already extinguished the lights she looked frantically around for something to use as a weapon. From the hall table she lifted her keys very slowly, stilling them in one palm to prevent their clinking together and, taking a collapsible umbrella in her other hand, she began, listening at every step, to climb up again.

The door into the drawing-room on the first floor was closed, no lights were showing. She flung it open, on to a silent room faintly illuminated by the street lamps. Up another floor. By now anticlimax had overtaken her alarm. She found, as she expected, nothing. Shamefaced at her over-reaction, she went back to collect her shoes, noticing that one of the pictures on the staircase was hanging slightly askew. She straightened it carefully.

(ii)

Helena did not go to Ingthorpe for several weeks after the Great-aunt's funeral. Eventually Mary's phone calls became plaintive at having no one to cook for and persuaded her to go down for a weekend. Her staying in London had been determined by the possibility, not even amounting to a probability, of seeing Robert. Her wait had been well rewarded, from her point of view, by the ringing of her doorbell (he had mislaid her keys some time ago, he explained) at one o'clock one Sunday morning. The unexpected joy of seeing him repaid three other barren weekends, working in the summer chill of London. Now her going to the country was decided by his suggestion that he should take the opportunity of admiring her inheritance by stopping for a few hours on Sunday afternoon on his way from his north Midlands constituency, where he usually spent his weekends, to catch an evening plane. To please Mary's craving for entertainment, she asked Marta and Richard and their children to come for lunch on Saturday.

Hearing Robert's voice on the Terrace of the House of Commons, a surprise even when she had teased herself with the chance of seeing him, had distracted Helena from the import of Richard's proposal. When, later, she gave it some thought she quailed a little at the idea of Marta's devastating energy being applied to her project. Helena wanted reflection; Marta would want action. There was, however, no respectable way in which she could forbid her involvement and so she could only accept it with good grace. She passed on to Marta sections of Great-aunt Fox's journals which she had brought down to London; since then she had heard nothing from her either about her plan of work or about her reaction to what she had read.

She arrived at Ingthorpe very late on Friday night and found to her amusement and surprise that Mary, still up and knitting at the late movie, had prepared the Great-aunt's bedroom for her.

'No good making shrines to the dead is what I say. The king is dead; long live the king. It's your house now and you may as well have the best room.'

Declining a ham sandwich or some cold rice pudding, Helena unpacked and made ready for bed. The king might be dead but Mary had made no changes. The room remained exactly as it was in the Great-aunt's day, as it had been designed in its modernist white of the 1920s. The piqué curtains were tied back and Helena raised the blinds on the long windows to look out on the dark garden, a real darkness, thick and furred, unlike the smoky orange of the London night. She left the blinds undrawn and was wakened by bird-song and the pre-dawn light flooding her room. Below her windows the balustrade of the terrace made a little rampart round the house which was lapped by the sea of the lawn. The contractors employed to mow had created perfect bands alternately silver and sage which reached to the ha-ha. Beyond, sheep were already at their work of grazing, grouped picturesquely under the clumps of century-old chestnuts. The Great-aunt had changed everything she could after 1925: her name, that of her son and her house; she gave up her profession which she had defended against her husband during his lifetime; yet she did not escape from the past in the most obvious way, she did not leave her home. There was nothing to suggest that before 1925 she had much interested herself in gardening; afterwards it became her life. Perhaps in the house and the garden lay her motive: her passion for them had already taken root, she could not leave them. Looking at the view of the calm ordering of nature, which the Great-aunt had supervised for more than half a century, Helena began to wonder whether she would be able to rid herself of Ingthorpe if her self-imposed conditions were not met. Would she allow herself to be satisfied with the court's verdict and accept that Diana Pollexfen was innocent and that there were no ghosts at Ingthorpe?

Great-aunt Fox's guilt or innocence did not interest Marta, as she explained to Helena as they sat under the cedar tree before lunch. She had no worries about her legacy; scrupulous as was her Swedish conscience it would not refuse an inheritance which would ultimately go to her children. The girls, Kristina and Anna, were angular and blonde. Rumoured in the family to be alarmingly intelligent, they did not permit this to be verified in normal social intercourse because they rarely spoke, except to one another in Swedish. They were very continental and formal in their behaviour, treating Helena with a strict courtesy which made her feel that she was almost as old as Great-aunt Fox.

'May we climb one of your trees?' Anna asked after they had politely sipped apple juice for some moments in the company of their elders.

'That one over there.' Kristina indicated the mulberry tree which, older than the present house and garden, had been incorporated by a bulge in the regular line of the ha-ha. They left to perch themselves in the crook of its branches, remote from adult life.

Marta's foot pushed relentlessly, rocking the hammock chair in which she sat. Her view of Diana Fox, she told Helena, was in feminist terms, a woman who had tried to make a career for herself and who had been hounded into retreat by the male world.

'I have no particular idea on the question of the murder,' she said broadmindedly. 'I am not so interested, as you are, in whether or not her acquittal was correct. I want to look at her whole life.'

'That's all to the good,' Helena said. 'The last thing I want to do is to force the evidence and if you are looking more widely you may produce a better perspective. The trouble is we don't have much about the murder in any case.'

'We need to work out who else might have had a motive to kill George Pollexfen and who else might have been able to do so.'

'Did you read that piece in the diaries where she says that no one else would have wanted to kill him?'

'She had a macabre sense of humour. How to take those journals? Do they strike you as having been written by an innocent woman?'

'Sometimes. Sometimes you read bits and you think only an innocent person could have been so stupid as to write this. In fact, she was lucky that the diaries were not found by the police and used as evidence. There are some statements which, if taken out of context, make her look as guilty as hell.'

'Yes, those are the ones easy to dismiss. More troubling is the sense in places that she is not telling the truth or rather that she is omitting part of the truth. Not because

she wished to mislead a reader but because she did not
even wish to acknowledge to herself something that she
knew or that she had done.' Helena felt this was pushing
intuition a bit far, then remembered her own first reaction
to reading the page that had fluttered out of the notebook.
*Today at half-past two in the afternoon I was acquitted of
the murder of my husband.* This person is lying. Such a
reaction had no logical validity, any more than her conviction, her desire, that the Great-aunt must be innocent. She
must have proof.

Mary came on to the terrace to call them in to lunch.
Marta waved to the girls in the mulberry tree and to
Richard who had carried his glass to admire a border of
flowering shrubs. In recent years, Helena recalled, he had
taken to gardening at their cottage and used to ring up the
Great-aunt to ask the name of the best variety of clematis
to order from his nursery. He stumped back across the
lawn in obedience to his wife's beckoning with his daughters running like drawings of stick children beside him.

It occurred to Helena that Richard's encouragement of
Marta's interest in the Great-aunt's life might be a tactic to
divert that ferocious energy away from himself. Gardening
was another symptom of the same condition: Marta suffered from hay fever so her rule over the world of nature
was necessarily less imperial. It must be exhausting for him
and for the girls to be the focus of that powerful will and
critical intelligence. For years Marta had been putting the
world to rights, lecturing her colleagues at work, her
friends around her dinner-table; now she concentrated on
the world in little, her family.

Mary had said, 'It'll be chicken and ice-cream then if
children are coming. That's what I always give them.'
What lay on the table was not immediately recognisable in
those simple terms. The chicken was a boned sausage, its

white flesh encircling a heart of green stuffing. The girls said nothing, picking dubiously at what had been made of normally edible food. The ice-cream, a bombe, white outside and chocolate within, met with more success and when lunch was over they professed themselves willing to walk round the lake with their father. Richard declined coffee and, leaving Helena and Marta on the terrace, the three of them, fortified with chocolates in their pockets, set off.

'Now we can get down to business,' Marta said, taking a pad out of her vast, soft bag from which almost anything, including a white rabbit, might have emerged. Helena, to regain the initiative, gave her a sketch of the characters and their subsequent history as they had been discovered by Simon. Marta listened, taking notes.

'You know how it is,' she said when Helena had finished. 'You have never heard a name before and suddenly you are sensitised to it and it leaps out at you everywhere. I found a book the other day, diaries and letters of a woman called Gwenola Orr, famous mostly for having been everyone's mistress, or at least sleeping around with artists and Balkan royalty and people like that, and finally making several marriages and coming to a thoroughly good end. Do you think there are still women who make fortunes by sex?' She looked for a moment as if she was about to plunge off down this fascinating byway, then decided to remain on track. 'Gwenola Orr shared a flat with Fanny Pollexfen in the Twenties and there was a little summary of Fanny's character and career. She, they, were amazing, really ruthless, fearless. They were often literally penniless but had absolutely no concern for the future, no prudence, no middle-class values. They sponged off others, men of course, borrowed money and never repaid it, stealing in fact, slept with men as a sort of currency, to repay a dinner or diamond ear-rings.' Marta's powerful disapproval radiated from her.

'So you think we have here someone who is more immoral, more likely to murder, than Diana Pollexfen?'

'Perhaps so. I know it is not evidence.'

'It certainly is not.'

'But it shows an attitude of mind.'

'I don't agree, much as I would like to. I think murder is committed as often by moral as immoral people. Killing is a crime off the scale, so that someone who does not cheat the Inland Revenue and is kind to children is just as likely or unlikely in extreme circumstances to murder as an amoral creature like Fanny Pollexfen. Still, it's interesting as background in building up a picture of the world in which Diana Pollexfen lived, the people she was surrounded by.'

'And a possible alternative criminal,' Marta insisted. 'Though I'm most interested in the one we have least information on, the Frenchman. I am sure he was her lover. We know that he and George Pollexfen detested one another; I think that relationship was at the bottom of everything. I should like to see a photograph of him, of them all in fact; you can tell a lot from a face.'

'I am not convinced he was her lover. It was Buckherd's theory and he seems to have based his idea on the spiteful housekeeper and on the need to make it a crime of passion to include the case in his book. And I'm surprised at the theory coming from you, Marta. You still see it as a *crime passionnel*, simply shifting the guilt from woman to man. I'd have thought that it would be more politically correct to keep Diana as the murderer-victim, defending her right to work.'

Marta's sense of humour, not her strongest trait, did not reach to self-mockery. She said rather stiffly, 'These are just hypotheses, Helena,' and drank the last of her coffee.

Helena contritely refilled her cup and said, 'There is a suggestion in the diaries that Cantegnac and George Pollexfen already knew one another in the war. Their hostility could date from that encounter and have nothing to do with Diana.'

'That's true. And it strengthens my case. It gives an additional or alternative line of motivation.'

'I can't find anything in the diaries to show that Diana ever found out what she wanted to know about the previous meeting between Cantegnac and her husband.'

'I haven't seen anything yet either. There is a hint that she suspected some confrontation in the war, actually at the Front. Then,' Marta continued implacably, 'there is the question of whether she suspected anyone else had done it or suspected that anyone knew she had done it.'

'I don't think there is anything to indicate she was afraid that someone knew something about her guilt. Yet clearly she refused to suspect anyone else either. She keeps saying that it is unthinkable that any of her friends could be murderers,' Helena said. Then she added, 'That could, of course, be because she knew quite well they weren't.'

'All her friendships seem to break down after she goes into prison and even after she is acquitted. Have you seen anything in the later journals about Pia or Arkadi Novikoff, or Edith Scrafton or Jonothon Pybus? And no Frenchman at all.'

'There's just so much of the journal. Have you looked at the whole collection in the Great-aunt's dressing-room? There are literally shelves of those notebooks. Also in some of the later volumes she writes weather reports and lists of plants in bloom or to be moved or ordered, nothing about personal relations at all.'

Across the lawns Richard, Kristina and Anna were

returning to the house, their fair skins reddened by the July sun. Marta's attention began to adjust itself.

'There's more to be got from the diaries and at least they should make a counterweight to Buckherd's chauvinist prejudice.'

'You had better take more of them away with you. I'll never have time to read them all.'

As she waved the Foxes goodbye at the end of the afternoon, Helena reflected that Marta was going to be a very useful researcher, dedicated, diligent, fertile in ideas, though evidently not thinking on the same lines as herself. She suspected that Marta's thesis was formulated and she was setting out to prove her case. Diana Pollexfen was being re-formed as a proto-feminist. As for Helena herself she had little sense of what had happened and why. She watched the information they were collecting, waiting and hoping that it would form itself into a pattern coherent and credible.

The following day, standing in the centre of the stable-yard, Helena waited fretfully for Robert. Weeks without him could pass and she could work, sleep, converse, if not without thought of him at least without disruption. The last few hours before a meeting were always ones of painful, agitated anticipation. He, who had for weeks or days been the peaceful background hum of her existence, suddenly became the only sound in her universe. It was for a few hours like being seventeen again and in love. Her concentration on any object was reduced to a few minutes, the palms of her hands were damp and her heart beat irregularly, jolting suddenly when her roaming attention realised that another sixty seconds had passed. Perhaps, she thought, as she pulled up a few stray blades of grass from between the cobbles and looked round for somewhere to dispose of them, this was why her curious relationship with

Robert remained so necessary to her after so many years. You could not go on being in love in this way if you had the unrestricted time and company of the beloved.

The house lay open and silent in the sun. Mary had been encouraged to take the Great-aunt's little car, which was normally used for shopping in Peterborough or Oakham market, to visit a friend in Leicester for the day. Helena looked at her watch; it had barely gone one. Robert could not be expected for at least three hours. She turned purposefully into the house and collected some keys from the kitchen dresser, returning through the yard to the tack room, when she climbed the stairs to the old photographic studio. She marvelled at the years she had been coming here and been unaware of its existence. It had changed since those days in the Twenties when Great-aunt Fox had worked there. No dark-room or developing equipment remained, no sign that the room had ever been used for anything other than storage.

Helena had already made an initial exploration of what was now the V & A's property, examining the boxes of glass negatives, all neatly labelled to correspond with the card indexes in the filing cabinets by the door. The room had been well fitted out with an elaborate system of catalogues, cabinets for glass negatives and prints, air conditioning, but the Great-aunt's energy had evidently diminished in the last decade or so: she had not got round to a computerised index.

In the catalogue Helena looked for Millard and found her work categorised by year up to 1931. The entry finished with the cryptic note 'From 1931–42 see Codrington.' She took down the references and began with 'Codrington 1933', a year chosen at random, curious to see what Diana Codrington had done when A.D. Millard no longer existed. It was evident that A.D. Millard had not ceased to work in 1925 even if her photography had been seen by no one. One glance at the folder showed that in the Great-aunt's life 1942, when she had lost her son, had been a greater watershed than her acquittal of murder seventeen years earlier. There was only one subject for 1933, a boy of about eleven or twelve, caught in movement, at play, at study, posed, asleep, dressed up. Although the photographs were detached, unsentimental, the obsessive love that had taken them was apparent in their intensity of focus; the child was the only subject in the world.

Opening the drawer of 'Millard 1925' was almost a relief, the tone very different. There were many studio portraits, faces, busts, half-length figures, the photography clear, elegant and witty. After flicking through them for ten minutes or so without finding anything that caught her attention, Helena stood up, glanced at her watch, picked up the keys. The far end of the room from the entrance formed the foot of an L. It was now filled with wide cabinets whose drawers were labelled with photographers' names and dates. This was where the dark-room had been in the days of the studio, with shelves on which the chemicals that had poisoned George Pollexfen had been kept. There had been tumblers here, too, and whisky presumably if that had been the disguise of George's poison. The studio had been a sociable place where one entertained, drank and talked as well as worked.

Why had Pollexfen come there that evening? To meet his wife was the obvious inference, made by Buckherd. Who else would occupy the studio? And he had died in the garden. They had walked out, he and Diana, he and the person he had come to meet, or alone. Helena cupped the keys in her palm, walking through the dimness of the tack room into the sunshine of the stableyard. He had walked along the southern range of buildings and through the small archway which led into the garden. Helena stood in the shade looking down the stone pathway to a seat under a pergola of roses. On her left was the wall of the kitchen garden against which fruit trees were espaliered. Sage and lavender leaned on to the flags whose warmth she could feel through the thin soles of her sandals. George Pollexfen had walked down here to die, for the seat at the end must have been where his body was found by Diana and Pia at ten o'clock that Monday morning. They had been walking 'in the shrubbery' according to Buckherd. Half-way down the paved walk there was a turning to her right, and a path wandered off through the thick band of shrubs and trees that separated this section of the garden from the lawns.

She walked along it until she was in sight of the house. Yes, that was right. They had perhaps started on the terrace, descending the shallow grey steps. She could see them in their shapeless dresses, Pia, who was travelling, in a hat of some kind, Diana bareheaded, looking at the ground as they walked and talked, of what? – their men, the child, their work, the past? They went to the lower limit of the shrubbery and turned on to this path. Then, hesitating, with one last subject to raise, one last question to ask, one that she had not had time or courage to mention all weekend, one of them – which one? – had swung away from the house again towards the apple walk. Helena followed them, her body mimicking her imagination. At what point would they have looked up, abandoned the prepared words for the cry of horror and alarm, to run down the walk to the figure lying in front of the seat?

Helena reached the pergola and sat down in its shade, looking back towards the stables. What had changed here in the sixty-five years since that day? The seat, large enough for two, was set into an old wall, stone, unlike the Victorian brick of the kitchen garden. The armpieces were planted with thick cushions of camomile. It was unlikely to have altered: its age and permanence seemed clear. The path itself was wrong. Buckherd described an indignant detail the letter etched in the gravel by the dying man's finger, the initial D which should in his view have administered the *coup de grâce* to Diana Pollexfen's defence, but which the skilful cross-examination of Hector Wallace had turned into an O or a Q or even a heel mark. She must have paved the gravelled walk then, and erased that accusing initial. Helena leaned back against the stone; how was she to reach beyond identification with the Great-aunt to some kind of objectivity, to proof?

Just then she heard an engine from beyond the house. Looking at her watch as she rose, she saw that she had cheated time and won. Two hours had passed and Robert was early. She reached the yard as his car came under the entrance opposite crowned with the estate clock touching three o'clock.

It was only later that evening when Mary, finding the keys abandoned on the hall table, came clucking to know if she had locked up the studio, that Helena remembered the photographs. As she was hurriedly replacing them in the drawer she found, at the bottom, one more folder, marked, 'developed June 1935'.

As soon as she opened it she recognised Pia Novikoff. She had seen no other image of her, nor read a description of her appearance, yet her character as she had understood it from Buckherd and the diaries made the identification unmistakable. She had a small face with wide eyes, a broad forehead and pointed chin; the expression was open to the camera, eager and unreserved. Helena fanned out the other photographs, studying the images carefully. What value could be placed on a portrait, the reading of a face in paint or celluloid? Was what she read there what the artist had intended to be visible, let alone what the character was in reality? As a lawyer, she had seen in court over and over again the influence that appearance could have in swaying the judge or the jury in their interpretation of the logic of facts. She had trained herself rigorously to give no value to either an attractive or repulsive appearance, to concentrate on deeds and on words.

The photographs before her were flattering in a particular manner. The photographer had not sought to make more beautiful but to heighten contrasts, to exaggerate traits, to dramatise. Since discovering the Great-aunt's past personae, Helena had read not only about Diana Pollexfen, accused of murder, but also of A.D. Millard, the photographer. She had not found much beyond short sections in books on early twentieth-century photography and one or two illustrations of her early architectural work, usually contrasted with her later portraits which tended to be regarded as less innovative and interesting.

There were two more photographs of women and three of men. Helena placed the three women side by side. The writer, Edith Scrafton, must be the aquiline profile, the other, Fanny Pollexfen; psychological stereotypes must be worth at least that much. Fanny's face, half turned towards the camera, was – Helena sought for a description – fleshy, her cheeks full, chin rounded, her mouth drawn up a little in natural good humour. Her eyes had an avidity which Pia's eagerness lacked. Helena laid aside this one, wondering how much of Marta's story about Fanny as a Bright Young Thing influenced her analysis of the face. Not a murderess's face, she thought, for it was too optimistic.

The three men were not difficult to identify: national types were sufficient aid to pick out Arkadi even without the strange black garment he was wearing. Helena suddenly realised that this was the original of the photograph in the Great-aunt's dressing-room. Dr Pybus had a solid, squarish physiognomy, a round, aggressive chin with his head held a little on one side. He had been photographed in his shirt-sleeves, from below, so that he leaned forward out of the picture in an enquiring fashion. Helena studied the Frenchman carefully. He was wholly lacking in the melancholy that in one way or another marked the other two. There was an arrogance in the jut of his chin and the tilt of his head. He had been a soldier, he could and would kill, Helena felt, for all her distrust of appearances.

There was one last photograph in the folder of a very different kind, a signed formal portrait of a man standing beside a desk, his left hand on a pile of books. She picked it up to regard the signature more closely. Of course, George Pollexfen, not taken by A.D. Millard. It was the birthday present she had commented on with such restraint in her diary. His face was composed; this was no photograph with pretensions to revelation of character. On the contrary, it aimed to depict a surface and to give that surface an extra coat of varnish. It showed a man who was a ruler. He imposed himself, without the natural arrogance that was evident in the Frenchman's portrait. It was not a weak face; the mouth was forceful and set. If she had been given the photographs without any previous knowledge of the personalities, she would not have chosen him as the victim. There was something faintly brutal about him; she might even have picked him out as the murderer. Proof of her poor judgement, or of the infinite deceptiveness of the human façade. She put the photographs back into their folder. The answer was not going to come by exercising psychological intuition. She needed proof.

She had explained her unease to Robert that afternoon,

her plan to establish for herself Great-aunt Fox's innocence. He, unlike her family, had made no exclamations about the idiocy or the impossibility of the task. He had listened to her evasive explanation and asked a few questions about how she and Marta were to go about it. His only comment had been that he would not have expected her, so supremely rational, to be moved to such a degree by emotion. Helena had said nothing to this, nothing of the presence that haunted the London house since the Great-aunt's death, and nothing of the organisation of her whole life, ruled by one emotion.

3

from *The Diaries of A.D. Millard*

edited by Marta Fox

Thursday 6th March 1919

It was raining as I arrived. Impossible to find a cab, as usual. When I finally got one I stepped off the kerb into a puddle and soaked my boots. Yet as I was driven across the Concorde and over the bridge even wet feet and vile weather could not stop my spirits rising. I left my things and went straight to see F. and Léonie who have a new apartment on the Ile de la Cité and a very cross *bonne* who refused to cook for us as we were so many. We went out to eat. I saw Gertrude, stouter and more manly than ever, and Alice in rue de Fleurus and J. full of malicious gossip of the Americans. F. had a new canvas of Matisse which he has hung badly.

Tuesday 11th March 1919

C.L. showed me prints of aerial photography which they used during the war and which filled me with new ideas.

He has promised to introduce me to a pilot he knows who flies from Le Bourget just north of Paris who will take me up with him. A.I. appeared today. He is staying with an old cousin and we crossed by chance in the rue du Dragon. We had coffee together, I could not stay as I had promised to meet K. in Montmartre. He looked at me with those dark eyes which do not see you but see things about you you do not know yourself, repulsive, compelling.

Wednesday 12th March 1919

A day lost. Lunch with A.I. No work, missed a rendezvous with P. in the evening. Nothing achieved except that I now remember why I cannot live here. Paris is seductive and I can be distracted from work or, worse, from life. Here one lives marginally, apart, and forgets that London exists. From midday I abandoned myself entirely to Paris and to A.I. We met at the café *d'en bas* from my hotel and lunched at a little restaurant nearby. It was heavenly, thick slices of jambon de campagne, coq au vin with blood in the sauce, a tarte au citron, red wine. I paid as I know A.I. is very short. Jono once told us of Arkadi in the old days: they drank only champagne at Cambridge, the Russians, every luxury was a part of ordinary consumption and now A.I. has to stay with his old cousin, sleeping on a sofa, and measure out a glass of gros rouge for a whole evening. Having been rich, rich, means that he has no pride where money is concerned and he took the roll of notes I passed to him to pay for lunch with complete unconcern. I had meant to visit Olga in the afternoon. A.I. walked with me down rue de Seine. At the entrance to the Luxembourg Gardens we were talking of Wittgenstein, who is a prisoner of war and whom Russell is trying to get released. The horror of it all is too much to contemplate. I abandoned

Olga and we walked in and sat on a pair of uncomfortable iron chairs. How the hours passed I don't know, what we talked of, where we walked. We had reached boulevard Arago by evening and went in to dine at a *restaurant populaire* where there was an *accordéoniste* and *chanteur*. It was there that I turned against the French. How can they, a people so rational, priding themselves on their balance, their reason, be so sentimental? The *chanteur* was singing of love. When one is in love, money does not matter. *Le portefeuille de mon amour n'est pas très lourde . . . un petit peu d'argent ou bien pas du tout. Pas besoin d'argent . . . du reste on s'en fou. On sera riche de tout notre amour.* Mooning like cattle of *amou-ou-ou-our.* The poor are worse than the rich in thinking money does not matter; they have to believe it, I suppose, to console themselves. *On s'en fou-ou-ou.* Love will last for ever; *amou-ou-ou-our, pou-ou-our, toujou-ou-ours.* Amid the loosening of wine, hair, smiles, faces in the hot atmosphere of alcohol and song something inside me hardened, became impatient. A. saw this and we left. We went back to the apartment of his old cousin in Passy. She was out. Of course the day ended badly. I shall leave at once. Paris has been a disaster. How could I let myself succumb to it?*

Thursday 13th March 1919

I arranged to leave tomorrow and ran around all day to see P. and others, whom I had missed. I left the hotel shiftily each time, turning left to avoid the café where I feared, I knew, A.I. must be. Then in the evening as I walked up

---

* A page was excised at this point. It is the only place in the manuscript at which A.D. Millard appears to have censored her own writing.

the boulevard planning to go to bed early before catching the first train I met Pia, Jono, Edith and A.I. with them. We dined together. In their company I suddenly felt very French in spite of having rejected Paris yesterday. They were so much the English ruling class abroad, disdainful, amused by the funny foreign ways, willing to be tolerant, to try new things because they are on holiday. E. in spite of being so clever, in spite of all her studies of French literature, her time driving an ambulance, speaks French v. badly with an English accent that she makes no effort to remove. Jono the same, in fact he speaks French as if it were English and then is enraged that no one understands him. P. speaks not at all and needs looking after. Like a child out for a treat with a godparent, she adores everything. Since I refused to be the dragoman and no one could understand Jono and Edith will not shine at Jono's expense, it was left to A.I. to lead, which he did with grace. He speaks impeccably, like a Frenchman of course. He evidently found Pia's excitement, her first time abroad since she was a child before the war, enchanting. My last evening in Paris. I shall not come back quickly. I recalled leaving in 1914, then so reluctantly, dining with Gaëtan, the atmosphere febrile with the war, death and love, heroism and sacrifice, so easy, so exciting when they are still words.

Monday 23rd July 1923

Everyone left early today. All the cars had gone by eleven and those for town decided to take an early train. Since then the house has been still. George has a dinner in town tonight and induced Fanny, who had threatened to stay for another two days before arriving early for her next Friday to Monday, to go with him to amuse him on the train. He took some trouble with his persuasion and I took it as a kindness to me that he did so. With George gone the house has another aspect, peaceful, feminine. Even the library becomes mine and I sit here looking out at the cedar and remember this is why I did it, why I married and why I am here. Not for the house itself for I had never been here when I agreed to marry George but to belong, and to have something – someone – to love. I thought it would be easiest to love someone who loved me, whose need was so easily fulfilled by me, a gift I could give.

When I was first in Europe, in Paris and then in London in 1914, I used to write to Edie. I used to write so often, sheet after sheet, a little incident took pages. It is easy to write when you both know what you mean, when all the assumptions and references are in place. But as mine changed the letters got shorter and rarer, as it became harder to explain from the beginning not only the what but the why. But the converse is not true: that when you share a life, the assumptions and references are shared. When I worked and was alone I wanted companionship and love. Now I have companionship of a kind and love of a kind I cannot work, or not as I did.

Saturday 20th June 1925

My thirtieth birthday. I received: a telegram from Mummie and Paps. They are cabling money for me and Peter to go to Sydney this winter. As if money were the problem. A book from Pia and Arkadi. A Degas sketch of a horse galloping from Gaëtan. An embossed white ceramic bowl from Edith. A pen from Jono. A shawl from Fanny. A photograph of himself, signed, from George. Peter drew a picture of a snake and, with Nurse's help, he too signed it; there is clearly something of his father in him, though thank God not much. My presents were given formally before dinner and I had to unwrap them and exclaim. I think I did it quite well. I think I did quite well altogether.

In the morning I rode with Jono. One is allowed to say nothing to him, to Edith, to anyone, about his leg and all I want to say is how remarkable it is, he is. He gives no sign that he is a crippled man, though he walks with a swaying, heaving gait, no, that's too strong, but definitely pulling somehow with his hip on the false leg which must be so heavy. But once in the saddle he is a centaur.

It is a terrible business for him, getting there, and he insists on doing it for himself, though he had conceded the mounting block and some help from the groom. It is forbidden to look. He does it in a very strange way. I did look, of course, from the shelter of the arch. He unclips something at the side of his knee to make the false leg bend and literally takes his false foot and puts it in the stirrup. Then, as if the whole wooden contraption were not attached to him, using his hands and a spring from the ankle he pulls himself upwards and swings his good leg over. The body has always been a terrible trial to Jono, as for most Englishmen, but worse because of not liking women. Oddly, the loss of his leg, the impossibility of doing so many physical things that he used to do, climbing and rowing, has actually made him more comfortable with himself. At King's, at the Cavendish, he is just a mind disembodied, a mathematical machine, that has no need of legs and on horseback he becomes part of the horse.

We rode through the fields to Black Down and back on the green lanes to Westhorp. A wind on the hill; the larks rising and singing, spiralling upwards and upwards until you expected the sound to become inaudible; thick shade and foaming cow parsley on the bridle path. It was a perfect morning and Jono the perfect companion. If only my birthday had begun and ended there. We rode side by side on the last mile home, walking. I was on Jono's right and on one occasion his leg clashed with mine, catching my ankle bone so that my eyes watered. It was like being struck by a heavy wedge.

Jono asked whether it was true George had never met Gaëtan before. When I thought about it last night, I supposed George was right, which he would be on something like that; they had not met before. Gaëtan did not come to our wedding; I have seen him half a dozen times in the last five years, with Pia, with Jono, in Paris, never with George. Then Jono said a peculiar thing. He said maybe they didn't know one another's names, but they certainly recognised one another; you don't know where or how? I could see that Jono was on one of his enquiries. He loves to know about personal relations, just as he loves to learn family trees, who is married to whom, who is someone's grandson or third cousin. It forms part of the encyclopaedic system of reference from which he can bring out some entirely unexpected piece of knowledge at an important moment.

He was hoping for some gossip, a sidelight from me, and it was humiliating to have to admit that I knew nothing and had not even guessed that there was something there to know. I hope I gave the impression that I knew something I did not wish to divulge; I am afraid Jono saw only too well that I was completely ignorant. Perhaps he'll let me know if he makes a discovery.

Pia came to my room at midnight to talk, as we talked in her room that evening ten years ago when Charlie was still alive and we had had our party presided over by Mrs Yaldwyn. Then we spoke about the future. I tried to explain to her that I wanted her here this weekend not to make a tradition but because I wanted to see her now. Past and present, Charlie, George, Arkadi, hovered almost visibly in her thoughts and, she is so transparent, I could see the impulses to mention one or the other and then the prohibitions that forbade. In the end it was George, who commanded her loyalty least, whom she could speak of. How could it go on, she wanted to know.

Pia is the only person I can talk to and how to talk to her about that? So I replied that it was not so bad. We didn't live together all the time and we usually managed well enough when we did. But this afternoon, Pia said. That was pretty bad. It was my own fault for not having shown him the studio earlier or at least told him about it more clearly. He could then have had a rage in private. I don't care. I have nothing to hide. It is rather he who should be ashamed of his displays of temper. I think they are getting worse; he used to try to hide them, and they are becoming harder to predict, though this one was inevitable. I tried to tell Pia I was used to his rages, could manage them. She just said, to live like that. But that thought, or its development, I could not contemplate: the idea that there could be an alternative.

I did not tell Pia that when I was on my way up to bed I went to the library to say good night to George, a politeness motivated by a wish to forestall him from visiting me here. I found him at his desk with his old Army pistol in front of him. He had evidently taken it out of wherever he keeps it, unwrapped it, loaded it. He said, rather strangely, that he was cleaning it. I am certain it was loaded. He was sitting with it, holding it in both hands, when I came in. He made no move to shoot me, though I am certain he would like to do so.

Then a knock on the door. I felt my skin grow clammy with fear; I idiotically thought it might be George to pursue his feud about the studio, or worse. The door opened and Edith came in. She was wearing a thick, flannel dressing-gown with an even thicker night-gown reaching to her feet, on a hot night in June. She looked radiant. I have so often felt raging impatience with Edith for being like all English academics and not taking any trouble with her appearance. Last night I thought, if you live a good life, perhaps you do not need to take trouble; goodness instead of cosmetics is the answer; do your duty and no wrinkle will mar your skin. If it weren't totally impossible I would have thought that Jono had rewarded her devotion.

Dear Edith, she came for reasons similar to Pia's. Not to reminisce; as an historian, she has no time for nostalgia, but to discover, no, even better, to reassure. She began by asking without preliminaries if he was often like that. Something about Edith's directness makes me evasive; where I will say outrageous things to shock the Yaldwyns Edith's cerebral calm and honesty which can face anything make me want to hide behind a few obfuscating platitudes. She took no notice of what I was saying. She just came to tell me, she said, that George should see a nerve specialist; he needed medical treatment. She could see I did not like the conversation and Edith is not one for girls' dorm gossips, like Pia, so she began to take herself off, stopping on her way out to say, it's something to do with Monsieur de Cantegnac. I'd keep them apart as much as possible.

Edith is very penetrating. I had seen that the studio was only a pretext or at least it was the occasion rather than the cause. She is right, it was Gaëtan's arrival which began the trouble this weekend. I cannot think why Gaëtan rather than Arkadi should arouse his rage, but George has never needed a reasonable cause for a display of temper.

George's presence looms over us all. Of course there was no possibility of having this weekend in his absence, but I realise I had imagined it without him, without his shadow cast on everyone else. His being here alters all relations, of each of my friends with me and with one another as well. Like thunder, he sours the milk. And he has become more thunderous in the last year. Before, he used to be more willing to be interested or pleased; now only people and occasions that directly bear on him, that he has chosen, have any power to lift the moroseness. He admits less and less of an area to me to choose my friends and activities. I suppose it is a reversion to type. The only solution is to wish he were not there.

He began the day in reasonable humour and was full of charm at breakfast; then something during the day worked on him and by the end of the afternoon he was black and angry. I did not go to church. He had already persuaded Fanny and Edith to accompany him and I suddenly felt I would hand over to them for one week the duty of sitting beside him on that rigid pew that has no sympathy for the human backside, feeling the chill, even in June, gradually penetrating their bones. I could imagine the Vicar bending with the sycophantic, mewling voice that gives George his due as a man and a landowner, Mrs Pollexfen's not unwell, I trust. To cap it, I said I would spend the time in the studio. Yesterday should have shown me that I should not rely on the presence of others to prevent a fit of fury, but I tried it none the less and got away with it. I hope now his first outrage is over, he will become used to the studio, though I can't pretend that use has made him any more accepting of my photography, for example. This morning he demanded I see him this evening in the studio. I could see it was for a minute financial and architectural inquisition and I simply refused to go. No doubt I shall have to face it next time he is up from London.

After they had left for church I did not go to the studio but took Gaëtan to see the horses. I wanted to find out from him what he knew of George, why his arrival had upset George, as Edith suggested. Two of the horses were in the near paddock, standing nose to tail under the big clump of trees, companionably swishing the flies away from one another's eyes. Gaëtan patted the shoulder of the big bay, smoothing his lovely velvety muzzle and blowing into his nostrils. Even the mare who is only about fourteen hands makes Gaëtan look small. He was asking me where I bought her and examining a little place on her fetlock while I was trying to work out whether it would be more successful to ask Gaëtan directly – or indirectly – or to let Jono do it, as he undoubtedly would, and then get it out of Jono which would be much easier. Jono loves to impart information, especially when there would be a little triumph in making me admit I had known nothing until he mentioned it to me yesterday.

But Gaëtan is more of a challenge. He lives a life of compartments, stepping from one room to another and closing the door carefully behind him. Only occasionally do you catch sight of something beyond as he passes between existences. I said it was strange to think that he had met both George and me, separately, in France before the war and then found us again afterwards, a double coincidence. Gaëtan has very thickly fringed eyes with light-grey irises; into which, because of his height, one looks down. I always find being taller than him disconcerting. He knows it and uses it for his greater success, for he imposes himself, Napoleonically, on his surroundings. I think this time I was more convincing than I had been with

Jono, even though I clearly got it wrong. No, he said, it was not then. He moved round, putting the little mare between us. There is an assumption that married people confide in one another. The unmarried don't know that it is possible never to speak to your spouse except with a third party present so that you have to learn quite simple things, like his plans for the next week, from conversations with others. So it wasn't before the war. I did not want to betray I knew nothing at all of what George thought, so I said, I thought it was a very long time ago.

Gaëtan slapped the bay on the rump and began to tramp across towards the gate to the far paddock where the mares and foals were at grass. I ran to catch up with him. It was long ago, he said. It was ten years ago. Where were you ten years ago today? What were you doing? Do you remember? I was suddenly furious. I had intended to get information from Gaëtan and he was facing me with an inquisition. He did not want to know the answer, it was rhetoric and evasion and it reminded me needlessly that ten years ago Mrs Yaldwyn and Pia and Jono and I together said goodbye to Charles. It was exactly the day after my birthday and a month later he was dead. The Yaldwyns do it endlessly, counting back, marking anniversaries. I hate it. I regretted that I had asked them all for this weekend. I don't want to be reminded of ten years ago or five years ago or fifteen years ago. The past is over. The only thing to do is to write it off and begin every day with a new life.

You can't remember at all, Gaëtan said, *tu ne te souviens pas du tout, de rien*. I remember what happened ten years ago down to the smallest detail. I've forgotten nothing. Whole days come back to me, every moment of the clock. I see everything I saw, I hear everything I heard until I am blind and deaf with the past. I remember the faces of the dead, or if they had no faces left, their hands, their torn uniforms, their wounds, their rat-eaten flesh. Of course I remember him. He refused to say any more. By the time we had reached the paddock gate he was speaking again about the horses. He has an extraordinary memory, for he recognised one he had advised me to buy two years ago when he was staying with Jono. So it will have to be Jono who finds out when George and Gaëtan met and I shall have to extract it from him because Gaëtan is not going to tell me, and it is not because he will not talk about the war but because I am George's wife.

Friday 31st July 1925

I was arrested three days ago and brought here to Holloway Gaol. By writing it down I try to make it believable, to realise that it is true. It is true and is no more unbelievable than my marrying George or persuading my parents to let me stay in Paris. It was not even unexpected. Felix Plews had warned me. He seemed to think that I had it in my power to prevent its happening, if I said something, produced someone to protect me. There was nothing I could do. I had answered all their questions, what more could be done? They arrested me at home in London. It was done with great correctness.

I remember seeing a great brawling man arrested in the street in Sydney once on our way back from school. I don't know what for, probably drunkenness among other crimes. For he was certainly drunk; he shouted and lurched, trying to strike the policeman who had already taken his arm. He did not succeed, tripping and falling, taking his captor with him, his great round-toed boot revealing a hole in the sole. There was something huge, solid and grotesque about the scene. My arrest was small, refined, mean. The policeman from Rutland who had come right at the start had travelled to London for the occasion to be with the Chief Inspector from Scotland Yard. They had sly, triumphal expressions as if to say, you can't put one over on us; we're not the kind to be taken in by a disreputable photographer masquerading as the wife of a Member of Parliament. Or perhaps it was, a little colonial. They knew all about me; they had certainly questioned me over and over again about my past, origins, work and I am still not sure which they found most reprehensible.

The Metropolitan one, James, made a little speech reciting that he was arresting me for the murder of my husband, George Pollexfen. When he had finished there was a pause; they were waiting for something and when I said, and what happens next? I could see that they were ready to add that to the evidence against me. I rang for Stanley and asked her to pack me an overnight bag. When I asked, where shall I go? What do I need? How long shall I be away? – things I needed to know – I saw that they were the wrong questions, all adding to the pile of my guilt. I finally understood that I could expect nothing from them when, after permitting me to send a telegram to Felix Plews to tell him what had happened and to ask him to come as soon as possible and get me out of their hands, they insisted on leaving at once, even though I explained that Peter was out with his nurse and would not return for another hour. They were pleased at last to find something that moved me, became more insistent on haste.

I saw then that what they had expected had been tears, confessions, pleas. It would have made no difference but they would have enjoyed it and perhaps been nicer to me, taking pleasure in a cruel power to humiliate. Once I was handed over to the authorities here I was no longer an individual, as I was to James and Starling, even if a despised one, and only by concentration on one thing have I been able to endure the petty tyranny, the rank smells, the hours of boredom, the noise, the inedible food.

I saw Felix Plews today. I had apparently the right to see him immediately but his being in the country and I in London caused what they call 'unavoidable delays'. He has at least arranged certain things. First Peter. He was able to tell me that Pia has come up from Oxfordshire and moved into Brook Street with him. She intends that his life should carry on as normal for him and has somehow fought off the Pollexfens' attempts to take him over.

A normal life without me; I have disappeared from those moments in his day when I broke into his routine with Nurse and Effie. First Papa goes, then Mummie. Or perhaps he doesn't see it like that. We came, we went, both of us; perhaps he just waits for us to come again. Time buckles and expands. For a little boy the future is two minutes from now and for me the future is three days and no further. That will be the appearance on Monday in the Magistrates' court when they will ask for bail, principally because of Peter, and I shall perhaps be able to go home.

Felix Plews is not optimistic; he is naturally pessimistic about everything. But I hope and I have faith in him to achieve it. I think he likes me. Which is rare. Men usually are attracted to me or dislike me, but they don't just like. Only dear Jono and that because of Charles. He has arranged things here, Felix Plews, obtaining books, paper and pencils for me, explaining to me what I may and may not expect, in some things more than I imagined, for I expected nothing.

Monday 3rd August 1925

The committal proceedings. No bail. I am here until I am

tried and when that will be will depend on the preparation of both prosecution and defence. So I am back here and the way out is now so terrifying to look at that I cannot bear to do it.

Sunday 16th August 1925

I don't think they can prove I murdered George. They just think I am the most likely person to have done it. It is a recognition, if covert, that logically life without George would be better than life with him and so anyone in my position would want to get rid of him. And empirically it is true. Life without George was better. Those six weeks between the funeral and my arrest were the best in my married life. The fear that what did happen might happen was ever present, but I did not really believe it and was happy. I did not think that those fools James and Starling would find out who really did it; neither did I think, until Felix Plews warned me, that they would actually fabricate a case against me. And life at Laughton at that time was life with the minor irritations and the major flaw removed.

Monday 24th August 1925

Felix Plews today brought to meet me the barrister whom he has engaged. The courts do not sit in August; no one is in London in August; I presume crime is not committed in August, as everyone who is anyone goes away. Felix Plews has said nothing about his own dedication to duty in working on my behalf in the holiday month for I don't think he regards it as anything extraordinary. Certainly I have never heard of him taking a holiday in any circumstances. He emphasised his fisherman skill in capturing for me a fine salmon like Hector Wallace.

Wallace is a Scotsman who has abandoned his national law for the capital, a kind of colonial too; and young, for a lawyer, that is to say in his forties. He has a firm-fleshed skin like an apple and very dark-brown eyes under tailored black eyebrows. He went through the points to be discussed in an impersonal businesslike fashion so it was almost possible to believe we were discussing somebody else's case. Then towards the end of our interview he said, have you any idea who murdered your husband, and when I said, none, he insisted, come, come, you know who was there that weekend, you know the circumstances of your husband's life, you must have some notion, a suspicion. I remained silent. Even privately, he went on, you must have speculated. You know you did not do it, so who did? Do you not say to yourself, who should be here in my place? I said, I do not think in that way. I find it hard enough to make myself understand that George is really dead. I cannot connect his death with any possible action by anyone I know.

I could see that he was becoming irritated; he was writing me down as a stupid woman who could not even be relied on to help herself. He said, you know, you must not see this in childish terms of telling tales on your friends. In any case, I am not the police and can do nothing to inculpate them. It is simply a little informal speculation that would provide me with a better understanding, a sense of direction within your story. I said, I cannot see why anyone, except me of course, would want to murder George. He saw the joke, but did not like it and his annoyance became obvious. Madam, he said, I have the job of protecting you and I see it is not only from the prosecution but from yourself. You do not yet seem to have come to a proper realisation of what will happen to you if I fail. You will be hanged and that will be that. Your beauty, your charm, your position will not save you. I shall lose a case and you your life, so I suggest you give me your co-operation.

I wanted to say nothing more, simply to refuse to speak, but I could see the agitation on poor Felix Plews's flabby, florid face. He had been so sure that this was the man we should have, so delighted to have engaged him that I agreed to discuss who might or might not have killed George. We got no further than we had already but the semblance of exchange, the giving of information, which amounted to nothing, seemed to please them both. For me, dressing up Jono or Pia in the role of a poisoner was more fantastic and time-wasting than any photographic session could ever have been. It bore no relation to reality whatsoever.

Eventually they went away, leaving me very depressed. I have behaved very stupidly, alienated the man whom it is most important I should impress, attract, have on my side, something I have never found difficult to do in the past, if I set my mind to it. The reality of what has happened still seems no stronger. I hang in limbo, in a purgatory waiting for judgement. It is a form of sleep walking. Nothing has any meaning or consequence, at least not ones I can face. I have to shut my mind to his words, if I fail, you will be hanged and that will be that.

Friday 28th August 1925

I have the right to receive letters but few people write to me. What can you say to a friend charged with her husband's murder, even if she protests her innocence; she would be bound to do that in any case. They must feel as I do when friends admire my books or my photographs. How can they say anything else? So what is the value of their praise? I would find it difficult myself; I try to put myself in their places and write, the weather is good; the raspberry crop is delicious. It is irrelevant to someone in gaol who may soon be dead. Pia does not write. I have news of Peter through Felix Plews who has struck up a friendship with Nurse. He clearly sits through hours of her inconsequential stories of Peter's doings in order to be able to tell me. But Pia does not write. Why does she not write? Can she believe me guilty?

Tuesday 8th September 1925

The police and Mr Wallace between them have convinced me. I must have done it. He said to me today, you seem to be working on the hypothesis that a random poisoner, who drops photographic chemicals in any glass of whisky that he happens upon, roams the English countryside. I tried, this time with conviction, to tell him that I do not know; I have no hypothesis, I just live with not knowing, like not believing in God, but not being convinced he does not exist. One has to live with ignorance. He is of course Calvinist and was truly shocked.

Wednesday 9th September 1925

However random and godless the world, I realise I have always secretly believed since childhood that my life had a purpose. It was moving towards an end, to achieve something. I keep looking back now to see if the signposts pointed here in a way I did not recognise when I passed them. I suddenly remembered just as I was falling asleep last night the hanged cat at Keelers Creek. The farmhand's boy whom I played with for the first week of the holiday whom I later avoided when he had appalled me with the carcass of a koala he had shot. He only wanted to impress, I see now, but I would have nothing more to do with him. So he killed the kitten I had petted and adopted as my own. He wrung its neck and then hung it on a gibbet in front of my window in revenge. What does that mean?

Monday 30th November 1925

It is impossible to tell what they think, the judge and the jury. Today was the day of the prosecution and I had to sit and listen to my life turned into a moral tale of someone whose sole purpose was to obtain a fortune by marriage or murder. The facts were not wrong in themselves, only that the interpretation of them or of the motivation that led to each action was as black as it could be. I could hardly believe the crass prejudices, that an Australian who marries an English gentleman, for example, must be poor and a fortune hunter.

The prosecutor is a passionless man called Angell; this I take as a bad omen. Right must be on his side. I would have hired him myself if I had known there existed a barrister with such a name. He recounts my ambition, my wiles, with the clear, unshocked tones of a man who has seen much wickedness and is above it all.

When he began to call his witnesses I saw another kind of accusation. Mrs Everett came into the witness box and, though she would not look at me, I saw she hated me. She described Gaëtan's visit as if he and George were fighting duels. Where does such hatred come from, and such imagination? She drew herself in as she spoke, priding herself on her pure conscience, poor but honest, plain but truthful. We all know that Beauty means Trouble; Handsome is as Handsome does. At the door as I came out was a crush of people. The police had to surround me to push through the crowd to the vehicle to take me to the cells. I did not know what they wanted: to gape at, to touch a monster? As I bent to get in, someone spat at me. In the evening there was a letter waiting for me from Nurse, enclosing one from Peter. He had drawn another snake.

There is a gap in A.D. Millard's diaries between 1942 when her son was killed in France and 1947. Though the reason for her ceasing to write is clear, what motivated her to resume on 9th April 1947 is not known.

Wednesday 9th April 1947

Rain during the night, mist in the early morning.
Narcissus on the south lawn cream and lemon at their best.
Temperature forty at eight a.m., rose to forty-nine in the afternoon.
Worked in kitchen garden a.m.
Sprayed apple and pear trees.

Monday 14th October 1991

Today I read Pia's obituary. She died last week and now it is too late. I cannot any longer debate whether or not to write to her. Every time I thought of doing so my will failed. Why should she care now? Perhaps she knew all along, as Arkadi did. Perhaps she guessed, as I think Jono must have done; his gift of Arkadi's books was so odd, so pointed, sent by his friend from America, when I had not seen him for so long. Arkadi had an extraordinarily acute observation for someone who seemed so unworldly and so hopelessly impractical. He would never be able to describe a woman's dress or the colour of the curtains or even what he had eaten for lunch, yet he had a capacity to follow someone's mind as it searched for a way out. I wonder when he knew, as that story showed that he did. At once or only long afterwards, with a godlike gaze seeing all in one comprehending vision, or by work, by piecing together all he could find out? He did not tell Pia, certainly. Now, after all these years, with Pia dead, I feel that the most important thing is that Edith should know.

4

Pia Novikoff's Testimony

Simon telephoned one afternoon to ask if he could stay with Helena for two nights. 'Can I use your spare bedroom?' was how he put it. 'I'm going to be a bit busy in the next couple of days.'

The single guest bedroom in the basement of her little house was as dark and uninviting as Helena could make it. Visitors limited her freedom. Now that most of her friends were married with families, she was rarely called upon to provide them with accommodation.

'I'll take you out to dinner to talk about the Great-aunt,' Simon had promised, without elaborating on what was suddenly causing his busyness. Helena agreed to his staying, mainly out of surprise at having been asked. As soon as she put down the receiver, she dialled Isobel's work number to ask what was going on. Ms Brunskill was in a meeting, she was told and after that she did not have time to try again. Simon offered no further explanation for his need for a bed in London and, since Helena could not take up his offer of dinner, she had no opportunity to question him.

On the second morning of his stay Simon was at the

dining-room table with muesli, a croissant, real coffee and a copy of *The Times* as Helena was gathering her keys and briefcase to leave. It occurred to her that her guest must have acquired all the ingredients for the meal himself, as she certainly had not bought them. 'I hope you were comfortable, Simon,' she said guiltily.

'Oh, yes, thank you. Your cleaning lady does a very good job.' Helena did wonder for a second what João could have done well, but lacked the interest to enquire.

'And is everything OK?' She peered inside her briefcase to check she had put in an umbrella.

'Yes, thanks.'

'And your meetings?'

'Meetings? Oh, yes, fine. Oh, Helena, something that might interest you, or perhaps Marta.'

'Marta?'

'About the Great-aunt,' Simon said patiently. 'Anyway. Yesterday I was walking along one of those streets between Piccadilly and Regent Street and I saw an exhibition that you might like. Pia Novikoff, the friend of the Great-aunt's. I didn't have time to go round it myself. You might find a portrait of the Great-aunt in youth there or something.'

'Pia Novikoff,' Helena repeated slowly. 'You don't know which gallery? Never mind, I can find it.'

'Yes, I took a card. Here, keep it.'

'Many thanks. I'll go this weekend. Simon, I must dash. Love to Isobel.'

'Of course. Does the cleaning lady come again today? Shall I leave the keys with her?'

'No, not today. Post them through the letter box.'

Helena gave the gallery's card to Sophie, her secretary, asking her to find out about the Novikoff exhibition and its opening times. She must, she told herself, make a plan.

Going to exhibitions of Pia Novikoff's paintings and reading about the wild and successful life of Fanny Pollexfen did not get her any closer to the core of Great-aunt Fox's life, the murder of her husband. It was all very interesting; it fleshed out her past before the Foxes; it reminded her, and having just undergone her birthday she was ready for such reminders, that the old had not always been old and that she would not always be young; but it was essentially peripheral.

One good thing about Simon's visit was that the presence had not manifested itself, or if it had, its fidgeting with her things, moving her books and pictures, touching her clothes in cupboards, went unnoticed in the minor disturbance of his presence.

As she was leaving for lunch Sophie put her head around Helena's door. 'You'll have to take an afternoon off.'

'Do I look that bad?'

'If you want to see that exhibition. People who buy pictures don't work and they go to the country at weekends, so the gallery is only open from ten to six on weekdays, or by special arrangement. Do you want a special arrangement?'

'No, thanks. I'll organise myself.'

The gallery was empty at five thirty on Friday evening when she entered, empty even of a pretty girl to offer a catalogue and ask her to sign a visitors' book. Helena began by walking round the first room which ran back a long way from the street. A spiral staircase descended to another hall below. Her eyes swept the walls. She did not know what she had been expecting or what she had hoped to find: whatever it was, she did not recognise it. The first works were drawings, still lifes and nudes, academic, student works; then a few landscapes, more nudes, in oils this time, the colours thick and dark. She picked her way down the stairs and went into the centre of the lower room hoping for a painting to stand out from the rest.

'Were you looking for something in particular?' The question which made her start came from the far corner where an elderly Indian was seated in a low leather chair.

'No, not really, or at least yes. I am looking for work she was doing in the mid-Twenties.'

The Indian got up awkwardly. He was tall and very thin with long, thick, white hair, pale skin and dark circles around his eyes. 'At that stage she was still selling her work. You've seen some other canvases from that time? Perhaps you collect them?'

'No, I haven't. I don't collect . . .' She suddenly realised that the paintings in the dining-room at Ingthorpe were Novikoffs; the style, the colours were the same as those she could see around her. 'Oh dear, I sound quite incoherent. I think I have just inherited some from my great-aunt and I wanted to know about the painter. I'd never heard of her before.'

'Few people have. She hasn't had an exhibition for over fifty years. Everyone thought she was dead, if they thought of her at all. She was a very remarkable painter and you should hang on to your paintings. They'll be worth a lot, if that's what interests you.'

'It's more her life than her work or its value that interests me.'

'Really? They are of course inseparable, in her more than in many painters. Unlike many artists working in her lifetime she was not concerned with abstraction; she did not paint myths or religious subjects, never fantasy. She painted what she could see, mostly the people around her. Look at this one.' He led her to a painting near the staircase. 'It's a good example of her style in the Forties and shows why it has been unfashionable for the whole of this century. She had the gift of an eye that saw the minutest detail from which she could not escape. It is detail of surface rendered with feeling for that surface itself, not with thought of its meaning. In selecting her subjects and then painting them in this way she achieved an astonishing and painful psychological clarity. Don't you find?'

Helena looked at the small painting of the torso of a naked child, rendered in flat, unemotional tones. It was unsentimental, even cruel. The child, a boy, was not attractive.

'He looks as if he has suffered,' the Indian was saying. 'He has been abandoned and knows that his rejection was because of his unworthiness.'

'Yes?' Helena bent close, stepped back. The painting, isolated from its companions by the Indian's choice, suddenly became compelling. 'She painted very sparingly, very drily. You can see the amazingly detailed vision, painted so lightly with so little.' He paused. 'You're not interested in this technical stuff, are you?'

'Not really. I'm interested in her.' Something about the child suddenly struck her. 'It's you, isn't it?' she said.

The Indian ignored her question. 'You need a catalogue to start with. Did they give you one?'

'There was no one there.'

'Oh no, I'm in charge, I remember.' He began to climb the stairs arthritically. 'The catalogue will tell you about her life. What do you want to know?'

'I want to know about her marriage to Arkadi Novikoff, her life, her friendships in the 1920s.'

The Indian walked across to the glass entrance and taking a key from the table drawer he locked it. 'I don't think I want anyone else today; we don't want to be interrupted.'

Helena made a note of where he dropped the key on the

desk. He collected a catalogue from a pile and hobbled over to a couple of uncomfortable-looking chairs.

'Where shall we start? I'll tell you about her and then you can ask me questions. The first thing you should know is that she was a great artist.' He sank down awkwardly and gazed with his melancholy, encircled eyes at Helena standing above him. 'Sit down. This is what you need.' He slapped the glossy brochure on his lap. 'But you need me even more. I wrote it. Everything there is to know about her, I know. I'm her son.'

Helena was startled. 'I didn't know she . . .' she began.

'She didn't. She had no children of her own. She adopted me in 1941 when I was twelve, a complicated story. I won't bore you with it. I just tell you I am her son as provenance or introduction. Look.' On the inside cover was a small photograph. Helena had time to peer at the pictures and name, Dr Ananda Ramasubramaniam, before he drew it back.

'Let me tell you her story. An outline. Her personality is much more complex. I couldn't tell you about that in under a week. Born 1895, died 1991. Father writer, mother half Italian, an amateur painter. Three brothers died in the First World War. She trained at the Slade in its great days. Settled in the 1920s in Oxfordshire where she lived for the rest of her life. Married Arkadi Novikoff in 1923, Russian-Jewish writer, separated from him in 1926. Exhibitions in London and Paris.' He was turning the pages of his catalogue as he spoke. 'The first in 1928, then in the Thirties, 1933, 1935, 1939. After that, nothing. She painted on commission after the war and there were a few discriminating people who knew her work, but she fell out of fashion and would not change for new fads. She wouldn't exhibit any more, she just painted and painted and put her work in a barn and so it has come to me.'

Helena began to feel that she could be sitting in the gallery all night while the son discoursed on his mother's genius. She must take his knowledge in hand.

'My interest is very specific,' she interrupted him. 'It concerns her friendship from roughly 1914 to 1925 or 1926 with my great-aunt who was A.D. Millard, the photographer, whose married name was Diana Pollexfen.'

'Ah yes, the murderess.'

'No.' Helena was surprised at her emphasis and the surge of indignation that accompanied it. 'Why do you say that? She was acquitted of murder.'

'So you are looking to vindicate your aunt. That's why you've come?'

'Yes, that's the reason. It looks as if you won't be able to help me.'

'It depends whether you want the truth, or at least the truth as Pia saw it. I have not been into that episode in great detail because I concentrate on her work, but I can tell you that she did not speak kindly of your aunt. Not that she spoke of her often and it was all long before my time, you understand. And she never talked of it voluntarily because it was all connected with the failure of her marriage with Novikoff. I only really learned a bit about it five years ago when I decided that one day I would write the biography of the truly extraordinary woman who was my mother. I then began to question her, to take notes. Sometimes she would answer me, sometimes not. It took me years to extract the story of her life from her.' He paused. 'And you? Are you doing the same thing: going to mount a retrospective of your aunt's work, writing a biography? She was another extraordinary woman, not good, not maternal, not warm, like Mama Pia, another type of woman altogether.'

'How can you say this? You know nothing about her. If

you could see her photographs of her son, for example.'

He pounced. 'So you have unpublished works, papers, letters?'

'My great-aunt left her photographic collection to the V & A.'

He looked at her sideways. 'And papers, correspondence, diaries, stuff like that?'

'She has only just died; I haven't looked through everything yet.' Helena reflected that evasion was an instinct with her. Then she relented. 'Possibly.'

'She didn't still live in that house, Laughton, where it all happened?'

'Yes, I own it now.'

'Well, well. She was like Pia, never moved, clung to what she had. I'm still in my mother's house, not on the same scale as yours, though. Well, my dear, perhaps we can do business?'

'What have you to offer?'

'Oh, I have letters, I certainly have letters from A.D. Millard; I have notes of my conversations with Pia. I have a lot that could interest you.'

'What about the murder?'

'The murder is peripheral to me; yes, I suppose the murder comes into it.'

'I have some journals,' Helena admitted.

'Diaries, covering what years?'

'Her life.'

'Her life? Does Pia figure?'

'Yes. As a friend rather than as a painter. There are photographs too.'

Dr Ramasubramaniam was fumbling in the breast pocket of his rumpled suit, to pull out a diary. 'You must come to see me in Oxfordshire, bringing something with you, of course. Everything you have. And your paintings, or photographs of them. I'd like to see them too. When can you make it? Monday, say?'

'It'll have to be next weekend. I can see it's no good coming to you hoping for proof of my great-aunt's innocence, so let me start now by asking one thing. What ended it? Why did they never see one another or communicate after the trial?'

'Murder was not something Pia would have approved of, even in a close friend.'

'She was innocent. She was proved innocent.'

'Though everyone thought she was guilty. She got away with it by being rich enough to buy a good counsel. I'm sorry. I agree it is strange, for Pia was the most loyal of individuals. I've never looked at that time with the murder as the central event. And A.D. Millard I have only thought of in connection with her influence on the painting. Look here.' He turned through his catalogue. 'It's only a sentence but it condenses years of thought.' He held the book up at some distance and read, almost declaimed, ' "In the immediate post-World War One period photography was an important influence on Pia Novikoff's development. While she rejected the 'artistic' effects of the Photo-Secessionists, the starkness of Paul Strand and the early A.D. Millard showed her the way in which bareness and apparent lack of commentary could strip down a portrait to its psychological basics . . ." ' He put it down abruptly and picked up the diary. 'What about a week tomorrow?'

Helena agreed the date provisionally, explaining that she would come with a cousin who was working on the subject with her, and would confirm the arrangement.

Dr Ramasubramaniam rose briskly. 'What luck, what luck. It was one of the eventualities which I hoped for when I arranged this exhibition, that further information would emerge and so it has. Now where . . .?'

Helena found the key for him and inserted it into the lock.

'Nervous of the mad professor, were you?' he said shrewdly. 'Don't worry, my dear, I'm harmless, comparatively.'

Helena rang Marta to see if she were free to join the expedition to Oxfordshire. 'It could be quite fun,' she wheedled when she sensed the hesitation at the other end of the line as Marta sorted through the weekend plans of the rest of the family. 'We could go out to lunch somewhere on the way. I mean somewhere delicious, not a pub.'

Whether she was drawn by the lunch to be eaten or the information to be gained Marta agreed. 'I must say I should like to meet Dr Ramasubramaniam.'

'You know of him, then?'

'Of course I do. Have you never heard of him? You are so blinkered, Helena. You think only of your work and a very narrow area of law at that. You have no interest in the wider worlds of art of politics or learning generally. You really should break out a little bit.'

Like everybody else, Helena considered that she was adequately cultivated and so was not annoyed by Marta's strictures, regarding them as having more to do with Marta than herself. 'So who is he, then? Instruct me.'

'He is an academic; originally, I think, a philosopher and historian; now he has become a sort of media pundit on modern society and culture. Deracinated Indian, very critical of India so they hate him in the subcontinent. He writes very provoking and critical books about western civilisation, too, so of course in our masochism we love him. Though the fact that he is deeply conservative makes the left find him hard to deal with. A sort of *enfant terrible* and media star combined.'

'It seems he was Pia Novikoff's adopted son. She would not sell or exhibit during her lifetime and he is determined to get recognition for her now.'

'He will certainly get her noticed, he is gifted for that. Whether that makes her a great painter is another matter.'

The directions to High Fold, as given to Helena over the telephone when she confirmed the meeting for the following Saturday, were complex and involuted, and so seemed the last few miles of the journey as they drove down narrower and narrower lanes guided by Marta reading out Helena's dictated notes. They had been invited for two o'clock and had abandoned plans for lunch other than a sandwich, eaten looking over a view of superb trees from the top of a whale-backed hill. They drove on, their faith failing them as they entered a large, deserted, modern farmyard, and only the word of a child on a pony encouraged them to take an unmetalled track which mounted the abrupt hillside with a refreshing directness of attack to which Helena and her car were unaccustomed. They eventually drew up beside a cottage built just below the brow of a hill with a wild garden in front and an orchard of curled and lichened fruit trees behind.

The front door which they had seen from the track faced the garden and the valley, and was entirely inaccessible. They approached and parked at the back of the house which consisted of a muddle of descending roofs of porches and outbuildings. Dr Ramasubramaniam, alert to their arrival, came out to meet them and to lead them inside.

As they stepped into the kitchen, Helena saw that the cottage, for more than sixty years the home of an unworldly woman, though it had been lovingly cared for, was untouched by the late twentieth century. The black-leaded range, the ceramic sink, the wooden table were authentically ancient with the wear of years to prove it. If Pia Novikoff had eschewed a lavish use of colour in her portraits, she used it plentifully in her decoration. They passed through a frescoed dining-room into a large living-room in which the frank colours of the oriental rugs layered on floor, chairs, table and benches competed with vibrant coral walls hung with as many paintings as could be unreasonably jigsawed together. Even the beams and cupboard doors were ornamented. Amid this anarchy of colour they sat down; Helena displaced a huge Burmese cat with a round, belligerent face, as she dropped into a kelim-draped chair which oozed stuffing from a wound below the arm rest.

Ramasubramaniam's papers and books were arranged in stacks on the floor, stalagmites of learning. In place of honour on the rug in front of an ottoman were several shoe boxes filled with file cards and bundles of letters tied with coloured tape. It appeared that these were put out rather as a pedlar might display one or two of his more enticing goods to trap his customers' attention. The image of the bazaar, aroused by the colour and the low divans laden with cushions on which they were invited to sit, was reinforced by Dr Ramasubramaniam himself who saw the core of the meeting, the exchange of information, as a trading operation.

There had been some disagreement between Marta and Helena about what and how much should be offered to the long R as Marta called him. Helena had suggested handing over the photographs and photocopies of the journals which made reference to the Novikoffs, especially for the period up to and just after Pollexfen's death. Marta was much more cautious. Though agreeing to do the photo-copying and to taking the copies with them, she wanted to be much more selective.

'We don't know what use he'll make of them.'

'Of course we don't. We can't expect to vet his work.'

'I think we should try to find out his general line and choose what we hand over to him.'

In the end they agreed to test the atmosphere of their meeting before giving everything unreservedly.

Dr Ramasubramaniam displayed a similar caution. He welcomed them with enthusiasm, but when he went back to the kitchen to make some coffee he returned hastily to see if they had started to examine his wares without his supervision. He picked up one bundle and placed it on the mantelshelf while he brought in three mugs of coffee and an open packet of ginger biscuits on a tray. He settled himself in what was clearly his own nest, an armchair which bulged and sagged like uncorseted female flesh, an impression strengthened by the faded chintz cover, spattered with dim roses like an old summer frock.

Marta leaned forward to take her mug; Helena sat back, nursing hers, content to allow Marta the direction of affairs. That Ramasubramaniam was susceptible to female charm Helena observed in his manner of looking both of them full in the eye, his vivacity, his smile, the pleasure of a man who likes women, perhaps too much for his own good. Marta, who would in theory have scorned the use of her femininity to gain an end, responded instinctively.

She began by ignoring the piles of manuscripts laid out for them, the folders of photocopies in her bag, and asked, 'Before we start on Diana and Pia, do tell us how you came to be adopted.'

The old advice, Helena thought, is always the best. Ask a man to talk about himself. The link, Ramasubramaniam explained, had been through his father who had read Law at Cambridge and had been a friend of Pia's brothers, Charlie and Francis. He had been caught between his admiration for European culture and his people's desire for independence. He had decided that the latter would not be gained unless he took advantage of the former for his son. He had brought the young Ananda to England in 1939 to enter him at Winchester in September. Trapped by the war, the father had remained in London where he had been killed by the bomb that fell on the Café de Paris. His wife had died when his son was born. Pia had been nominated as the boy's guardian in England, with no thought that she would ever be called upon to do more than appear at school events and make room for him amid her pictures and animals in the holidays. When she asked if she could adopt him formally, he had agreed.

Marta let him speak at length, without interruption, of his adoptive parent, her importance to his intellectual development, before bringing him back to her relationship with A.D. Millard. She produced from her bag some papers, selected as bargaining counters, tempters to be offered at appropriate points in the exchanges.

'We have journals written by Diana, our great-aunt, throughout her life. This entry, you see, is for Christmas 1914 which she spent with your mother's family. There are descriptions and comments on all three brothers, a bit on Pia herself, her mother, Jonothon Pybus, a cousin. Did you know that Charles Yaldwyn was in love with Diana?'

Ramasubramaniam, too, was leaning forward by now, his hands out to take the copy. 'No, no, I didn't know. She really didn't like to talk about A.D. Millard.'

'It was obviously one of those intensely romantic relationships of the very young. Diana was nineteen, Charles must have been about twenty-one. He would have been in his last year at Cambridge if he had not volunteered.'

Ramasubramaniam was reading the paper avidly. He had recognised its purpose and when he had finished he

said, 'If she wrote like this every day you must have a mine
of treasures. Now what have I got for you? I have letters,
of a later date, letters from Diana Pollexfen,' and letters to
and from Arkadi Novikoff which might have a bearing on
what you're interested in. In a general way.' He selected a
letter, already marked with a spill of paper, and passed it
across to Marta. 'That's a letter from Diana Pollexfen
about the birth of her son, asking Pia to be godmother.'

The commerce went on; papers were opened, glanced
at, laid aside on piles, read aloud.

'How they lived,' Marta exclaimed. 'Such contrasts. So
much leisure, so little comfort. No electricity, no central
heating, no running water, and the food. Listen to this:
"Aldous and Maria called this morning and stayed until
after tea. Maynard and James arrived after lunch. They
quarrelled. Mrs B made toad in the hole for lunch.
Fortunately I had bought a cake at Fullers' yesterday when
I went to see Fanny." '

Helena, who had watched, listened and read the various
papers as they passed back and forth, asked, 'And the
rupture of 1926. Was it final? Did you find any sign of their
having renewed their friendship later?'

'No, not at all. As I told you, she was reluctant to speak
about your great-aunt and I don't think they ever made
contact again.'

'It couldn't have been because she thought Diana had
murdered her husband. It sounds so implausible. Pia
Novikoff was the sort of person to defend her friends right
or wrong, wasn't she? Perhaps even more if they were
wrong.'

Dr Ramasubramaniam looked shifty. 'No, it wasn't
because of the murder, I misled you there. It seems that
the murder was an irrelevance as far as she was concerned.
No, the end of the relationship was about something else.

It's very important in Pia's life because it was the root of the ending of her marriage. The timing, coinciding with the trial, was purely chance. The murder was unconnected, as far as I know. Though Diana Pollexfen was not.'

'Diana caused the ending of Pia's marriage? Worse and worse. First they make her a murderess, now a home-wrecker of her best friend,' Marta exclaimed.

'Are you saying that Diana Pollexfen and Arkadi Novikoff had an affair?' Helena asked.

Ramasubramaniam paused. 'It probably has nothing to do with what you want to know . . .' He stopped again.

For years he had not known of Arkadi's existence, had been barely conscious that his adoptive mother had even been married. The opening of the concentration camps in the last months of the war, the newsreels and photographs of the emaciated survivors, had affected Pia grievously. She had not explained to him whom she sought in her frantic attempts through the Red Cross, through Jewish friends, through Army contacts to find out names of returnees from that limbo of horror. Only much later, forty years later, when he at last realised that, as an historian, he had in her memory an archive of a lifetime that he must use in a different, personal history, did he learn that it was her husband she had been seeking. She had discovered Arkadi's arrest in Paris in 1942 and deportation to Dachau. His subsequent history was without detail; his end unrecorded.

It was one long night that she had talked to him about Arkadi Novikoff's fate. In that story of suffering endured, she had retraced her own cruelty to Arkadi and she was able to retell it, marvelling at how hard she had been, how she had been unable to accept imperfection.

At the moment of dawning consciousness at Laughton, she had reproached herself for her naivety, stupidity, blindness, complacency. How had she not seen, or guessed, what had happened? It had not been wilful, or even a subconscious self-blinding. She could not have helped it. She could never see what was not before her eyes. And when she did see it, then she saw everything in its minutest detail.

She had begun to see the weekend that George Pollexfen had died. She was not sure when he was thought to have taken the poison; she always imagined that it had been at the same moment that she had seen Arkadi and Diana together.

They had separately and simultaneously entered the hall, from opposite sides, walking towards one another, without hesitation or embarrassment. Arkadi had paused; Diana had passed him without a check. He had put out his hand which had barely clasped her waist, and fallen away as she moved on. Arkadi had never, in Pia's knowledge, touched Diana beyond the social gesture of a kiss on the cheek, a shake of the hand. Yet that momentary touch implied a physical familiarity reaching far beyond such boundaries. And Diana did not react; her manner spoke of an acceptance of the fact, at the same time as a rejection of his gesture. Her face had not changed its expression and her voice, the light 'Good night, dear Arkadi', could have been overheard by anyone, Pia herself, without shock.

All this Pia had described to her son, sixty years later; still the long, hollow hand, the movement of the fine cotton over skin, remained in her mind's eye.

She remembered, too, that at first she had not understood what she had seen. It seemed that Arkadi was asking and Diana rejecting; he was in love with her; she was refusing him. But there was a lack of passion in both of them that had puzzled her as she lay, feigning sleep so that she should not have to speak to Arkadi, trying to decide which of them to ask.

In the morning she had decided she would speak to Diana. She felt infinitely less afraid of causing damage to their friendship than to her marriage; ultimately it mattered less and it was also more robust. She could confess the most outrageous fears and Diana would not be moved.

The words were never spoken, the questions never asked, that day or later. George Pollexfen's body, as stiff in death as he was obdurate in life, had inserted itself between Diana and the accusation, and it was several days later that Arkadi had forced the question from her.

They had dined with some friends in Kensington Square and were walking back to Chelsea after midnight. He had seen her perturbation of mind and attributed it to that sprawled figure at the end of the apple walk.

He put his arm around her shoulders and said, 'It was a terrible shock for you, my angel.'

Pia had halted under a street light in Old Church Street. 'It was a shock but not the shock you are thinking of. It was before that. I have to ask you, Arkadi, about you and Diana.'

As Pia had told the story to her son she had broken off there, her knobbed hand smoothing back a crinkled tress from her forehead with a paint-dabbed knuckle.

'If I had ever given you advice, Ananda, the one thing I would have said is: don't speak. Understand; say nothing. Words are weapons; they wound; they can never be taken back and, even when they heal, they leave a scar. Understanding evolves silently. I understood the essential between Diana and Arkadi in the one gesture I had seen. I did not need to know more. And when I did know the truth, which was not what I imagined it to be, I said things that could not be forgiven.'

What she had imagined, she explained to her son, was the most banal and obvious interpretation. Diana and Arkadi were in love, they were sleeping with one another. At that time she was tortured by uncertainty, she wanted proof, not ocular proof, which she thought she had, but intellectual proof, proof in so many words.

'I wanted to know and I wanted Arkadi. Even then common sense told me that I was more likely to keep Arkadi if I gave up the desire for proof, but I could not stop myself. That moment under the lamp on Old Church Street is the greatest regret of my life. Have you ever seen Arkadi? I put away my paintings of him. They're somewhere in the barn. I may get them out now to show you. He had a face of great delicacy, intelligence, humour, but his strengths were his weaknesses. He was too humane, respecting the autonomy of others, accepting what they said when they did not mean what they said. What I wanted him to say, what I was prepared for him to say was, "Yes, I'm having an affair with Diana. That's how it is. There's nothing you can do about it," and I would have cried and reproached him and he would have stayed with me and I would have had the moral upper hand. Oh, the ease of banal adultery. It wasn't that at all.'

As she said, 'You and Diana' to Arkadi, Pia had seen in his eyes a relief, a recognition that she knew.

'How . . .?' was all he said.

Pia, speaking with great speed, described the hand touching Diana's passing form at Laughton Hall. He made no attempt to deny the act or its meaning.

'But it is not what you think, Pia, and it has no bearing on us at all.' And, fatally, Arkadi told the truth. 'What it came down to was this.'

Pia had stooped forward to put more logs on the fire

and the warm light had thrown her features into sharp chiaroscuro.

'Arkadi and Diana had fallen in love when they first met in London at the end of the war, the first one, I get so muddled nowadays. Diana had refused to marry him, but she slept with him. Arkadi was really very conventional and this should have shown him that he was dealing with someone who was able to ignore the rules and do what she wanted.'

Ramasubramaniam turned to Helena. 'I think this is why I said "the murderess". Pia never said that Diana Pollexfen killed her husband, what she said was . . .' He consulted the notes that were scribbled on little cards contained in one of the shoe boxes on his lap. ' ". . . Diana didn't give a damn. I was always afraid of her, a little, for that reason. You never knew what she might do or say. She never hesitated out of regard for other people's sensibilities. She had a heart like a diamond." '

'Do go on,' Marta urged Ramasubramaniam. 'What did Arkadi reveal that was so terrible? If your mother was prepared to accept infidelity, what was it that she could not accept?'

Ramasubramaniam sighed, hesitated. 'I wonder if I shall be able to make you understand. When she told me she was completely convincing.'

It all went back to that visit to Paris in 1919. Diana had been to the battlefields to take photographs and then went to Paris where she had lived until August 1914. She installed herself in a little hotel in rue des Sts Pères. Arkadi on impulse had followed her, commandeering a camp bed in the minute flat of a refugee cousin in the Sixteenth Arrondissement. He waited for whenever Diana would give him an hour or a minute, lingering with a newspaper and a glass of wine in the café next to her hotel where she would join him. He had abandoned his policy of taking what she would give while waiting for a change of heart. One evening in a little restaurant in a street he would avoid for the rest of his life, he attempted to force a desired future.

He did not say as much to Pia as he confessed under the plane tree in Old Church Street; nevertheless she understood that if he had done things differently he might have won. He lost. They quarrelled. Diana told him with a fierce coldness that she would never marry him because he could not support her and she was not going to support him: here she did not mean financially. She would take on the world, marry a man in the world. She must have money, and more than money, a place, a role. And Arkadi accepted what she said.

'Pia', said Ramasubramaniam, 'was revolted. She was revolted by Diana's cold-hearted choice of the world. She had not much liked her friend's marriage, but she had excused it to herself with the thought that love was inexplicable and if it had led Diana to marry a blockhead like Pollexfen this had to be accepted. That she had married a blockhead like Pollexfen merely for his money and position was unforgivable. She could not forgive Arkadi, either, for his defeat, his acceptance of what Diana had said, for still loving her, for taking herself, Pia, as second best, Diana's friend. You can see her nature here: idealism and romanticism which are hardly of this world, but entirely of hers; totally uncompromising.'

In the silence that followed, the Burmese which had been sitting in front of the fireplace, as if one of the audience of his dead mistress's past, yawned and lashed its tail. Marta was scribbling furiously.

'This comes from your conversations with her? Nothing in the letters or papers?'

'No, no letters to Arkadi were recoverable, of course. I found none from him later than 1925. She told me all this one night, here. We sat until three or four in the morning. I understood; it seemed quite reasonable to behave as she did, to cast off her husband for his failure with another woman. It was only afterwards I thought about that poor sod caught between the two of them . . .'

Helena was reflecting that the actions of Pia and Arkadi were not so much incomprehensible as alien. She would have accepted where Pia resisted and resisted where Arkadi accepted. 'I wonder if Diana, too, tried to find Arkadi at the end of the war or even earlier,' she said. 'I must look in the diaries for that period.'

Marta looked up at this. 'I think she probably did. In fact, I have even wondered whether Peter's death in France in 1942 was not connected with Arkadi. There are several letters from Arkadi Novikoff among the Great-aunt's papers, written from Paris in the Thirties. This brings Arkadi into the front rank of possible murderers,' Marta commented. 'I had been concentrating on the Frenchman.'

Ramasubramaniam leaned back in his chair, sprawling like a child in his mother's lap, gazing up at the smoke-grimed ceiling. He took a fragment of biscuit from the arm of his chair and crammed it into his mouth as he talked. Crumbs gathered at the corners of his lips. 'I didn't know Arkadi. I didn't even know of his existence until years after his death, but I can tell you he was a herbivore.' There was a pause. Seeing that they were not going to question him, he made the definition unasked. 'The herbivores, intellectuals, writers, the middle-class liberals, Brahmins, are the natural prey of the carnivores, the fierce, ruthless, the upper classes, Kshatriyas. They're not distributed in the population by class alone, of course; they're defined by temperament. Historically, there is a lot in what I say. I did some work on the ecology of nomads and it has been found that meat-eaters, which is what pastoral people always are, consume a high level of tryptophan in their diet that is necessary for the manufacture of serotonin which acts as a neurotransmitter to the parts of the brain that control aggression. So there may be something in the theory of martial races after all. You should read my book on the Golden Horde. Poor Arkadi was certainly a herbivore. I can't see that he would have the, what? – the energy or the detachment to have killed someone. He was probably too profoundly moral as well.'

'Pah.' Marta made a harsh little Scandinavian sound of disagreement. 'Your psychology is nonsense. Murder can as easily be the action of the weak driven to the limit as the violence of the strong. Who is to say who would or would not do such a thing? In any case I would have thought a poisoning was herbivore murder, done at a distance, unwitnessed by the murderer, very theoretical. So your reasoning works as well for me as against me. However, I still keep my Frenchman in mind. I feel he may have been a carnivore.'

'And who is your Frenchman?'

'A certain Gaëtan du Breuilh de Cantegnac who was a friend of Diana Pollexfen and was present at Laughton Hall on the weekend of the murder. The accounts of the trial and the diaries, you'll see, suggest that he did not get on well with George Pollexfen.'

'Ah, yes, I know of him. He died a long time ago, just after the war or in the early Fifties. His wife used to write to Pia. Have you spoken to her?'

This time both Helena and Marta reacted satisfactorily.

'Spoken to her? She's still alive?'

'Yes, at least she was last year.' His bargaining instinct told him that he had come across an item of value and he immediately withdrew it a little. 'Now we are being side-tracked. We ought to return to our papers.'

'Have you met her? How old is she?'

'They are all a great age, these old women. She could go at any time. I had a letter from her on Pia's death, written in a very shaky hand admittedly, with every sign that she was in good mental form.'

'And you have her address?'

'Oh yes, I have her address.'

Marta and Ramasubramaniam began their trade in earnest at this point. Helena could see that Marta was willing now to exchange everything. What they were getting in return appeared to be letters, mostly dated earlier than 1925. As Marta handed over her photocopies of the journals, several thick folders-worth, she said, 'And now that address, Dr Ramasubramaniam, of Madame de Cantegnac.'

As they drove away in the evening sunlight, leaving the tall, bowed Indian waving at the back door, Helena glimpsed him in her rear-view mirror, as complacent as the Burmese cat. 'He's had a good afternoon,' she commented. 'He doesn't yet realise how much those early diaries contain about both the Yaldwyn family and the painting, the Slade, everything.'

'Do you think we gave it away?' Marta asked anxiously. She was recovering now from the effect of Ramasubramaniam's personality.

'He got more than we did, more to the point, I mean. We learned a lot in terms of background. It's always that: more about the characters who surrounded the Great-aunt and not about her, or her husband.'

'Madame de Cantegnac is a find. She may have letters,

papers, all kinds of information from her husband.'

'She may have been years younger than him and know nothing about his life before their marriage.'

'Helena, don't be so negative. We're going to Paris to find her.'

'Are we?'

'Yes. And we won't announce ourselves beforehand. That would give her time to decide that she was tired and didn't want to make the effort to face the past. We'll go for a weekend and just ring up, as if we were passing.'

'We'd better find out if she's still alive first.'

'I suppose so. I'll check and then make all the arrangements. What weekends are you free?'

5

Gaëtan de Cantegnac's Testimony

Helena was looking forward to August. It was a time of year when the pressure of work eased and she was usually able to go through the backlog that had accumulated during the months of the spring and summer. That period of comparative calm was always preceded by intense activity as her partners, about to depart for the beaches of the Mediterranean or the hills of Wales, cleared their own desks, finally dropping the troublesome remnants into her in-tray on their last evening in the office.

She herself never made holiday arrangements in advance: she waited to see what Robert's plans would be. In some years no meeting was possible and she had even come to enjoy the quiet and dusty City, to take a perverse pleasure in working through the holiday month. Sometimes, ingenuity and readiness to fly anywhere for a weekend contrived a couple of days somewhere obscure in Europe, one year in Bagni di Lucca, another, most oddly, in Berne, best of all when Robert found a week of his time and she borrowed a friend's villa, of an extreme simplicity, on a Greek island. This year she still did not know what she would be doing and her partners had made the assumption, barely confirming it with her, that she would be at work throughout August. If nothing else, she thought, this year there was Ingthorpe for the weekends. Parliament was due to rise on 26th July. Robert was leaving for France at the beginning of August to join his wife at Avignon at the festival, then to go with friends to their house in the Vaucluse for three weeks. He might be free for three days in Paris at the end of the month.

He would be landing about now and in the official car should make it back to London by ten. Downstairs, her fridge, for once, was full, stacked with the ingredients for dinner without effort, bought on her way home from work. She was waiting for him in the drawing-room, a room of sterile calm entered only by João. She tried to remember when she had last sat there; it must have been when Simon and Isobel, Richard and Marta came, soon after the Great-aunt died and she had decided to find out the truth about George Pollexfen's murder. Opposite her on the other side of the lifeless, gas-fired coals was a little bergère chair which matched the one in which she sat. Its cream linen cushion was concave, as if the presence had been sitting in it. Could it have been enough substance to weigh down a seat? Would ghostly buttocks hollow out a feather cushion? Helena, feeling the madness of metaphysics rising, leapt up and shook out the cushion, smoothing away the signs of where João had rested from his hoovering.

To distract herself she carried up from the basement bedroom one of the Novikoff paintings which she had retrieved from Ingthorpe. She unwrapped it from the bubble paper in which Mary had protected it and walked around trying it out in different positions in the room. It was a little landscape, grey, wintry, empty, which she found very attractive for its monochrome spareness. She propped it on a table and stepped back to admire it. The search for the Great-aunt's past was producing a number of unexpected gains, not least the discovery of these paintings. However, A.D. Millard and Diana Pollexfen remained as elusive as ever. The people who surrounded her had developed flesh and life from the journals, from Ramasubramaniam, from the glimpses of Fanny Pollexfen and Jonothon Pybus caught in published diaries and biographies; the Great-aunt and her relations with her husband were no clearer. There was always a gulf between accounts of the ruthless young adventuress of the 1920s and Helena's own memories of the Great-aunt in old age, in retreat from the world.

The journals which traversed that gulf did nothing to explain it, for as she read extracts from different decades, Helena could not decide whether she was reading an honest account meant for no eyes but the writer's, a work of fiction, or of self-deception. Did anyone keep a diary meaning no one else to read it? She doubted it. It might be written as therapy, a means of objectifying one's life for one's self, but the act of writing, however secret, implied a reader, known or unknown, one day, sooner or later.

Thinking of her own life, she knew she could never write down the most important part of it. A journal that set down the external events, the meetings, lunches, phone calls, drinks, dinners, concerts, would give only a fraction of her life. Even if she noted conversations, thoughts, incidents, the fundamental element could not be mentioned: the way that the world was full of reverberations, the sound of a certain thread of music overheard through an open car window drawn up beside her at traffic lights, a painting they had stood in front of, together, in Florence seen on a poster lying scuffed and discarded in the gutter, even the sight of two teenagers lying entwined on the grass, all of these referred to Robert, a middle-aged man with greying hair and a thickening waist. She could not risk a document so compromising to Robert, whose life as a politician had to appear to fulfil a model unattained by most of the population. Nor could she confess even to herself what she felt and confront, by writing it down, what she was doing.

She tried to judge from her own flinching from a diary what this suggested about Diana's journals. Had she written a diary which omitted the fundamental truth of her life or was she much more courageous than Helena herself? Only in one unexpected aspect did Helena find that her thoughts met those of the Great-aunt in the diaries: her struggle with her husband to be allowed to work.

It was clear from the journals that after her marriage Diana Pollexfen realised that her calculations had been incorrect. She gained a social respectability that she had lacked before; the marginal and insecure colonial had found a place in the centre of English upper-class life, but the price she had to pay was not the one she had been prepared for, a loveless marriage, but the sacrifice of what presumably she had done it for: her photography. The complaints in the diary had shown George Pollexfen's campaign against her work to have been relentless. They had married with different and opposing purposes and had clashed within months of their wedding. Helena, whose career had been a smooth progression from school to partnership in her law firm, began to see the reason for the encouragement she had always received from the Great-aunt. The balance between working and emotional lives was as difficult for her as it had been for Diana Pollexfen and the solution that she had found in Robert sixty-five years later was as unbalanced in its way as the Great-aunt's marriage for status in 1920.

She was coming to think that her cousins were right; her project was futile. The evidence did not lend itself to judgement. It was not possible to make up her mind with any security about what had happened. Understanding the relations between the friends present that June weekend in 1925 was making it no easier to prove the Great-aunt's innocence. Arkadi Novikoff had reason to envy George Pollexfen. Would this drive him, five years after his defeat in love, to poison his rival? It was just possible, but it was certainly not convincing enough to release her from her unease.

The phone rang. She picked up the receiver knowing that cancellation of that evening's meeting was the inevitable import. She composed her voice; never to betray disappointment was a cardinal rule. She was able, therefore, to reply to Marta without a sign of the relief that flooded her.

'You know I can't possibly go to Paris before September. The girls are on holiday from next week and we leave immediately for Sweden, then to Cambridgeshire. And in any case the French are all away in August. There's nobody in Paris at all. So we should put it off, don't you think?'

'I may have to go in any case. But you're right; no one will be there. We'll go later.'

Dr Ramasubramaniam's account of Arkadi and Diana in Paris in 1919 had given her her first opportunity to test the honesty of the Great-aunt's journals. The day after Marta's call she returned to Ingthorpe to closet herself in the Great-aunt's dressing-room, searching for a trace of the relationship which had hitherto escaped her. The idea of the hidden link between Diana and Arkadi haunted her. In her readings of the diaries hitherto Arkadi Novikoff had hardly struck her as an important character. She had seen him simply in terms of Pia's husband. She had now, however, read extensively in the period before Diana's marriage and she told herself she could simply have failed to discover the passages that revealed the link between the two of them. An impatient excitement drove her, too fast, up the A1 towards Ingthorpe. She felt that what she would discover today would provide her with a litmus test for Diana's openness to herself. Yet she doubted whether she would find anything. She did not even note in her diary her next meeting with Robert, superstitiously retaining it only in her memory: the last weekend in August in Paris. Would Diana Pollexfen really have written openly about the man she was said to have loved but refused to marry, a diary that her husband might have found and read?

At Ingthorpe her first hour had to be spent with Mary and she was released only by the latter's need to get on with lunch.

'Very light, Helena. Just a few peas from the garden with bacon and hyssop. And there are a few artichokes which I boiled last night. You go up, dear, and look at your papers. I'll call you about one and we'll have a good chat at lunch.'

Ramasubramaniam's account had placed the visit to Paris in 1919. Helena identified the ledgers covering the period and installed herself on the day bed. The first thing she found was there had been an incision, something she had not previously observed. A whole page, covering a day in March 1919, had been cut away cleanly with a sharp blade. She read with a feverish concentration, skimming the pages until her eye fell on the initials of A.I., Arkadi Izakovitch.

Mary called her at lunch-time and she and Helena sat down together in the kitchen, in front of two plates on each of which reposed an artichoke heart and a huge flat mushroom piled with a grey and green mixture. Lunch was long. While Helena's mind brooded on the diaries upstairs, she gave the forefront of her attention to Mary and her stories of her youngest niece, who was threatening to drop out of university.

'She says what's the use with unemployment and all that.'

Helena, feeling aged, was shocked. 'What's the alternative? Better to be unemployed, if that's really what'll happen, with a degree than without. But she'll find a job; she's so bright, intelligent.'

'It's not so easy. She wants to live in London with her boyfriend and be a model.'

'That's fantasy, Mary. To succeed as a model must be much more difficult than finding a job with a good degree.' She recalled the niece, Elspeth, who had stayed with Mary during her summer holidays. Last year she had been a luscious twenty-year-old, beautiful, but surely not sufficiently anorectic to qualify as a potential model. She had cast blankly lascivious glances at any male within eyeshot and Helena remembered thinking that the demands of nature were so cruel to young women, calling them to find a mate when reason and their parents were telling them to sit exams, find a job.

'She's coming to stay in a week or so. If you're up here then you could talk to her, Helena.'

'I don't think she'll find much in my life to recommend my advice to her.'

'Well, you earn good money at least.'

'Of course I'll talk to her if the occasion arises. But advice never does much good, especially on choices like that. Perhaps her boyfriend will throw her over and she will drown herself in her work to get over it.'

Helena went back to her reading when Mary allowed her

to and did not put the diaries down until around seven when she went out into the garden. The day had been overcast and the skies still hung over the trees in the park.

Her close reading of Diana's journal with Ramasubramaniam's biographical notes about Pia as a touchstone had revealed one thing to her. They were written for a reader: Diana herself. Diana had selected events for recording. She did not omit things in their entirety, but the significance of events was not made apparent to a common reader. Why should they be? The real reader, rereader, was the writer herself to whom the weight of each incident was immediately recalled. It was only by linkage, the juxtaposition of incidents and thoughts that, with some external knowledge, the underlying meaning of events could be read. She suspected that the one excision had related in some unequivocal way to something of Diana's affair with Arkadi and that she had taken it out, perhaps at the time of her marriage, perhaps later, as simply too painful a reminder of what she had rejected in her contempt for sentimental French songs about love and poverty.

August was a dusty, peaceful month. Helena's spirit was soothed by much clearing and cleaning out. At the office her non-urgent tray subsided to the molehill of a few sheets of paper instead of towering as a mountain that threatened to turn into a landslip and engulf her.

At home João had taken his family back to Portugal for the holidays and the substitute he had provided worked with a new broom's fierceness, eradicating all trace of the presence, which, Helena observed, also took its leave in August. This, too, comforted her, convincing her that she had been suffering from a combination of overwork, grief and an overactive imagination and that everything she had noticed that betrayed a presence had been nothing more nor less than João's attempts to prove to her that he really visited the house and cleaned it in her absence.

At Ingthorpe Mary had her nieces to stay and organised them as part of her team to open the gardens which had been the highlight of the Great-aunt's year. She insisted that Helena come for the event and ask to lunch those local gardening worthies who had always been invited. Helena felt the tendrils of habit locking her into the web of Ingthorpe life and wondered again if she would have the courage to break free.

And throughout it all the thought of three days in Paris at the end of the month.

As Marta had pointed out, the chances of finding Madame de Cantegnac in the capital during the holiday month were remote. Nevertheless, Helena prepared papers and photographs of Gaëtan de Cantegnac which she thought would serve as an initial gambit in her approach to the old woman and would nudge her memory, if that were needed, calling up any stories she might have heard of her husband's past. She studied the Frenchman's appearance in Diana's image. He was slight and erect with a head wholly out of proportion with his narrow shoulders: thick, dark hair, long face, melancholy, downward-sloping eyebrows. Beside him stood, half turned away, a woman, much taller than him, stooping as if faintly embarrassed by her height. The thin face was that of Edith Scrafton, the untraceable member of the party that weekend.

With this memento in her bag Helena flew to Paris. In the Place de la Concorde holiday makers in shorts and sandals gazed at the obelisk; not a Parisian was to be seen on the boulevard St Germain; the *boulangeries* displayed *Fermeture Annuelle* signs. The same pleasure that she felt in working at weekends or holidays, Helena felt in coming to Paris in August. She liked the sense that life was going on elsewhere, that she was seeing the secret, the abandoned aspect of the city, like wandering around an empty house when the inhabitants were away. In fact, it was like being the presence in her own house when she was at work: touching the books, opening the cupboards, reading the letters piled on the desk. The presence was her *doppelgänger*, the Great-aunt haunting her niece to whom she had handed on her possessions. Diana Pollexfen had lived that solitary life in the empty house of her murdered husband, always a visitor, someone with a new name. With a conscious effort Helena put the Great-aunt, Ingthorpe, the haunted Chelsea house, out of her mind and paid the taxi that had now stopped in the rue St Simon.

She thought no more about any of these things for the next two days. Life of the surface dropped away and she lived the secret life. Only when Robert had left for London did she bring out her folder of documents about Gaëtan du Breuilh de Cantegnac and look up the address and phone number given to her by Dr Ramasubramaniam.

Her call was answered by a woman whose voice Helena judged as of late middle age, not that of a ninety-year-old. She listened to Helena's explanation and request and then said, 'It is my mother-in-law that you are talking of. I don't know if . . . She is very frail, you know. I'll speak to her. I'm sorry, what did you say your name was? And your great-aunt's?'

Helena hesitated between Diana's surnames. She was not sure whether the name Diana Pollexfen would decide Madame de Cantegnac against seeing her, or whether it would mean nothing to her. In the end Pollexfen seemed the only sensible one to give. If its effects were too clearly negative Marta would curse her. She would have then to try writing. The receiver at the other end was put down and Helena heard high-heeled shoes receding on a wooden floor, a door closing. After some considerable time the sounds were repeated in reverse, the door closed, the shoes tapped closer.

'I'm sorry to have kept you waiting. My mother-in-law will be very pleased to see you. You said you were only here today, so can I suggest this afternoon after lunch, about two. Do you have our address? I must give you the entry code.'

Helena noted the directions for entry to the building in the rue de Grenelle and was about to ring off when the younger Madame de Cantegnac said, 'Maman seemed very excited when she heard of you. Can I just ask you, is it a visit of courtesy or do you have some information to give her? I mean, that is, she is very aged, she should not be shocked, or overstimulated.'

'I have no news to give her. I have some photographs of her husband that I thought she might like to see. My great-aunt, who died recently, was a friend of Monsieur de Cantegnac in the 1920s and I was hoping that your mother-in-law might have information to give me, about, er, the connection between the two families.'

The rue de Grenelle was deserted at five minutes to two, cars parked asymetrically, like cats asleep in the sun. The air lay heavily, trapped in the canyon of the narrow street; the sun shone on the shuttered upper windows of the northern side and Helena, walking in the shade from the Sèvres-Babylone Métro, imagined the drowsy life behind them, replete with lunch and red wine. She found the house she sought without difficulty, its common blue number indicated huge grey doors, their paint peeling. The single bell was marked *Sonnez et Poussez*. She pushed the porter's door set into the *porte-cochère*, and found herself confronted by modern glass doors where she applied the code she had been given. Once inside the building she walked through a cool tunnel leading to a courtyard where a spreading plane tree occupied a central position, its trunk so twisted and gnarled that it must have been planted to give shade from an eighteenth-century sun. She entered a staircase on the far side and took a minuscule lift to the second floor. She had barely touched the bell before the door flew open and she was face to face with a well-kept woman of about sixty.

'Madame de Cantegnac,' she said, holding out her hand. The daughter-in-law had iron-grey hair, cut and set in a stiff protective helmet. The hand that took Helena's was garnished with old-fashioned rings. The younger Madame de Cantegnac had a look of energy and discontent as if the demands made on her had never been enough for her capacity for action.

'Mademoiselle Fox, *bonjour*. Maman is ready to meet you.' Her voice was loud, as if to be overheard. She lowered it, 'Remember, please, what I told you this morning. Not too much excitement. Come this way.'

The house was very old. The hall through which they passed was low, irregular in shape, leading into a drawing-room, also low and long, scattered with little gold chairs arranged in stiff social groups.

'Maman, here is Mademoiselle Fox to see you.'

The golden light, reflected up from the dark, polished floor, distracted Helena's vision for a moment. Then she saw, beside the stone fireplace filled with a pot of white gardenias, lost in a wing chair, the aged Madame de Cantegnac. And recognised her immediately.

'Miss Fox, do come in. Forgive me for not getting up. This wretched hip of mine really cripples me.' They had been speaking French until Madame de Cantegnac used English, the English of an Englishwoman.

Helena approached, shook hands, sat down in the chair

opposite her hostess. The old woman was very bent, the joints of her body at ankle, knee, hip and neck were sharp. She was thin to emaciation and wearing what, for all its skilfully contrived artlessness, could only have been a wig. Beneath it she regarded Helena with hazy, almost colourless, grey eyes, gazing from a face dominated by one feature still recognisable from photographs of sixty-five years ago, a scimitar nose.

'I can see you are surprised,' she said. 'You did not know I was English.' Helena murmured agreement. 'Nor, perhaps, that I, too, was a friend of your great-aunt's.'

'Now that I see you, I know who you are. I did not realise that Edith Scrafton had married Gaëtan de Cantegnac.'

'It was at the Pollexfens' at Laughton Hall that I met my husband. It was the weekend that Diana's husband died. Do you know about that story? And after that I never went there again.'

Helena was rapidly rearranging her ideas of what to ask and what was to be learnt from Edith Scrafton rather than the expected Madame de Cantegnac.

'And when did your great-aunt die?' her hostess continued.

'Earlier this year, in June.'

'Only in June?' She sounded disappointed, though it was hard to know whether it was at lost opportunities for reunion or because her own longevity looked less remarkable. 'She would have been ninety, perhaps. She was certainly younger than me.'

'Ninety-seven.'

'Ninety-seven. I am ninety-eight and in really excellent health. I intend to make at least a hundred.'

'I hope you will.' Helena took out the photographs she had brought, presenting the one of her hostess with her future husband taken by Diana on the terrace at Laughton. Madame de Cantegnac took it and glanced at it briefly.

'Ah yes. The clothes we wore in those days. That cloche hat. This must have been taken in Normandy.'

Helena began to feel that a living witness was not more reliable or helpful than diaries, letters, photographs or American authors.

'Did you stay in contact with my great-aunt after your marriage?' she asked. 'Did she come to see you here in France?'

'I didn't hear from her for a long time after I married. I wrote to her when I heard that Peter had died, after the war. He was a wonderful boy. I met him during the war when he came to get Arkadi out; I didn't have any reply. Then I had a letter quite recently.'

The combination of apparent coherence and real confusion was extremely difficult to deal with, Helena felt.

'The loss of a child. I cannot think of anything worse. It is something you can never ever recover from. It must have been the most terrible thing that ever happened to her.'

Helena was wondering whether to abandon the attempt on Madame de Cantegnac's memory when the old woman said to her sharply, 'And now, why did you want to see me? Young women do not usually spend their time in Paris visiting unknown friends of their dead great-aunts.'

'I don't know what you know about my great-aunt's life after her husband was . . . died. In 1949 she married my great-uncle and when my parents died about fifteen years ago she more or less adopted me. She left me her house and money when she died. The strange thing is that we, that is my family, didn't know anything about her previous life. I was not aware that she had had a son. I had no idea that she was born in Australia. I had never heard about the murder of her husband.'

'And you wanted to find out what I knew about her past? The story of her trial was a shock, I suppose.'

'Yes. I am now the owner of her husband's house and of money which originally, I suppose, came from him. And it all leads back to that weekend in June 1925 which you spent at Laughton Hall.'

'That weekend. I remember that weekend so well.' She looked as if she had woken up suddenly. 'The photograph. It was taken that weekend. It was not Normandy. We went riding together.'

Madame de Cantegnac's memories of the Laughton Hall weekend were of a totally unexpected nature. The days preceding the murder, which Buckherd had depicted as filled with tension between husband and wife, she viewed aureoled in a golden haze.

'The weather was hot, English heat, not like the Mediterranean, so there was always a little breath of air. The sky was blue. The house was like a little jewel in the middle of all that lush greenery. It was a paradise to go there. I lived near Cambridge, you know. Our house was dark, cedars in the garden, dark-brown paint. You can't imagine the gloom of the Victorian and Edwardian past that hung over us in those days. They talk of the golden age of the Edwardians; they don't know what it was like. How hard it was to cast off that past. The dead that lay in their trenches. And that white house at Laughton, so young, so gay. Diana gathered there such interesting people. She was my model in many respects when I married and came to live here in Paris. I always wanted our house in Normandy to have that elegance, humour, charm of Laughton.'

The old woman held the photograph of herself and her husband in youth in hands whose slack skin lay over the bones like loose-fitting crepe gloves. Nothing, not sixty-five years, five children, a world war, Gaëtan's death, nothing could erase those days. The force and fascination of Gaëtan's gaze, his charm, her first sense of overwhelming sexual attraction. How had she arrived at such an age, thirty-one she had been then, without ever experiencing it before? No moment in her life had been comparable with the realisation that he was rearranging his plans at the end of the day to accompany her and Jono to Cambridge because of her. She sighed.

'Did Diana ever come to see you in Paris or in Normandy?' Helena asked again. The old woman seemed both more distant and more focused as she talked about the Twenties.

'No, she never did. She did not come to our wedding. I never saw her again, in fact, after that summer.'

'Why was that? Was there some disagreement? You and your husband had both been such close friends of hers.'

There ensued another of the longish pauses during which Madame de Cantegnac placed herself in that far time, searching for fleeting motives and serious reasons that had long since been buried at the foundation of her later life.

'It was Diana,' she said eventually. 'She refused to see us. I always had a terrible sense of guilt. She was arrested, you know. When she was in prison I was abroad with my parents. We always went to Switzerland in August and I did not know what had happened. When I returned and discovered she was in Holloway . . . and then she was moved to Bedford Gaol. I went to visit her but I was not permitted to see her. I wrote but received no answer. I should have done something; I should have insisted. It was all so shocking. I was engaged to be married. I was finishing a book. My parents were very difficult.' Helena saw that the grey eyes were magnified through a lens of tears. 'All this is so trivial in comparison with a friend in prison standing trial for her life. So when, later, Diana never replied to our letters and invitations, refused all contact, I felt, I knew, it was because of my failure to support her.'

'You know,' Helena said, 'that after the trial she changed her name, her son's name, the name of her house. She cut herself off from all her old friends.'

'Yes, I know. I knew Pia Novikoff hardly saw her again. But that was something else. There were other reasons there: Arkadi.'

'You knew about Diana and Arkadi?'

'What was there to know? I know Arkadi loved Diana.'

'And George Pollexfen?' Helena suddenly asked. 'What sort of man was he?' Then, unable to contain herself longer, 'Did she kill him?'

What was for Helena the crucial question seemed for Edith de Cantegnac one that she had barely considered. She looked puzzled, less by the substance of the question and more by Helena's intense desire to know the answer.

'I don't know,' she said eventually. 'It is something that I have been content to leave open. That is, I accepted the court's verdict that she was innocent and that this left the murder unsolved. It is a terrifying thing to say about anyone, but I must say it: Diana could have done it. I never had a burning sense of indignation when she was put on trial because I did not feel, as one would about some people in that situation, that she could *never* have done it. If I had imagined it, I would not have thought of her using poison. I would have said that she would have used a dagger, a slender, pointed, jewelled dagger, snatched up in fury. Poison has a slyness that I do not associate with her, and photographic poison is so obvious, isn't it? It looks more as if might have been someone trying to pin the blame on Diana. So perhaps, on balance, I would say she didn't do it. With Diana one always had the feeling that she could do anything. You look surprised, you disagree? She did not appear so to you?'

'No, she was absorbed by her garden. Very retiring. She never gave the impression of wanting to step outside her frame.'

'We change. We remain the same but we change. I am not the Edith Scrafton of those days. I look back and I see someone else, not myself, quite separate. A fool in many ways. I feel impatient with her folly, a lucky fool.'

At that moment the younger Madame de Cantegnac came in, carrying a tray on which were placed two minute coffee cups rimmed with gold, monogrammed GBC, and a whole chocolate cake. She poured coffee from a battered aluminium percolator, cut tiny slices of the cake.

'You are not tired, Maman? You should have your rest soon.' Good manners compelled Helena, against her wishes, to say, 'I hope I have not stayed too long. I must go.'

To her relief the old woman said, 'No, no. I am not tired at all. We are talking of people that I have not seen for more than half a century, Henriette. The problem of living so long, the problem of success you might say, apart from being a nuisance to your relatives . . .'

'No, no, Maman.'

'. . . is that there is no one left of one's own age. All dead long ago. Even my eldest son, Henriette's husband, is dead. And there is no one interested in the past.' With her coffee spoon she cut off crumbs, mouse nibblings, from the Reine de Saba and consumed them with an eager greed. 'We still have a lot to talk about.'

'I shall leave you then, Maman. I leave the coffee here. Mademoiselle Fox will re-serve you if you want it, either of you.'

She left with her dignified, heavy gait; as the door closed behind her Helena said, 'And George Pollexfen? Did you know him well? What sort of man was he? He is the most difficult character to learn about. He had the most public, the most official personality, and is the hardest one to understand.'

Edith de Cantegnac sucked the coffee spoon, mumbling the chocolate cake in her mouth. 'I knew him only when Diana married him. He was not at all the sort of person I met at my parents' house. Later here in France, I went out, met politicians, personalities; then I did not. He was a façade, a correct façade. He was a man made by other people's regard of him. He was like Bishop Berkeley's cow: he existed when others looked at him; when they looked away, he vanished. He was not authentic. I never understood how someone like Diana could have married him. And then, once she had married him, to submit as she did to all the conventional behaviour he demanded.'

She raised her coffee cup and replaced it. Helena offered to refill it. 'I shouldn't. It is very stimulating, but since you are here I shall.' She sipped the thick black liquid. 'Of course I became a conventional French wife when I married. I studied others to see how to do it; my husband was someone worth doing it for. We had a fundamental understanding. They had nothing, underneath, George and Diana, not even sex, though I did not understand that at the time. Only afterwards, when I was married myself, did I see that, in addition to everything else, or rather in subtraction, there was not even a good physical rapport between them. It is something you can only recognise, I think, if as we say here, *on est bien dans sa peau*. And even on the surface he was not always . . . kind to her.' She paused, as if thinking of some specific examples of this unkindness. 'And when I think that Diana might have married Gaëtan, if she had wished it. There was some deep lack of judgement somewhere in her. Or a longing for an ideal that she thought she could buy with such a marriage.'

'Was your husband, before he knew you, in love with my great-aunt?'

'You mean were they lovers?' Helena was amused to see how French the old Englishwoman had become. 'No, never. That's what my husband told me and I believe him. You think I am naive, perhaps? No. I think he would have liked to have been, so I think when he said, with his regret not entirely concealed, that he was not, that it was so.'

She had been jealous of Diana, in retrospect. Gaëtan had been delighted. He found every sign of passion in his English stick of a female a tribute to his own charm. She had challenged him once after their marriage, on a train. Where had they been going? Why had Diana come to her mind? It was probably when she was pregnant. Only in those times did hormonal turbulence lead to emotional conversations, tears, which she detested but could not help and which, she thought, Gaëtan actually enjoyed.

In those early days of her marriage the terrible fear of losing him would sometimes overwhelm her, fear that his casual and occasional infidelity would one day mean, not the ending of her marriage, for she had been in France long enough by then to know that was an impossibility, but an ending of their intimacy. Perhaps she had dredged up Diana in order not to mention the more trivial episodes that she suspected, doubted, knew existed. And Gaëtan's laughter, the little chagrin that she identified beneath the laughter, convinced her: Diana had once turned him down. More fool her.

'In the accounts of the trial there was speculation about Mrs Pollexfen's French lover and about the fact that he did not come to testify at the trial.'

'Yes? He did not go, of course, because Diana most urgently insisted that he should not. And what could he say? He had no evidence to give. Neither he nor I was there when George died.'

'Why did Diana persuade him not to come?'

'Because she knew that nothing he could say would help.'

'And what did your husband think of George Pollexfen?'

There followed another of Edith de Cantegnac's long silences. The sun shone obliquely through the trees in the courtyard, leaving a shifting pattern on the polished floor. Helena could see that the old woman was tired; she breathed deeply with a heaving of her narrow, flattened chest, as if out of the bottom of her lungs she drew emotions and memories that had long been drowned there. She was remembering.

She was remembering the war. *We shall remember them.* In every village of France in the square in front of the church or the *mairie* was an ugly little cross remembering them, listing the children who died for France, Henri Rey, Joseph Lator, Celestin Isscartier, Bernard Martin, Richard Martin. But we don't remember, thank God; to recall those things would make life unendurable. So memory is drowned, eradicating whole weeks, months of existence, four years out. In the fields of northern France the earth sifted down into the shell holes and regrew its thick green fur; the blasted trees were swathed in wild clematis and the new ones hung with festoons of mistletoe.

For a moment she remembered herself when young. That puritanical, idealistic young woman in the thick serge suit and peaked cap that gripped her head too tightly. The predominating memory was of dirt, filth that engrimed everything. Yet the yellow mud that dried as hard as a pastry crust on boots and hems was clean, pure, in comparison with the filth that oozed from within human-kind: the bodies left for days under fire blew up with it, their guts gushed out from them, the ambulances swilled with blood and water, vomit and urine. Even among the women; sweat-stiffened shirts and menstrual rags piled in the washrooms. And nature had been pitifully tortured by man's brutality; the countryside ripped by trenches like bayonet strokes through flesh; the trees with branches dangling like broken limbs still attached only by a shred of muscle and skin; the dying horse which no one had bothered to shoot, its black eye filmed with grey, one hoof still pawing itself upright; the lost dog curled in the doorway when she stumbled into her billet at two o'clock in the morning.

It was sanity not to remember, for memory brought a sort of madness. She was too old now to feel anything more than a constriction in the throat at the thought of the horror of it. She had survived, that was all that mattered, survived and forgotten. For those who, afterwards, could not forget or could not forget quickly enough there had been an abyss beneath them into which they could plunge without warning. She remembered George Pollexfen's tormenting of his wife. His subtle contradiction of her words, her joy, her work. He had made her suffer for something that was making him ill. He would have passed as perfectly fit, A1; no sliver of shrapnel had been lodged permanently within his muscles, no rush of gas had stripped the lining from his lungs; nevertheless, he had been seriously unwell. She had seen it most clearly the weekend he died. She had tried to tell Diana who had refused what she had offered. And afterwards it was not relevant.

She and Gaëtan that weekend in their first discovery of one another had found out each other's war, but barely. The time, the Front, the corps, that was enough, the rest went unsaid, for it was not necessary. Each knew what the other must have seen and endured. No search to understand there; acceptance was total.

So it had only been many years later that she had learned more about George Pollexfen, some time in the Thirties, after the birth of the children, after the financial difficulties, when Chantilly had to be sold, in the period she thought of as the best time of her life, before the next war when Gaëtan had gone off to England for four years, when she had lived in Normandy with the children and billeted Germans and all the moral shuffling and accommodation of Occupation. Oh, it had been the best time, when habit and trust and forgiveness opened locked doors. She had not thought of Laughton, of Diana and George, for literally years. What had brought about that extraordinary confidence that Gaëtan had made?

They had walked out into the park after dinner. She remembered the huge leaves, thick and pale, of early summer. It must have been one of the May holidays, *Ascension* or *Pentecôte*, for they normally remained in Paris until the children finished school for the summer. Gaëtan had recalled the first time they had met and she had been transported back to Laughton.

He had come late to Diana's birthday weekend, arriving during dinner. He had not noticed her at first, though they had been placed next to one another, for he had given all his attention to his host. His first words to George Pollexfen had shown that they had met before, that is, Gaëtan had claimed previous acquaintance, Pollexfen had denied it.

They sat under the vast horse-chestnut looking back at

the rhythmical forms of their grey house. Open windows on the top floor indicated where the children slept under an English regime of fresh air.

'How did you know him?' Edith had asked idly. She did not really care. The connection between Diana and her husband would never now be renewed.

'I knew him because he was responsible for the deaths of a hundred or so of my men.' Gaëtan spoke quietly, as if about another life. There was no anger, hardly even pain.

'How?' Her exclamation was emphatic, horrified.

'It must have been some time in 1916. It was at Vic, near Maricourt, a sort of elbow bent outwards, the junction between the English XIII Corps and the French XX. I was liaison officer there then because I spoke English well and could communicate with them. We were losing thousands of men a week at Verdun at the time and were taking men out of the Somme trenches, so we were maintaining our line with very small numbers, never properly reinforced. I knew that the joint was the weak point in that area of the Front and for weeks I had been writing to the HQ that we could not hold and that the English must move to cover us. I had very good relations with the English and I hoped to get their High Command to agree. One day they sent from Haig's Headquarters Pollexfen, that arrogant bastard, who came to see it on the ground. Denied my assessment of the situation. Saw no need to bring round more English troops to cover the Butte. The very next day the German bombardment began. We knew at once what that meant, but it was too late to get help for the first onslaught. We lost hundreds in a few hours. Finally, the decision was taken to withdraw from the salient by a few hundred metres, not more.

'The English had several companies being held in reserve. They should have been brought up to help us on the Butte but Pollexfen had advised Haig and the English Headquarters that they should not be used in support of the French. I know this. It is not chauvinism. I am not blaming our losses on the English, I am simply saying what was so. Pollexfen told me this himself. I remember a terrible confrontation with him in the English Battalion Headquarters. He, of course, remained calm throughout while I fulfilled all his prejudices about the Latins by becoming impassioned. It was strange we did not recognise one another at once when we met at Laughton but, as you know, one did not always look – normal – under conditions like that.'

Daylight had faded as Gaëtan talked. Lamplight had filled one or two of the upper windows of the house in precise golden rectangles. Edith had sat with her long legs stretched out in front of her, her large feet crossed at the ankles. It was only thus, looking across the unmown grass at her grey house, its two towers with their conical navy slate roofs, at the golden windows of the children's bedrooms, that she could contemplate those twenty-year-old memories.

For her it had always been night. She must have driven her ambulance from the casualty clearing stations to the rear hospitals in daylight hundreds of times; she could only remember the night duties, the blackness lit up by the Verey lights, the rain that darkened the evening skies.

'We met again, a year later perhaps, at the Bois de Lencourt,' Gaëtan went on. 'That time we were not in confrontation, we were witnesses of one of those amazing acts of courage and comradeship that took place all the time at the Front but were so rarely recorded. I wrote of it in my diary and after I met Pollexfen all those years later, I looked it up to remind myself of it.'

In the sequence of the diary the date and the place were

named. The purpose of the events of that day in the pattern of the war would have been only apparent on the vast maps of the Front pinned up in the headquarters or in the ministries of Paris and London. Perhaps there had been no purpose, or a purpose so small as to be of no moment, a little diversionary event with no hope of reaching the named goal, simply undertaken to occupy a German company, divert some German artillery fire so that their shells were not directed elsewhere. There had been many dead in the fighting of the past few days and an English company was bringing in the dead, work that they had been doing during the night. It was early morning and the German bombardment had begun again. At intervals the shells would cease for a period, then resume. In the moments of comparative quiet, cries could be heard out on the wire.

'He must have been there for at least a day and been left for dead. He had recovered consciousness and his calls, not even for help, just calls, were so desolate, so hopeless. Everyone longed for the bombardment to begin again to drown the sound. It was not a plea, because how could you ask someone to kill themselves in attempting to rescue you? Even to put the top of your kepi over the parapet was to ask for death. A little man, as small as me, a sergeant, came running along the trench calling out he would have to go to him, who would come with him? Of course, no one would. I reassured him that by evening in the dark someone, I if I were still there, would come out with him to find his friend.

' "He's not my friend. I don't know who he is. I would not leave a dog like that." He would not take the reassurance. Suddenly he leapt up to the edge of the trench and kicking on one of the supports, stepped out. I expected to see him fall back instantly. I ran to a look-out post where I could see what happened. It was there I found George Pollexfen who had come from I don't know where and who climbed up to watch, like me. The sergeant scuttled, doubled up like a child playing a game not wanting to be seen, jumping and darting, not to avoid shots, for though the Germans did shoot at him, they were doing it for fun, waiting to see what he was up to, but to find footholds on that land ploughed by shells. When he reached the man on the wire he disappeared from sight, from mine and from the Germans' too I should think, into a bomb crater and there was no sign of him or sound from the dying man for a long time. I had given them up, thinking he had been hit or was going to stay there with his comrade until it was dark and safer to emerge, when I saw movement some way from where he had entered the crater. He had hooked the body of the wounded man on to his back and was crawling with him towards us. The distance was no more than a hundred metres; he disappeared at times from our view entirely and every metre was painful to watch. What it must have been to undertake. I was there when he at last reached the English lines. The company was kept very busy with return fire in support of the Nottinghamshires in the Bois de Lencourt. So it was George Pollexfen and I who received the sergeant and his burden who, we saw, under the blood and filth that encased him, was a captain of the Worcesters who had been in the advance here two days earlier.

'It was an heroic act, there was no doubt, but I had seen other acts of madness and courage. When I came to Laughton on that occasion when I first saw you, *ma chère*, I knew I had met him, no, met is not really the word for those encounters of the war. It implies an introduction, a correct way of making oneself known. I knew Pollexfen and I had come across one another. At first I remembered the row, the disadvantage of passion and fury in the face of inflexible calm, bovine unresponsiveness. Then later I remembered the sergeant, watching that act of heroism, of receiving the wounded man back into the trenches.'

It had been Jono who had supplied the link and the understanding. Jono had seen that they had recognised one another, recognition with hostility, and had said to him as they stood on the terrace at Laughton on Saturday evening, their cigars filming the air like gunsmoke, 'Did you come across Pollexfen when he was on Haig's staff? I see that you knew him before.'

He began to tell Jono about the meeting at Vic on the Somme in 1916. Then he remembered the second encounter and the sergeant, how he and Pollexfen had received him and the wounded captain with tenderness into the trench which was no longer a place of horror but home, a place of refuge from the dangers outside. He was momentarily overcome by the vividness of the memory and began to recount it, though it had little to do with Pollexfen.

'I often wonder what became of that sergeant.'

Jono was propped against the balustrade, tapping his false leg with his stick, wood idly rapping on wood.

'Bois de Lencourt,' he repeated. 'That's where George got his DSO. Rescued a captain of the 8th Worcesters from the wire in broad daylight.'

Gaëtan said nothing; the connection was made immediately. How could two captains of the 8th Worcesters be rescued from the wire in circumstances of exceptional bravery at Bois de Lencourt? Though it was impossible to guess how Pollexfen had got away with his cheating, Gaëtan was certain that he had guessed right. It was written on Pollexfen's face. When he had arrived, Pollexfen had remembered their cradling of the anonymous captain of the 8th Worcesters, not the angry exchange at Battalion Headquarters. The fury and self-justification which Gaëtan had divined in him verified his guess. He glanced at Jono whose calmly shuttered face showed no sign of what he had made of Gaëtan's story.

He had never spoken of that surmise until he sat with his wife under the horse-chestnuts in Normandy.

'Can it really be true?' Edith asked. 'Could he get away with someone else's courage?'

Gaëtan shrugged. 'Who knows how it was done; that company was virtually wiped out that very day in a big German bombardment. But I know he knew I knew. Do you remember on the Sunday morning before church you joined us in the hall at Laughton? We had just spoken about where we had met previously. I wanted to mention the Bois de Lencourt to him to see what his reaction would be.'

'You did not say anything about the sergeant or the captain of the Worcesters?'

'No, it was not necessary.'

Edith shook her head. 'He was a very sick man, I thought, he had an unreasoning violence about him. He was often vile to Diana. I could never understand why she put up with it. Do you remember that awful outburst about the photographic studio she had created? I suppose it was shell-shock.'

They stood up to continue their evening walk. 'And Jono? What did he make of it?'

'Jono? He made the same assumption as me, of that I am certain; we never spoke of it.'

Helena was much afraid that the younger Madame de Cantegnac would reproach her when she returned. The old woman's afternoon of reliving her past, her visualisation of the May evening in Normandy with her husband and the calling up of their experiences in the war had affected her as a great physical effort would have done. She was

breathing fast and shallowly now; the deeper, more rumi-
native rhythm had quickened as she had entered into her
story. Her hands, eyes, face had moved and her voice had
changed its tone and expression as if she were taking on
the personality of whomever she was speaking of at the
time. She leaned back in her chair and closed her eyes for a
moment. Helena felt a real anxiety that she had placed an
excessive strain on her hostess.

'I am afraid this has tired you out. Shall I call your
daughter-in-law?'

'No, no thank you. She is very good to me and indeed
without her I don't know how I should manage. I should
have to move in with one of my daughters, which is not a
prospect to please. But she does fuss, Henriette I mean.'
With a bony hand, the knuckles peaked like gothic spires,
she sought a handkerchief in her sleeve. 'It is tiring to think
of the past in that way, following a line through many
years. I think of the past very often, normally little
incidents come to me at random. They swim up out of the
tank of their own volition. And the past is so vivid, it is
quite painful to recall. All old people say this, of course. I
remember my own poor, plaintive old mother, who was
much younger than I am now, saying how clear the days of
the 1860s were in her memory. I can see the horse-
chestnut, the avenue of *tilleul*, the lights in the house, in
1938 I suppose it was, more clearly than I can see out of
that window now. And not just see, but hear the shuffling
of the leaves, the purring of the nightjar, smell the lime
flowers. And yet I find it difficult to remember what
happened last week, or when I last saw my youngest
granddaughter. Was Diana like that? Tell me about her.'

'If she lived in the past,' Helena said, 'she did it secretly.
As I explained to you, her lives as Diana Millard, Diana
Pollexfen, Diana Codrington – that was the name she took

after her husband's death – were quite unknown to us.'

'That is less unusual than you appear to think, my dear. It happens that Diana's life was exceptionally fragmented. But what do you think my granddaughters or my great-granddaughters know of my life? I am simply *grand'mère*. I have been very old for a very long time. They probably are not aware of the books I wrote, of what I did in the second war, let alone the first.'

Helena nodded, acknowledging the truth of what was said. 'But the revelation of your past to your grandchildren would not lay open a murder.'

'No. Some appalling things, no doubt, for the angel of judgement to weigh up, but not a murder.'

The door opened and the solid step of Henriette de Cantegnac approached them. Her mother-in-law regarded her.

'You look rested, Henriette. I hope that you slept.'

'Too long, *Maman*. I meant to have five minutes only. And you have evidently spent your time in gruesome conversation. I heard "murder" as I came in.'

Helena gathered up her bag, stood to shake hands. As she was leaving the old woman spoke again.

'If I think of anything that will be more useful to you I shall write to you. I am afraid you have learned very little. It has been a great pleasure for me.'

6

Jonothon Pybus's Testimony

When she returned home from Paris late at night Helena did not permit herself to look for signs of the presence's activity in her absence. She dropped her bags in the hall and went to her study to make notes of her conversation with Edith de Cantegnac. It was too late to ring Marta and she was glad to put off speaking to her and countering the reproaches she knew she would meet.

'Helena, we were going to go together in September,' Marta said vexedly the following evening. 'I am disappointed. It's years since I was in Paris. You know it is not a place one goes with children. It would have been such a pleasure for me.'

'I'm sorry, Marta.'

'And I need to hear everything she said. It would have been so useful.'

'I'm sorry, Marta.'

'We can hardly expect an old woman to repeat such an interview.'

'Marta, I have extensive notes which I shall hand over to you in toto.'

'And just what were you doing in Paris, Helena?'

'I had to go in any case. I simply tried her on the off-chance. As you said, it was very unlikely she would have been there in August. But there she was. And I thought I should go ahead. She is very old, Marta. She could die on us at any moment.'

'You had better come and tell me all about it. Come on Saturday. We are still in Cambridgeshire. You can then go to Ingthorpe. I'll expect you for lunch.'

Helena agreed meekly, feeling that she had got off comparatively lightly. Marta's guilt-making capacity was much greater than she had displayed in that conversation.

Clunch House was a thickset building with small windows and the tight, enclosed aspect of the Fenlands. Its natural character was thwarted by Marta's determinedly Scandinavian life there. In the summer the doors and windows stood open to the damp sunlight even though wood-burning stoves, and even discreet oil-fired central heating, had to work at the same time to evaporate the moisture that seeped up from the ground as well as permeating the air above.

Sudden pleasure, an extra pleasure, she told herself, rose in Helena as she parked her car beside the overgrown laurel hedge and recognised the Volvo that belonged to Isobel and Simon. Though not particularly warm, the day was fine and she found Simon and Richard sitting in the garden while the children played in the long grass of the orchard. The two men made a somewhat incongruous pair, often coupled in child-minding or on holiday expeditions by their wives' friendship rather than because they were cousins. Helena frequently marvelled at men's capacity to tolerate those with whom they had little in common and to spend time amicably when thrown together by external events, selecting from their range of interests ones that more or less matched. She usually talked to Richard of politics, his life cutting through Robert's and allowing her sidelights on to it. She thought of him as bookish and cultivated, a fanatical concert-goer in spite of the unsocial hours of his profession. He and Simon, however, never spoke of either politics or music, bringing out cricket, City gossip and incomprehensible schoolboyish jokes which ran for years.

Richard was sprawling in a deck-chair, exposing soft white belly flesh through gaps in a shirt that was old, and now too small. He gave the impression of someone whose normal posture was maintained by his dark suits and striped shirts; once into old clothes he had no sense of what was wearable and immediately looked like a tramp. In contrast, Simon was dressed for play in a grown-up version of his twins' jeans and sweatshirts, looking tanned and energetic. He had just returned from three weeks in Turkey spent with the twins in the grandeur of a smart hotel.

'No self-catering for him,' Richard was mocking him.

'The girls liked it.'

'The excuses made in the name of children.'

Isobel had been too busy to accompany them and had booked the holiday, through her secretary, after one reading of an article in the travel pages of a Saturday paper.

As Helena arrived, Isobel, who had been helping Marta in the kitchen, came out to summon the children and to greet Helena. She carried the wine bottle inside, thereby ensuring that the men followed.

Marta was placing dishes of fish and vegetables, soused, smoked and pickled, on the table, amid them radishes, tomatoes and bunches of fresh herbs.

'All from Daddy's garden,' one of the girls explained.

'The lettuces have bolted,' said the other and they stifled

inexplicable laughter at the outrageousness and unseemliness either of the lettuces or of mentioning them. Helena watched them passing dishes to Isobel's twins, helping themselves. The young were so impossibly beautiful and graceful, with a beauty and grace never again attainable. Even as they made discontented faces at a reproach of one or other mother, who watched their table manners with critical eyes, their features had a softness and radiance which they would lose, when? In five years, perhaps; by the time they were fifteen certainly. In the past the young had been preserved in their immaturity until much later. Helena remembered eating lunch with Simon and Richard, their parents, and Great-aunt Fox, at the oval table at Ingthorpe. Far from innocent plans and thoughts had teemed in their heads behind the silence that was more or less enforced on children at those old-fashioned meals. The innocence of childhood, a myth only of the forgetful and childless, had long been exploded; the serenity of old age, too.

'Where did you stay, Helena?' Marta was asking. 'I want to make myself sick by knowing what I missed. And tell what you ate, too. Everything.'

'Marta, I am sorry. We'll go together anyway. A girls' jaunt, one weekend. Isobel could come, too, if she weren't so busy.'

'Mummy.'

'Don't interrupt, darling.'

'I haven't had my pill.'

'Oh, no. Simon, could you find them? They're somewhere upstairs in my washbag or suitcase.'

'Can't Nickie go herself? In Mummy's bag in her bathroom. You know what they look like.'

'No, Simon. I don't want . . . I asked you.'

'I know you asked me and I've told Nick to get them.'

'Simon . . . Oh, damn it, I'll do it myself, like everything else.'

'No, sit still,' Simon snarled and leaped up clumsily.

Nicola, her beauty as innocently unconscious as ever, ignored the disturbance she had caused. Slow by just a second, Helena began to answer Marta's question.

'Rue St Simon was where I stayed and I had several delicious meals. I am afraid Marta won't approve. I have to confess I had foie gras.'

Simon had returned by now and was dispensing pills to one of the twins. Attention flickered away from Helena's fresh foie gras cooked with apples, though she kept on talking through the distraction, which was made less by Simon's fussy opening of the childproof top and pouring of extra water, Nicola's elaborate tossing of her chin and swallowing with repeated ripplings of her throat muscles, than by Isobel's intense concentration on the performance until it had finished and Simon was about to place the pills on the mantelshelf.

'Not there, Simon. We'll only forget them.'

With great care, Simon put the bottle on the table beside his daughter. 'When you have finished your lunch you can put them back in Mummy's washbag in the bathroom.' He sat down deliberately and picked up his napkin. Isobel looked as if she were going to insist on the pills' being returned to their place at once; Helena lurched desperately on to a description of the display of good things at Hédiard, where she had gone to buy a present for Marta, and no pause intervened for Isobel to issue her ukase.

After lunch Marta ordered everybody off to the lake to read or punt, saying that she must take serious notes from Helena who would stay and help her wash up. Simon looked momentarily rebellious, but the easy obedience of Richard made the loading of the entire party with all its paraphernalia into the Volvo straightforward.

Helena and Marta went back into the kitchen to gather up the plates from which the arrears of the summer pudding had been scraped.

'What's the matter with Isobel and Simon?' Helena said. 'Have they been at one another's throats since they arrived?' She regretted what she had said; it only invited a prolonged psychoanalysis of both partners and their faulty relationship from Marta which she felt it was disloyal to Isobel to listen to.

Marta did not respond as Helena had expected. 'Who knows what goes on within a couple?' she said. 'I've given up speculation why one pair suddenly breaks apart for no sufficient – at least to me – reason and another remains together through violence and misery. And why, too,' she was bending down to file plates into the dishwasher and suddenly glared sideways and upwards at Helena standing at the sink, 'some people decide to have no intimate life and just to be old aunties at the age of thirty.'

Helena smiled tranquilly. She had no fears of Marta's perspicacity. Theory blinkered and offered her protection.

'I'm afraid the mystery of the couple is even more impenetrable in the past.' She picked up a pan that held the remains of potato and dill glued to its sides. She scraped a bit off with a fingernail and ate it thoughtfully with a morsel of herring and sour cream. She tipped the rest of the herring into a smaller bowl and looked for the cling film.

'Edith de Cantegnac said much the same thing about Diana and George Pollexfen.' She put on red rubber gloves and began to scour the potato pan. 'Even when the evidence is before you, you can't understand it.'

'I suppose it puts paid to the French lover as a motive or as an accomplice.'

'I think so. Of course, she would be bound, even at this distance, out of loyalty to her husband, to reject all ideas of his complicity in the murder. I didn't even suggest it. I did put his relationship with Diana to her. She considered it a possibility. I think her husband probably always had a glad eye, so it was not a new idea in itself. She thought Diana had refused him a long time ago. So there goes the French lover. There goes the lover entirely. Arkadi's out; Gaëtan's out; Dr Pybus was never in the running.'

Marta shut the fridge on the last of the leftovers and pressed the button on the dishwasher. Above the roar of the water she said, 'I'll get my papers.' They installed themselves outside in the chilly sunshine. The grass shivered constantly in the cold draughts that ran through it. Helena pulled on another sweater.

'Why don't you go to Italy for the summer? England is so cold.'

'Nonsense.' Marta, who was wearing only a T-shirt and jeans, settled into her deck-chair, opening herself to the primrose pale light. 'If it wasn't Cambridgeshire, I would have to find a house on a Baltic island and the Baltic is now very polluted. I have no patience with all this heat. All that would happen would be that the girls would spend all day indoors watching videos because it was too hot to play outside. Now tell me about Cantegnac's story of George Pollexfen and the sergeant.' She was plucking the petals off a basketful of roses and tipping them on to a sheet to make pot pourri.

Helena, who had only sketched the story on the telephone, told it now in detail. She thought of the old woman reliving the golden evening in Normandy in 1938 when Gaëtan de Cantegnac had himself relived the muddy banality of the sergeant's heroism in 1917 at the Bois de Lencourt. Each account in its setting added something to the story; the reason for its being told, its reception by its audience had curled another circle of petals, now stripped off to be dried for their essential fragrance. Marta listened in silence, making no comment until Helena had finished.

'I don't see that your visit has got you anywhere, do you? What you have told me is fascinating for me. But for you? Gaëtan de Cantegnac is now less likely as an accomplice or alternative murderer. If Cantegnac had been found filled with cyanide, one might now say that Pollexfen had done it to avoid being found out as a fraud. It's strange. One can think of reasons why Pollexfen might have wanted to kill Arkadi and now the Frenchman, but not the other way round. He is essentially a killer, not a victim.'

'One is reduced to saying what the Great-aunt wrote in her diary, that there was a mysterious poisoner abroad.'

'Or one could blame the servants. The housekeeper, for example.'

'No, no. They would have poisoned Diana, rather than George Pollexfen. Fraud that he was, he was everything they expected of a master, but she was not the genuine article and they clearly despised her.'

In the early evening Helena set off for Ingthorpe to have supper with Mary. As she drove she brooded simultaneously on the Great-aunt's past and Isobel's present. Every couple, she told herself platitudinously, had their ups and downs, periods of difficulty: every cliché in the magazine journalists' dictionary. She felt unsafe; Isobel's competence, her command of every area of life, had always been a reassurance to Helena. She could not compete and did not want to; if Isobel could control everything, home, husband, children, business, to perfection there was no reason why she, Helena, should not more or less manage half that list. Signs of

Isobel's life cracking undermined her.

Helena felt she had got off very lightly for the sin of her illicit trip to Paris, without seeking to account for it beyond luck and a period of good humour in the switchback of Marta's moods. The good humour was more than a passing event. A week later Helena met Richard at a reception for lawyers and legislators which combined exchanges of views with consumption of wine, of the anonymous white or red variety, and unappetising gobbets of food. Her cousin, catching sight of her entrance, late, made his way across the floor of the crowded City hall to speak to her. His progress was slow as there were many who required a word in the ear, a pat on the shoulder or a clasp of the hand on his way. Helena, who had been instantly captured by a colleague for whom she felt equally boredom and guilt at winning, most unjustifiably, a case in which he had been acting for the other side, saw Richard's intention and could only wait with impatience for his arrival to release her from her unwelcome companion. When he at last arrived it was of Marta that he wished to speak.

'She's been working on the Great-aunt for all she's worth; it takes a lot of pressure off the children. Too much parental interest can be – well, too much. Anyhow, Ram has now become an important collaborator.'

'Ram?'

'Dr Ramasubramaniam. What is he? Cultural historian? Philosopher? I thought you introduced them. He is giving Marta a lot of theoretical background in which to place the events of Great-aunt Fox's life. I doubt if in the end her best friend would recognise her, so I don't think you need to worry too much.'

'Is Marta already planning her book? We don't know the answer yet.'

'Oh, I don't think an answer to a simple question like,

did she murder her husband? has any significance for Marta and Ram. They don't need an answer, the point is to search, not to find. However, Ram has put Marta on to some more material. Has she told you about it yet?'

'There was something on my answerphone a day or so ago from her but I'm afraid I've not returned her call yet.'

'Oh well, I'll let her tell you about the trip she's planning. She's acquired a lap dog in preparation for it. You know, one of those computers that you carry around with you and then plug into your telephone. I'll move on. I just wanted you to know what a godsend Great-aunt Fox has turned out to be.'

Helena's curiosity was sufficiently aroused to telephone Marta from the office the next day. There was a note of triumph, of one-upmanship, in Marta's voice as she said, 'Ram told me about a cache of Pybus papers in the library at Johns Hopkins at Baltimore and now, by coincidence, Richard is going on a trip to Washington before the party conference. So I'm going with him and I shall go to Baltimore for two days to check them.'

'What sort of papers are they?' Helena asked sceptically. 'How did they get to Baltimore?'

'You remember that stuff that Simon found out for us about Pybus. He spent the last ten years or so of his life in the States. When he died or committed suicide or whatever, all his property and papers went to another American scientist, a German, Jewish, very distinguished, who later won the Nobel prize for physics. He, the Nobel prize winner, eventually died and left all his papers to Johns Hopkins and Pybus's are among them. Ram knows all about this because Pybus corresponded with Pia apparently and through his contacts in America he heard about this collection.'

'I hope you have a lovely time. Is it really going to be useful?'

Marta was not put out, even by this undermining remark. 'I am told there are private letters as well as scientific papers and I am going as much to look at stuff about Pia for Ram as to see about Great-aunt Fox. Really, Helena,' Marta's voice sharpened a little, 'the question of the murder is nothing, or at least very small indeed. You must have a wider perspective.'

Helena laughed. 'No, no, *you* must have the wider perspective, Marta. I leave the academic stratosphere to you. My concern is very simple and very personal.'

Marta sounded mollified by this definition of their areas of interest. 'Who knows, I may find all kinds of information for you.'

'And what about the children?' Kristina and Anna had been for years Marta's resented reason for not travelling with Richard when the occasion arose.

'I've not quite sorted that out. They'll stay with friends for the weekdays and go to school with them.'

'What about letting them come to Ingthorpe with me for the weekend? Mary will be overjoyed.'

Marta's good humour was restored to its previous level of benevolence at this suggestion and Helena, putting down the phone, was glad that the American visit would so quickly cancel out her own journey across the Channel. Though she was doubtful of the chances of the visit turning up anything of any relevance at all, it would give pleasure to Marta and that seemed object enough.

She was sufficiently interested, however, in Marta's plan to look up the references given to her months ago by Simon about Dr Jonothon Pybus. She was glad that she had noted them meticulously in her notebook for that month. Without them it would have taken days to reassemble all the pieces. Even the very brief hours she had spent in tracking down references in libraries or reading through the manifold volumes of Diana's journals had taught her how long and fruitless research could be. Hours spent with the eye passing vertically down page after page seeking a key word or name, finding nothing and at the end the uncomfortable uncertainty as to whether the blank drawn was really because there was nothing there or because in a second's inattention, blinded by the numbing boredom of it all, she had failed to pick out the essential passage.

This experience made her all the more doubtful that Marta had any chance at all of finding anything about Diana Pollexfen or Pia Novikoff in two days in Baltimore. Perhaps her purpose was to report on the collections to Dr Ramasubramaniam and go back with him at a later date. Helena could imagine the two of them in an American university library, Ramasubramaniam with a pile of shoe boxes sprouting minutely coded index cards, Marta beside him with her computer on her knee.

Her own notes about Pybus came closer to Ramasubramaniam's system than to Marta's high technology. Her folder labelled *Pybus* contained a sheaf of photocopies supplied by Simon or taken by herself after an evening in the British Museum. Simon, a most assiduous researcher (after all, he had the time, she thought ungratefully), had copied snippets from a good number of sources, carefully annotating each sheet with the title, author and page of his source. As Helena sat one evening turning over these sheets, Pybus began to emerge in his own right, separating himself from the pawkily humorous, observant shadow of a persona with which she had endowed him up till then.

Unlike Pia, who was quintessentially English, and Diana

and Arkadi, who were Francophile foreigners, Dr Pybus, for all the loss of his leg in the First World War, was oriented towards Germany, a German speaker and passionate lover of German science and German music. In an account of the escape of Jewish intellectuals from Hitler's Germany in the 1930s his name occurred again and again. He had fought British Government indifference, used his contacts to find posts for his German friends in the States. The Nobel prize winner, Jakob Winter, whose collection Marta was going to consult, was one of those whom Jono had helped.

None of the material focused directly on Jono himself so none of it answered the question that formed in Helena's mind. Where lay the origin of his Communism? Did it lie in the wounds of the First World War or in the attachments he had made during his time in Germany in the Twenties? Was it simply a form of anti-Nazism or was it a theoretical construct, a desire for formal order in politics to mimic the beauty and order of physics?

Marta and Richard departed two weeks later in a flurry of letters about keys to the London house, instructions on its workings; addresses of every workman concerned with its upkeep, arrangements for the girls covering every moment of their parents' absence with even more minute explanations about collecting and returning them for their weekend at Ingthorpe. With such a battery of information to work on Helena did not anticipate hearing from Marta during the week she was away and, when the phone rang when she was asleep one night, it was not Marta's voice she expected to hear. Marta, breathless with news, was not even put out when Helena, looking blearily at the little enamelled clock, told her it was three in the morning.

'Oh. I thought the time went the other way. Never mind.

If it did I wouldn't have got hold of you, so it is all to the good.'

'Why do you need to get hold of me so urgently in any case?'

'Because I thought you were desperate to know. I've solved it. I know who did it.'

'Did what?'

'Helena, you are being exceptionally stupid today. The murder of George Pollexfen. I thought that was your overriding concern. You're obviously not in the least interested in the wider context, the way the characters fit into a broader cultural framework. You just want to solve the mystery. Well, I've done it.'

Helena was silent, collecting her wits. She was not sure whether at three in the morning she wanted to know all that badly.

'So who was it did it?' she asked with a sleep-ridden lack of grammar.

'Pybus.'

'Pybus?'

'Yes. This is a gold-mine, a treasure trove. There's so much stuff I can hardly begin to tell you. I was going to ring Ram but if it is three o'clock with you I'll wait until the morning. What a good thing I rang you first. There's masses of stuff about Pia as well.'

'And how do you know it was Pybus?'

'There are letters, dozens of them. He was being black-mailed. He committed suicide because of it.'

'A bit late in the day, surely.'

'Why?'

'He didn't die until '51 or '52.'

'Helena, why are you being so obstructive? I thought you'd be delighted.'

'But why did he do it?'

'It's to do with the war. All that stuff you got from Edith de Cantegnac. I'm telling you, I've got all the proof here. I'll fax you tomorrow.'

Helena put the phone down wearily and lay back on her pillows. Pybus? Why would he have wanted to kill Pollexfen? And would he have been able to watch someone he knew to be innocent on trial for her life and say nothing? She supposed if he were capable of murder he would certainly have been capable of that. But how did it fit with the picture of someone who almost ruined himself financially to help his Jewish friends in the Thirties, who worked on Little Boy and Fat Man in the Forties, in order to defeat Hitler? There was an inconsistency or rather an incompatibility, for it was in seemliness rather than in logic that the disjunction was felt. Helena prepared herself, sceptically, for Marta's fax.

It, or rather they, did not begin to arrive until late in the afternoon. Marta had evidently gone to bed after calling Helena and had not applied herself to forwarding her proof until the following day. Once started, the material poured across the Atlantic. It began with Sophie entering Helena's office with several sheets of curling fax paper.

'Helena, do you know what this is about? It's marked to you, but it looks very odd. I don't recognise it at all.'

The first sheet was in manuscript, small, crabbed writing, almost gothic in its illegibility, across which Marta had scrawled 'For Helena: Proof at last. This is what you've been waiting for. M.'

'It's from my cousin who's doing some research in America. You'd better gather them into one folder and give them all to me to take home.'

She was surprised at the reluctance she felt to read the faxes. This was not how she wanted to reach understanding. She held the slick paper in her hands with a sensation of distaste for a moment before permitting her eyes to study the first document. It consisted of a single page from the middle of what seemed to be a letter.

. . . weigh in the balance the men I've saved – you above all – and those I've killed, from the Somme to Hiroshima. The nameless, faceless ones, the unknown, weigh heaviest, though they should be the easiest to dismiss. After all, it was the conscious acceptance of guilt in the necessary murder, vindicated by collective assent. But I can't accept that now; the mud-clogged dead of High Wood, the melted flesh of Nagasaki, haunt me. Awake or asleep, I see them. Yet for the one death for which I should feel individual responsibility, George Pollexfen's, I feel no guilt at all. In fact, I feel a hardening and self-justification, just as I felt at the time – I told you – when I confronted him just before he died and accused him of stealing other men's deeds, cashing in on the innocent and insignificant. Thinking about it still makes my blood boil: in Pollexfen's actions are summed up all that stinks in England, class and advantage, useless ceremony and symbols. I can't feel guilty about his death. At least I looked Pollexfen in the eye, that night in Diana's studio, and told him what a shit he was. It was not death launched from miles away, impersonal, obscene.

It was a document that demanded thought. Helena put it away with subsequent sheets from Marta to read later. She was relieved. The admission of guilt carried no conviction. She had been half afraid that Marta's proof would convince her, would be real proof, showing the who, the how, the why. This did nothing of the kind.

That evening she sat down at the table at home with a plate of baked beans and a piece of toast in front of her and lined up the transparent folder of faxes beside her place. Marta's letter which had followed hard on the heels of the photocopy, running out of the machine in hot explanation, was a series of instructions about how to understand what she had found.

It seems to have been written just before his death in 1952, she had scrawled, *when he was under threat of deportation as an undesirable alien – because of his Communist sympathies. It was McCarthy time – so he was very worried about his friends in the scientific community, many of whom had been fellow-travellers at the very least just because they were anti-Nazi and he was obviously contemplating suicide already. He took an overdose of some kind a week or so later. I think this letter, which was written to his friend Winter, shows that he was in a deep depression which led to his suicide. He had obviously already confessed murdering Pollexfen to Winter before – a pity he isn't still alive, Winter – but felt justified because of Pollexfen's dishonourable conduct. The 'stealing other men's deeds' must refer to the story Edith de Cantegnac told you. What about the 'necessary murder' bit? Is that a quotation? In Pybus's case the revulsion from Pollexfen would have been reinforced by his Marxist world view that placed him as capitalist and social exploiter . . .*

Helena finished her baked beans, wiping the last morsel of toast around her plate to sop up the juice. No hope of anything else: the cupboard was bare. Tomorrow she must . . . Her mind turned gratefully from writing shopping lists to destroying Marta's thesis. She dismissed the wider perspective that Marta was so fond of and imagined Pybus on that June night.

The Rolls that had been taking Pybus, Edith and Gaëtan to Cambridge had turned back in its course for Jono to retrieve some papers. She could imagine the journey, Jono and Gaëtan talking, Edith silent, transfigured by Gaëtan, brave enough even to announce to her parents her absence whenever he would wish it the following day. Jono suddenly realising, or pretending to realise, that a folder of papers was missing. Was it contrived? Did the papers exist at all? Were they neatly packed in his bags all the time or had he really mislaid them?

When they returned to Laughton it would have been early evening, still light. Diana and Fanny in the drawing-room; Peter already in bed; no sign of George. Edith offering to help Jono in his search and being irritably rebuffed. Did he not want her help because there were no papers to find or because he could jealously sense the current of attraction between his friend and Edith, or just because Edith always irritated him? He had been left to make his own investigations into the lost documents, looking round the drawing-room, questioning Mrs Everett, laboriously climbing to his bedroom, disappearing on to the terrace, limping through the shrubbery to the stable-yard. Why had he gone to the studio? There was no rendezvous, Helena was sure. How could he have contrived to return at any given time? He had gone there in search of his folder and found . . . Presumably he had found George Pollexfen waiting for his interview with Diana, the one she claimed in her diary, written before George's death had been discovered, that she had refused to attend.

So they had met unexpectedly and something had propelled Jono into mentioning what he had learned or deduced from his conversation with Gaëtan. He must have accused Pollexfen of obtaining his DSO by fraud, of passing off the deeds of the unknown sergeant as his own. She could see them in the studio under the white eaves, the light of the almost interminable summer evening still percolating through the north windows, the room filled with the inhibited contempt, fury, hatred, of two Englishmen whose feelings were rarely openly expressed.

They moved, the puppets of her imagination, facing one another in antagonism, striding around the room, tapping on the table with suppressed rage. She could imagine the shock to Pollexfen that what he feared the Frenchman knew was now known to Pybus also. Marta was right; Pollexfen looked less like a victim than a killer cornered. Had Pybus seen in George the representative of all he hated and despised? Was he already a Communist in 1925, Helena wondered? Marta's wider perspective was so wide as perhaps to be telescoping different stages of Pybus's life. It was more likely that he developed his Communist sympathies as a result of a period in Germany and the rise of Nazi power in the Thirties. Had a well-connected Cambridge scientist already espoused the cause of the proletariat by the early Twenties? It seemed implausible.

Even if he were not already a Communist, the attitudes which were to make him one were already in place. He might have seen it as another 'necessary murder' to avenge Gaëtan's dead Chasseurs as well as the cheated soldier. Had Pybus stood with his back to his victim, mixing him a lethal dose composed from one of Diana's photographic chemicals, blandly handed him the glass containing the revenge for the nameless, unrewarded sergeant? She could not make her puppet concoct the mixture, which Jono as a scientist would have well known how to do, and leave it in the whisky glass, still less hand it to his companion. They remained locked in accusation; Pybus refused to act.

By the time she went to bed she had convinced herself that Marta was wrong. Pybus might accept guilt but, she felt sure, he was not the murderer.

Part Five

THE JUDGEMENT

The Day of Judgement, Helena found, comes without a blast of trumpets; you are there without realising it. The first warning sign that the time was near came from an unexpected quarter.

When Helena arrived at Ingthorpe late on Friday night, Mary was sitting at the kitchen table listening to the Book at Bedtime on the radio and knitting a cardigan which had exactly the same texture as her woolly grey head. Helena often wondered whether she had perfected some system for spinning her own hair into wool. She stood up as Helena entered, piercing the grey ball with her needles. 'There you are,' she said. 'I wondered if they would ever let you go. Take your bag up to your room and when you come down I'll give you a bowl of soup, and something to eat. You won't have eaten much at lunch, so I thought you'd want a bite now. Off you go.'

Helena dutifully climbed the stairs, coiling round the marquetry table with its bowl of white roses. She wondered why the presence, so closely associated in her mind with the Great-aunt, never manifested itself here at Ingthorpe. The house was kept by Mary as it always had been. The flowers from the garden were placed twice a week in their traditional bowls in their accustomed places. The dust was removed, the wood, silver, brass polished. The books lay waiting for someone to open them up and read them. Nothing here moved, remaining eerily the same. The presence would feel at home. While in London, in the restless shifting of things, the distressed being gave an indication of something unsettled, unresolved.

Helena's feeling that everything at Ingthorpe was unchangeably tranquil was in error. When she entered the kitchen she found that Mary had put out a bowl of beetroot soup. Helena sighed with pleasure as she plunged her spoon into the astonishingly pink surface flecked with the green of chives. She sat down opposite Mary, then, about to take her first mouthful, became aware of the tension of the housekeeper's regard. She lowered her hand. 'What's the matter?'

'Go on, eat, eat.' She would not speak until Helena had sipped and then she said, 'Now Helena, you know you're going to have to make up your mind what you're going to do: I want to make my plans.'

Helena once again put down her spoon. The pink soup which had seemed so cheerful now had a bilious and sinister tint. 'Of course you must, Mary dear. What do you want to do? You mustn't feel that you have to wait for me to decide. Do you want to look for another job? Is your sister wanting you to go to live with her?'

'I don't know yet. But I want to know what your plans are. If staying here is possible, I'd want to know.'

'I don't think I can tell you yet. You see, the money isn't sorted out completely, so I don't know what I can afford or what . . .' Helena's voice trailed off.

Mary was relentless, insistent. 'I need to know, Helena. It's the uncertainty, you know. I need to be sure what I'm doing at my age. I need some security.'

Helena went up to bed realising the time had come for a verdict. But she was not ready. It was not the money that prevented her from deciding what to do. It was true that the estate was not yet settled and she knew that the circuitous workings of her own profession meant that it would be some considerable time yet before it was tidied up and put away. However, from what Stringer had told her, she knew that if she wanted to she could afford to keep Ingthorpe and Mary. The question was, would she? There was, she thought, something uncomfortable about trying to sit in judgement on her great-aunt, deciding whether or not she could accept her legacy and doing it, moreover, in her very room. She turned off the lights and raised the lower sash of one of the long windows. She sat on the floor and looked out at the darkened garden. The sky was clear and a spattering of stars lay on it. She tried to reflect on what she had learned since beginning her enquiry into the Great-aunt's life and George Pollexfen's death.

Extraordinarily, against her expectations, what had emerged were not new facts, those fixed points of a timetable about which there could be little argument. She had thought these would form a skeleton of events, a skeleton still in existence when the more ephemeral flesh of mixed emotion, motive, desire, had rotted away in the intervening years. From those facts she had hoped to read the past and uncover a truth which had been hidden.

The evidence had been quite other. Nothing new in terms of the occurrences of that weekend had appeared. The details that she had learned from Diana's diaries and from the biased Buckherd had not been significantly altered by anything she had discovered subsequently. Only the pattern of relationships that meshed those events had come into focus, bound Diana into a context which made it harder, not easier, to judge whether or not she was guilty.

She had come to see, if nothing else, that the proof that she wanted was unlikely to emerge, and she would have to be satisfied with an arbitrary decision and live with the resultant guilt, either of rejecting her inheritance and having condemned her beloved great-aunt of murder, or of having accepted the legacy of murder. She could see a balance, like St Michael's in Charlton church; it hung in her mind's eye, the scales absolutely level. She must set a deadline. And she must speak to Robert. Taking those two decisions did not make her feel any more at ease and her distressed mind turned to her other worry: Isobel and Simon.

Something had gone wrong; she could make a guess at what, but she could not think of what to do to help matters. She would have an opportunity to talk to Isobel soon, for her friend had seen a window, as she put it, and had persuaded Helena to go with her to Crete for ten days. They would relax and swim in the hotel's heated pool. The children were back at school and Simon would cope at home. What good talking about it would do she could not imagine; it was the folk remedy always recommended in such cases. Helena had little faith in it, though she had no alternative to offer.

She returned to London with no decision taken. Now she felt that, as she was not competent to judge, and was unlikely to learn anything that would make it easier, her decision was simply to choose whether to abandon her quest, accept her legacy and forget about that death in the garden in June 1925, or whether to wait until something revealed the judgement to her. She had to deal with Mary's reasonable request. She had to worry about Simon and Isobel.

Everything began in the normal way. Even for Diana the day of her judgement must have had the banality of prison routine: the warders calling her at six a.m., the prison breakfast of bread and margarine. For Helena, the alarm, breakfasting on a hasty cup of Nescafé, the walk to the tube, gathering her thoughts about the problems on her agenda, everything was as usual as yesterday and last week. It was a day of passage, a mid-week day, on the way to better things, seeing Robert at the weekend, the holiday in Crete next week. An ordinary day, a little better than normal: Robert had rung from Rome at six thirty while she was cleaning her teeth and on an air of spearmint she had explained Mary's ultimatum. He would be back this afternoon, he said; they would talk at the weekend and she would decide by the time she got back from Xania. Helena, like many women who ruled their own lives, adored being told what to do when there was no obligation to follow the advice given. She felt calmer. She would talk to Robert and to Isobel and she would be able to decide.

In the evening, as she walked home the usual shadow fell, the anticipation of what she might find, or believe she had found, in the movements of the Great-aunt's alter ego around the house. It was not João's day so her nervous alertness to any foreign presence was heightened.

She passed a bookshop, its doors wide open, and without forethought or hesitation she turned inside as if her steps had been leading her there all along. She would buy some paperbacks for her holiday which would delay by an hour the placing of her key in the lock of her door. She had assembled a small pile of novels and biographies and was wandering through the Art and Design section when she stumbled on Simon. He was crouching beside a book-case like a sick hare in a field and it was only as she exclaimed almost in horror, that she realised he was flicking through a large volume taken from a lower shelf.

'Simon, what are you doing here?'

He got up awkwardly, shutting the book. He kissed her

cheek and said, 'The same as you I expect: not going home.'

'I've just come from the office. I'm buying books for next week. It's a pity you can't come too. It should be lovely in Crete in September, not too hot . . .' She found herself babbling and stopped.

'I could come. What's to stop me? No reason at all. I've no proper job and an excellent nanny. I've not been invited, that's all.'

Helena's sense of peace always bestowed by bookshops and libraries, deriving from the order, the stored knowledge, the potential, was shattered. She put down her selection and said, helplessly in the face of unhappiness, 'You do sound down in the mouth. Come and have a drink. We won't go home. We'll go to a pub. You need distraction and noise and people to cheer you up.'

Simon did not show any sign of relishing any of these suggestions; after a moment's hesitation, he said grudgingly, 'OK. Why not?' and followed Helena out of the shop.

They went into the first bar they came to, filled with the young and their noise. Helena felt as if she had a casualty on her hands, as if she had come across an accident and had never learned first aid. While she could not walk away from a friend's unhappiness, she was conscious of her own distaste for confidences and advice. Panic at exposed distress filled her. If only Isobel were here; if only they could be normal. They must be normal. She would buy him something to eat; she would take him to a film. These were normal activities: the body took over, absorbing the food, the story, nourishment and ideas; the cells worked at something external and so the mind did not brood on its wrongs, multiplying them.

It was a sign of Simon's depression that he sat down

gloomily and let Helena order the drinks. Food, she thought, running her eye down the list on the blackboard behind the bar, the most basic solace. The female answer to a problem, eat it. She ordered chilli con carne for Simon because it looked heavy and filling and whitebait for herself for the opposite reason. She put Simon's gin down in front of him and saw that he had recovered from his solitary misery at least sufficiently for ordinary conversation.

How much men needed women, she thought. Spinsters like herself – she rather relished the archaism – might be eccentric but they managed their lives well, with their passions for cats, gardens and good works. Simon, on the other hand, required the constant grooming attention of a woman. While he had had Isobel's love, he had thrived. Now that she was overloaded with work and irritable with him he was like a neglected pet.

Simon took a large swig of his gin. 'How are you getting on with the detective work? Have you proved the Great-aunt's innocence yet?'

Helena seized the subject gratefully and elaborated on what she and Marta had discovered. Simon listened with what was very evidently only half his mind. She could see that not so very far below the surface was a source of pain and disturbance which he could not leave.

When she paused he said, 'So you haven't actually found that irrefutable proof that you were hoping for?'

'No, and now I begin to doubt if I ever shall.'

'I forgot to say to you at that weekend at Richard's that I found some books which would interest you. You remember I told you Arkadi Novikoff had written a couple of novels, or books of short stories rather, in the Twenties, after he had split up with his wife? Before I went away with the twins there was a church fête and on the bookstall I

found both of them. Matching editions with the dust
jackets, by Paul Nash incidentally. I got them for 50p
each.'

'How marvellous. Have you read them? Are they
romans-à-clef?'

'If you mean is there an account of a country house
murder with an unexpected denouement in which it is
revealed that the butler poisoned his master, the answer is
no. There are several interesting portraits of women who I
think must be his wife, Diana and possibly Fanny
Pollexfen.'

'How did he depict them? How did you recognise them?'

'The essence of his stories is the same. There are certain
people, men, artists, who have a sensitivity which enables
them to see the world in a particular way and which
incapacitates them from succeeding. Success in art, in love,
in life, goes to those coarse-grained natures who are able
to seize opportunities and to trample over their more
discerning but less pushy contemporaries. And in his world
the coarse-natured are women. There is something in
women's make-up that makes them more ruthless and less
spiritual than men.'

The chilli con carne and whitebait arrived. Helena
observed that Simon was less interested in food than he
used to be. He ate without the relish and concentration
which he formerly dedicated to his nourishment. Instead,
he seemed much exercised by Arkadi Novikoff's short
stories, as if they in some way reflected his own dilemmas,
or his own views of the world.

'There is one story about a woman poet, whom the
central character helps and encourages, less because her
work is good, in fact it's lousy, but because he is sorry for
her.'

'If it were real life it would be because he wanted to go

to bed with her,' said Helena cynically.

'No, his motives are pure. Then the poetess launches herself on the world, is well received, critically acclaimed, a financial success. The world admires the meretricious, success goes to the coarse, violent and unworthy.'

'Does she get her come-uppance, the poetess? Is she punished, even by a realisation of the worthlessness of what she had achieved?'

'Of course not. She has everything her heart could desire: money, position, acclaim, a husband too, and is perfectly satisfied. It ends tragically, naturally. How he must have hated his wife.'

'Simon, what about a film? Would that amuse you? We could just catch the last performance.' Helena had no idea what was on. To watch other people's emotional problems on celluloid without having to intervene seemed a much better idea than acting as confidante.

Simon gave the suggestion barely a moment's considera- tion. 'No,' he said. 'I'm fine here. Let me get you another drink.' He carried the glasses back to their table, still absorbed in the story of Arkadi Novikoff.

'They say that writing is the activity of the powerless. Not journalism; they have plenty of power, journalists; I mean writing novels. But I think it's an exercise of great power. What a revenge on his wife. She chucked him out, wouldn't have anything more to do with him and went on living very comfortably, thank you, as she always had, and he was left, abandoned, without anything. Ended up in Dachau. At least he was able to put his point of view, show her up.'

Helena could not avoid it any longer; the bitterness in his voice was too clear. 'Oh, Simon, what is the matter? Things can't be as bad as that for you, surely?'

He was suddenly aware of how much he had allowed to

be seen by thinking aloud in her presence. 'Nothing's the matter,' he said. 'Nothing at all. I was just talking about Arkadi and Pia Novikoff. I know it's not immediately relevant to the Great-aunt; it's more background material. I just thought it might be useful to you.'

Helena's directness had changed the mode of their conversation. She saw, with relief, that he was not going to tell her that Isobel didn't understand him. Though, thought Helena, she clearly didn't.

He looked at his watch. 'Time to go,' he said. 'I've bored you enough for the evening. What about that short story? Shall I send you the books?'

Amid the thoughts that had occupied the surface of her mind as Simon had been talking, her concern for him and for Isobel, her terror that he would tell her openly things that she did not want to hear about their marriage, she had recognised something in the story he had been telling. The realisation that she had been told something important, been given a key to the Great-aunt's story, if she could only see how to insert it into the lock, made her react with alacrity to Simon's signals of departure. They walked together down the King's Road.

'Shall we get you a taxi?' she asked, looking over her shoulder.

'No, no. I'll walk to the tube. I'm very economical with Isobel's money. It'll do me good.'

'In that case, I'll say goodbye here. Good night, Simon. Thank you very much for that story of Arkadi Novikoff. It was very interesting indeed.'

She turned into a side street and concentrated on Simon's words, *How he must have hated his wife*, which had acted strangely upon her, like the flare of a match in darkness, allowing her to see how the diverse shapes which she had been attempting to understand by touch alone were related to one another. In that moment, things which she had fumblingly comprehended in part were suddenly revealed to view.

How he must have hated his wife. The short story had struck Simon because of its correspondence with his own position. His rage and jealousy of Isobel's success must be all the greater, because he could not console himself with his artistic inviolability. Without even that refuge, which Arkadi had had, Simon was indeed desolate, left without any form of significance in his own eyes, even the impotent revenge of writing.

How he must have hated his wife. In the flare of intuition it had come to Helena that the story was not about Arkadi and Pia, or only secondarily. It was about Diana and George. *How he must have hated his wife.* The evidence that she had seen, the letters that had passed between Pia and Arkadi in the Twenties, between Diana and Arkadi in the Thirties, were not filled with rancour and a desire to hurt. Her judgement of Arkadi was that he was not a vengeful man. He was, also, too much of an artist simply to write out his own life as a short story.

Helena had walked slowly, her mind absorbed by what Simon had suddenly shown her. She inserted her key into the lock of her front door, still thinking of the meaning of what she had just recognised, and as she opened the door she was drawn violently back to the present.

The house was dark but she knew, knew, that this time the presence was there. Not that someone had been there in her absence, but was there at that instant. She stood on the doormat, her own foreshortened shadow falling before her.

The layers of noise separated themselves into the intermittent sound of traffic on the King's Road and St Leonard's Terrace; footsteps and voices a long way away at the far end of Radnor Walk; the faint throbbing of the music of the rock-loving daughter of a neighbour issuing from an upper window five houses down the street; the beating of her own blood which she felt as a hammer in her chest, a clock in her wrists, a flow in her ears; and the sound of the latch on the door of the drawing-room releasing itself into its bed.

Helena calmly closed the front door and without turning on the lights began to mount the stairs, her way illuminated only by the moon which shone through the window on the half-landing. She wondered, later, what she had been expecting to meet. The presence was so closely linked in her mind with the Great-aunt's death that she realised that she had half anticipated some ghostly confrontation. Her courage surprised her, even then, though since the ghost was, she thought, one essentially well disposed towards her, she had perhaps no need to feel afraid.

She opened the drawing-room door. Here, too, no lamp was lit. The street lights threw two long rectangles like sheets over the furniture, the strict lines of the windows distorted by their fall over the various shapes in the room, all colour bleached from them, as if sculpted in pale stone: the beaded footstool; the sloped front on the escritoire; the horizontal surface of a work table on which were the ruffled shapes of a bowl of roses; the two bergère chairs on either side of the fireplace, in one of which sat a woman.

It was not, of course, Diana Fox, in either living or ghostly form. She was small, plumpish; her hair, worn loose to her shoulders, was curly and untidy, framing a round face out of which jutted an unexpected chin. It was a face whose structure was hidden deep below the flesh, whose features were not carved from bone but modelled in soft and pliable clay, the substance tweaked at the last moment to produce that chin.

Helena recognised her at once, even in that dim light. Long ago, when she had first met Robert, Helena had seen photographs of an election campaign in which his wife had appeared, smiling faintly, as if at something that did not concern her, but which she was glad had pleased him. It was a rare appearance: Sara Occam was never again to be seen in the press photographs which Helena studied so avidly. Now she was sitting with her hands resting lightly on the arms of her chair, gazing abstractedly out of the window. 'I wondered if you would get back while I was here tonight. I somehow thought you would,' she said.

Helena walked to the companion chair and sat down. Her knees were trembling and she had the sensation that she might faint. The horror could not have been greater if it had been the Great-aunt who had been sitting there.

'I would have been earlier, then I met a friend in a bookshop and went with him to have supper in a pub. It was all a bit unexpected.' She felt she had to apologise, as if for breaking an engagement.

'It doesn't matter, now. I kept hoping we would meet here. But of course you are so busy these days.'

There was a short pause. Helena's panic had subsided. One reason why she had chosen her branch of the law was that she liked plenty of time for reflection and could not think on her feet as one needed to do at the Bar. Now she felt a frozen calm. No plan or response to what was happening came into her mind. She would simply react.

'Have you been here long?' Helena's evident lack of understanding made her visitor impatient. 'Have you lived here long?'

'In this house? About eight years. It was a total ruin when I bought it.'

'You have done it up very well. I feel very comfortable

when I come here, soothed.' She looked round approvingly.

This is mad, Helena thought. It is impossible to sit here and talk about decorating houses.

'I like your books, pictures, and your music especially. Do you play an instrument?'

'Not really. I learned the piano at school, but I don't practise now. No time.'

'I knew you were musical. I have always taken an interest in you, you know. I saw you at the opera in the spring. I used to sing. I began to train as a singer, but, well, other things happen in life and I did not have the courage or perseverance to persist. That means I wasn't good enough, I suppose. Did you enjoy it?'

'The opera? What was it?' A memory struck her, a disc playing on the night of her birthday. 'Was it *Lucia?* Yes, yes, I did.'

It seemed their meeting was to be one of trivial conversation, the exchanges one makes on first acquaintance, establishing a map of overlapping interests and connections.

'I go all the time. It is the supreme art form, don't you think? My greatest regret is that my marriage ended my singing career. You cannot combine being the wife of a politician and an opera singer. It is not just the music, you know. It is the story, too, which is so important. People like my husband mock the librettos of operas, saying that they are indulgent fantasies, incredible rigmaroles.'

Helena could hear Robert's voice, dismissive, amused, unserious.

'But, as in everything else, he is wrong. Opera expresses passions which exist within us but which only the very brave or the mad have the courage to live. As he may very well find, one day.' She leaned forward a little in her earnestness. A car drove slowly past the house and its lights drifted over the visitor's face, circling upwards as the sound of its engine reached its crescendo and was cut off as it turned out of the street. 'People . . .' Somehow the contempt in her voice for people who did not understand opera was merged with an emotional force associated with Robert.

'People think of only one or two arias which they take quite out of context, without significance. It's like waving coloured rattles in front of a baby. It's very pretty, but what does it mean? You have to understand the whole. And he is incapable of that. He simply has no idea of the meaning.'

Helena's heart leaped to Robert's defence, thinking of the moment standing together in the Louvre a month ago when he had touched her hand, as they stood together in front of Poussin's shepherds faced with a tomb. She had known that he had shared her fear of loss and death.

'So many women live under the shadow of a man,' Sara Occam was saying, 'who prevents them from being what they should be and doing what they are capable of doing, so they grow deformed and blighted.'

Helena did not at first know what element to respond to in this speech, the general, the personal or the artistic.

'Should they not step out of the shadow,' she asked tentatively, 'cut the bonds to free them if the situation is intolerable?'

'That does not deal with the guilt. Guilt should be punished.'

'Can we take on ourselves the right to punish?'

'Can a lawyer ask that?'

'Especially a lawyer. In law, punishment is abstracted, depersonalised. The law is the collective right to punish, it takes the spirit of revenge out of the punishment. Or one can wait for St Michael's scales on the day of judgement . . .'

Sara waved her hands in front of her face as if pushing off a lot of irrelevancies. 'No, no. You are talking about questions of social misbehaviour, dealt with by Law and Church. I mean someone who is a stone on your heart, who has taken your time and wasted your life. That demands a punishment which no one else can give. You must take it yourself.'

'No, no,' Helena echoed her vehemence. She felt as if she were talking to someone in a foreign language that neither of them spoke. 'You must free yourself. You must not think in terms of punishment and revenge.'

We are all blinded by our spectacles. What we put on to help us see, corrects not to an abstract clarity but to our own vision. Helena was filled with fear for Robert. The danger had arrived, as always, on the least protected front. She might have expected from Sara Occam reproaches, demands, which would have been hard to rebuff. What she had never foreseen was that she would be his wife's weapon for his destruction.

Sara Occam was looking at her with an expression of aroused interest, as if curious to see the passion she had awakened. She waited to see if Helena had more to say. Then she stood up.

'You're quite right, my dear. "You must free yourself." I shall remember those words. It is right that you should show me how to act. And now I must go. My husband,' she spoke of him, as if he were someone Helena had not yet met, 'gets back very late. I like to be home first. He hates coming to an empty house.'

She walked to the head of the stairs with the confidence of someone in her own home. In the hall she picked up a set of keys which were lying beside Helena's, where she always put them on the little table, and let herself out of the front door.

Helena's heart was racing with terror. She heard a car slowing down, its ticking engine revealing it as a taxi. Sara Occam would be getting into it now; the note changed; it moved off. And once home, what would she do? When would she act? Helena had no doubt at all that she would have her revenge. Their meeting would precipitate an action that Robert's wife had been brooding on for a long time. She could imagine her sitting down at her telephone with her address book and calling that friend or cousin from the web of family and acquaintance, and dispassionately recounting the scandal of her husband's private life. It would appear first as a few sentences in a gossip column; the hints would grow bolder, the enemies gather, the stories multiply, a filthy comet of the imagination with a tail of smears and innuendo. At a certain point Robert would be forced to resign with his achievements sneered at and his future destroyed. It had happened so many times before. How could she have let him take such a gamble which placed everything, future and past, in the scales, balanced against present pleasure? She did not even think of what it would mean for herself, not from selflessness, rather because she knew that for her, her self-image, her chaste and hard-working persona, would be utterly overthrown in ways that she could not bear to think of. She sat on the stairs in the still unlit house to control her horror.

There was only one thing to do, something she had never done in eight years. She must ring Robert. She switched on lights as she went downstairs and picked up the receiver.

She got through to his office. No, the Minister was not there; he was at an official dinner. Was it urgent? Who should he say was calling? What was the message? He would try to contact him. He would certainly be asked to call before he left for home.

Helena put down the phone and began to move restlessly around the room waiting for the return call. She drew curtains, turned on lights, a kettle, music.

Not quite obliterated by later events, still echoing, sounding faintly in counterpoint to the crisis overwhelming her, was Simon's voice, *How he must have hated his wife*. George Pollexfen, married to A.D. Millard, a brilliant and talented photographer, had thought somehow to capture that brilliance and talent, and had found that it had escaped him, that he lived alongside it, as hollow as he had always been. The phone had barely begun to ring when she reached it.

'Helena?' Robert's voice was perfectly level, betraying no surprise at the abandonment of eight years' caution. She assumed that he was surrounded by his people and was pleased to hear that her voice sounded as quotidian as his own.

'I've just seen your wife. I found her here. I'm at home. She had some keys.'

'Ah yes, the lost keys. I wondered . . .'

She remembered the doorbell at one in the morning, months ago, just after the Great-aunt died.

'How was she? How did she seem?' They could have been talking about a mutual friend. The madness of the evening grew on Helena.

'Well, strange.'

'How?'

'We talked about opera.'

'*Lucia de Lammermoor*?'

'Yes, how did you know? What I rang to say was, I think she wants to harm you. She knows, I mean clearly she knows, and she talked about punishment and this is the most obvious way of doing it.'

Robert was silent as if considering what to do. 'Thank you for letting me know. I'll go straight home now. It may not be that, but it may be worse.'

Helena decided to submit herself to the discipline of preparing for bed, but sleep was impossible to attain. Once she admitted as much, she made a selection of the Great-aunt's diaries. How easy it had been calmly to read of the emotions and crises of the past when her mind was at ease. Only now when her own heart was in an anguish of anxiety did she really invest what she read with the distress that the Great-aunt must have felt in the weeks and months in prison when she did not know how long her future was. It was too painful. She put back the much studied 1925 volume.

Simon had said that Arkadi had published his short stories . . . when was it? In 1933 he had moved to Paris. It was before that, because subsequently he had written in French. In 1928 and 1931. She wondered if Diana had come across them, if Arkadi had even sent her copies. She had not bothered to look in the library at Ingthorpe. Not knowing the month of publication, she skimmed through the closely written pages of 1928 looking for the title or Arkadi's name.

The diaries in the years after the trial had changed their character. There were no more pages of self-analysis, of feelings, even of reflection. The Great-aunt had written to impose a framework on her life. Each day noted activities, usually involving her son or her garden: she reported the transplantation of an *Andromeda floribunda* to a new, more favourable, site; the arrival of a governess for Peter; the annual clipping of the yew hedge; Peter's hatred of Latin homework; what she had for lunch; Peter's love of anchovy toast after his afternoon ride; mulching the roses;

what she wore; the weather; the temperature, *maxima* and *minima*. Only the surface. Books she listed: only the titles, without comment on their substance. Arkadi Novikoff's short stories were not mentioned.

The enamelled clock showed her it was five past three. Impossible to place Robert. What had he found when he reached home? Was he lying, as he should be, asleep and at peace beside his wife; or awake, open-eyed in the darkness, contemplating the appalling publicity that would appear week by week in the months up to Christmas, wondering whether to resign before disaster happened, or to face it out in the hope of surviving? She decided that she must try once again to sleep and was replacing a ledger in the shelves when she remembered Marta's saying that she had seen a reference to Arkadi and Pia very late on, in the last year of the Great-aunt's life, a page which she had photocopied to give to Ramasubramaniam. She took out the final volume written in the sprawling, childlike hand of the very old. Opening it towards the end, her eye lighted on her own name. She had regarded the journals as historical documents, or legal ones, evidence in the case, to such a degree that she had never looked at them for her own part in the Great-aunt's life.

Helena for lunch, Great-aunt Fox had written for Sunday 27th January. *Mary made lamb with juniper berries. H. had been to see the* Nozze *performed in a private house in Derbyshire. She insisted on playing the last act to me on the gramophone. The moment of forgiveness is so terrible I could hardly bear it. I cannot forgive myself that I never wrote to Pia.*

She remembered that lunch when the Great-aunt had seemed tired and very aged. She had recounted her week to amuse her; had found the old records in their soft shabby covers and played the last act to share her pleasure, discovering to her dismay that the Great-aunt had shed tears. She had accounted for them as the easy, sentimental emotion of the very old, overcome by beauty.

Sleep forgotten now, Helena looked further back, searching in the autumn around the time of Pia's death in October. Under the date Monday 14th October 1991, she found the reference which told her what she must do in the morning.

She slept fitfully, the journal lying beside her on the other half of her bed. The enamel clock was no comfort when she awoke, the minute pendulum wagged maddeningly, imperviously. Robert must ring soon. By eight o'clock, she decided that there was no point in working at home as she had thought to do; he could reach her as easily in the office and she took herself off to the City. As she walked to the tube she tried to convince herself that nothing had happened. He would not phone to tell her nothing and that was precisely what the future held, if they were lucky. She stopped in the sudden realisation that she might never speak to him or see him again.

With this melancholy idea now a conviction, she recklessly dealt with immediate matters, left instructions for her morning's meetings to be postponed and took a taxi back to the West End. At the London Library she looked up Novikoff, Arkadi Izakovitch, in the catalogue and discovered to her relief that the two volumes of short stories, forgotten and unread, had not been weeded out. Crouching in the stacks, she ran her hands over the dusty tops of the books until she found Arkadi's. Unlike Simon's copies they had no dust jackets. Their covers were black, cloth-bound, worn, the thick beige endpapers freckled with the fine pointillism of age. She checked them out and took the tube back to the City.

Sophie, worried by Helena's unusual behaviour, said to

her warningly as she passed through the outer office, 'You have an appointment at two thirty which I couldn't cancel. You'll have to see them; they had already set off from Leeds when I called.'

Helena glanced at her watch. 'All right, I'll see them. But until then, no visitors, no phone calls. Keep Henry off my back, will you? Tell him I'm busy. And, oh Sophie, when you go out to lunch will you bring me a sandwich and an apple?'

She kicked off her shoes and sat down in one of the easy chairs by the window with her knees drawn up to begin her reading of Arkadi's stories.

When Sophie came in at half-past one with her lunch in a paper bag she was still curled up in the chair. She had skimmed the two books, identified Simon's short story and was reading it with a concentration which had nothing in common with her usual businesslike focus on her legal papers, nor her rapid reading of novels and biographies. The words which others had read in the past, racing through to occupy an hour, or more attentively to understand the author's ideas, carried for her echoes of the lives of Great-aunt Fox, of Pia, of George Pollexfen and of Fanny, of Arkadi himself. Among those resonances was Simon's and Isobel's troubled relationship.

As she read she became more and more convinced that Simon was wrong; Arkadi was not writing about himself. Simon's reading of the main character had been influenced by his self-identification with him. Nor was he seen as uncritically as Simon had implied. In fact Arkadi had left open to question whether his hero was really an unrecognised genius or an untalented man jealous of the success given to a woman. The ending, Helena thought, was, as Simon had said, tragic but unexpectedly weak. The hero killed himself by drowning, swimming out to sea. It was not what Helena had anticipated from Simon's account.

She inserted a slip of paper into the book and took the sandwich from Sophie.

'Helena, are you all right?'

'Of course I'm all right. Now. I'll get back to work. You'd better bring me those files for the two-thirty meeting.'

'I'll get them for you. Here's your apple. And I got you a *Standard*. You can look at it with your coffee.'

Helena extracted the sandwiches from their triangular coffin and lifted a corner of the flaccid bread to see what extraordinary combination of ingredients Sophie had chosen for her: chicken tikka and cottage cheese was by sight the best estimate, to be confirmed by taste. Sophie had placed the newspaper on the coffee table in front of her. It was folded horizontally in four and the third band from the top lay uppermost, partially obscured by the sandwich casing. Through the distorting transparency of the plastic Helena read a headline, backwards because the paper was upside down. EDICIUS

It was in that moment, as her eye and brain made the effort to correct her reversed vision, like understanding the past, which is also approached from the wrong direction, that the disparate ideas on which she had been speculating since yesterday evening suddenly flew together at one point as if a magnet had been placed amid iron filings. She had already thought, Simon, Simon, are you all right? She had a sudden vision of him lying face down in the garden at Ingthorpe, one hand outstretched in accusation, like George. How did Arkadi know? She leaned forward to pick up the newspaper and her eye simultaneously finished the inverted headline, *Minister's Wife Attempts Suicide*.

It occupied barely an inch of column space. *Mrs Sara*

Occam, wife of Robert Occam, Minister of State at the Foreign Office, was rushed to St Thomas's Hospital last night, suffering from a drug overdose. She had been discovered by her husband on his return to their West London home. She was said by a hospital spokesman this morning to be 'very poorly'. Mrs Occam, who is on the Board of the Royal Opera House, has been an indefatigable worker for the schizophrenics' charity Two Minds.

It was Sophie who picked up the fallen sandwiches, the pink chicken and white curd which had tumbled over the rugs that covered the bare boards of the office floor. She swept the newspaper into a dustbin bag along with the paper wrapping, cellophane packet and the rest of the debris of Helena's lunch, while Helena prepared for the afternoon's meeting.

The effort to suppress her thoughts about Robert and his wife, about Simon, and George Pollexfen and Arkadi, was so great that a fragment would from time to time detach itself from the submerged mass and surface among her explanations of the complex case on which the legal advisor and two food scientists of a large company had come to consult her. She could only stop for a moment, if she was speaking, and, as though wrenching a steering wheel, redirect her attention to matters in hand. Not until the meeting was over and she had made her notes was she able to take the phone and make the one contact that was possible to her. It rang for a long time and she was on the point of putting the receiver down when one of the twins answered. Daddy, she said, was out.

'When did he go, Nickie, or is it Charlie?' Helena asked urgently.

Charlotte thought for a moment before replying, 'It's Charlie. He was here for breakfast. Then we went to school. He wasn't here when we got back.'

'Will you ask him to ring me when he comes in? Say it's a bit urgent.'

'OK. Or Mummy too?'

'Er, yes. Mummy, if she gets in first.'

The child's voice restored Helena's sense of reality. What did she propose to say to Isobel when she returned her call? Or Simon, for that matter? How did you say to someone, don't kill yourself. Don't let him kill himself. As long as he had not done it already, was not lying in the garden filled with drugs and alcohol, like George Pollexfen, or Sara Occam. Worry about Simon consumed her and she gratefully indulged it, for it prevented her from imagining Sara Occam going home last night, opening her bathroom cabinet and, with that same distant calm with which she had conducted their conversation, selecting the pills that she would consume handful by handful, sitting on the edge of her bed.

Simon, Simon, he must be all right. Arkadi had been able to write out his resentment of Pia, to forgive her in creativity: Simon had lamented not having that recourse. Yet he had other things to draw him back: his children for example. He did not suffer from schizophrenia like Sara Occam, shell-shock like George Pollexfen.

'Helena, I'm off now. Are you sure you're OK? You look most peculiar.'

'Sophie. Yes, I'm fine. At least, I have a lousy head-ache, but I'm fine. See you tomorrow. Don't worry, I'll get that.'

'Helena, what's the matter? Charlie said it was urgent.'

'Isobel.'

'Yes, Helena, what is it?'

'Where's Simon?'

'Simon's here. Do you want him? We're in the car on the way to dinner. He's driving. You sound most odd.'

'No. It's . . . I've got a migraine, that's all. A terrible day and something's come up. You'll be furious. I can't go to Crete next week.'

'Helena.'

'I know, I know. I can't help it. Look, this is my idea.' It had only just come to her. 'Simon must go instead. You need a holiday, so don't cancel it. Take Simon. He can drive you around and find all the good restaurants and take your photograph.'

There was silence at the other end, a silence filled with static. Then Isobel said, 'I'll see. Perhaps. We'll talk about it. Oh, there's a bridge coming up. I'll . . .' She was cut off. Helena leaned back in her chair. If she could just get herself into a taxi. She must go home and lie down. She mustn't think. She must get home.

She took a taxi, leaning back into a corner with her eyes closed. Her mind circled like a fairground machine with sickening swoops from present to past, rushing through broken images of George and Jono in the studio; the body in the apple walk; the rows of blue jars ranged neatly on shelves above the dark-room sink, one item missing from a perfect line; braking violently as the past fused with the present, a fist of pills from a small brown pot crammed into the mouth.

She felt as if she were suffering from travel sickness as the taxi drew up at her yellow front door. She paid the driver and staggered inside, her hands fumbling with her keys, shutting the door as if she could thus shut off her mind. She ran down the stairs, stumbling over the mail lying on the doormat, and threw up in the loo. Her forehead was damp and her own face peered back at her from the mirror, ghostly grey. No need to look for signs of the presence. She crawled upstairs, her hands pattering on the stair carpet like a dog, and lay down on her bed without taking off her clothes.

The room was dark when she regained consciousness, the windows, uncurtained, making orange-black holes in the wall. She was cold; her knees, as she lowered her feet to the floor, trembled; but the flashing lights, the sickness, had gone, leaving her weightless, emptied. It was three in the morning. Why was it, she thought, that whenever she woke with worry or guilt in the night it was always exactly three o'clock? She undressed slowly, bathed, went downstairs to make herself a herbal tea. She pressed the playback on the answerphone which responded only with the anonymous clicks of those who would not speak. Robert?

At last installed in bed with her sheets moulding her like a shroud, she decided she would be ill. She would phone Sophie in the morning. It would be the first time she had been ill since she had had flu eight years ago, just after she had met Robert. He had come to visit her, she remembered, the first time he had come to the house and found her ill in bed amid the builders' rubble. Beside her on the pillow lay the mail that she must have picked up without realising it as she came in. The top envelope was written in a large foreign hand; on the stamp she recognised Marianne. The characters moved with a slow swimming motion over the thick blue paper, tied together in words only in a most tenuous fashion. It was too soon to hope to read. She lay back and turned off the light again.

So she had found the answer that she had been seeking. The Great-aunt was not a murderess. George Pollexfen had committed suicide, deliberately trying to throw blame on his wife so that she would be accused, perhaps executed, for murder.

Isobel had said that it would do her good to learn that life is not as cut and dried as lawyers like to make it. She could not have imagined that it would be her husband's words, *How he must have hated his wife*, that had illuminated the past. Or that an attempted suicide in the present would have eventually revealed the motives of the past.

As protection against the present Helena began to reconstruct the past. The puppets this time moved with lives of their own.

She began with those three days in June as they had been lived by George Pollexfen. In the accounts of Diana's diaries, of Pia and Edith de Cantegnac, he was a peripheral figure until, by dying, he forced himself into the centre of their attention. But there was another story, George's own, in which his death was not an unexpected, inexplicable act of violence, cutting into the tranquillity of a garden in June. For George his death was the inevitable culmination of a long wait. It had begun in the war with the anonymous sergeant who could not bear the sound of another man's pain, who had preferred to die than listen hour after hour to the cries of agony of the captain of the Worcesters out in no man's land. George had stolen another man's actions and he must have always lived with the fear that one day his fraud would be uncovered. When he had seen Gaëtan de Cantegnac arrive at his own dinner-table, he had known it would be soon.

Helena imagined George's living the hollow years that followed the war in which he forgot his theft for weeks on end and then was brought face to face with genuine heroism or tragedy and reminded of what he had taken and what he had lost.

In some respects George was stereotypically honourable: he had accepted the demands of courage and heroism placed on him by his role as officer and gentleman, and his fraud had grown out of that acceptance. He had not known how to reject the call to leadership and fruitless courage in impossible circumstances. Instead of rebelling against the slaughter of the war, he had remained convinced that the world was right and he was wrong: his revulsion and fear were signs of his own cowardice and failure. The war had frayed his personality to breaking point. He had sacrificed his personal honour in order to maintain the façade of the hero and perhaps that paradox was the swivel on which turned his feelings for Diana, who would not accept the part he and convention assigned to her. *She had been a stone on his heart, taking his time and wasting his life. That demands a punishment which no one else can impose. You must make it yourself.*

She fell asleep at last and was only awakened by the telephone. Fumbling for the receiver, she saw that she had overslept; it was eight o'clock.

Marta, whose metabolism functioned well first thing in the morning in spite of jet lag, wanted a reaction to her material on Pybus. 'You're in bed, Helena,' she said accusingly. 'You're lying down. I can tell by your voice. I thought I would just catch you before you left for work.'

'I'm ill,' said Helena firmly. She was going to maintain her decision of the early hours.

'Ill? You're never ill. What's the matter? Anyway, never mind about that. What do you think about my findings in Baltimore?'

The past was still easier to deal with than the present; Helena roused herself sufficiently to cope with Marta. The last thing she wanted was to have visits to her sickbed. 'No, Marta. It wasn't Pybus. I know what happened. I've worked it out.'

'You mean you had a blinding flash of insight and no evidence?'

'Something like that. Listen, it was George himself. Do you remember saying he was more a killer than a victim?

He was both. He committed suicide and tried to make it look as if Diana killed him.'

For once Marta was silent as she absorbed this idea.

'Jono was involved as a sort of precipitating cause,' Helena went on. 'Jono knew what had happened, or realised it later. There's a bit in the diaries, very late on, when the Great-aunt says that she thought that Jono knew, because he sent her, via Winter, copies of Arkadi's short stories. Of course, when we first read them, we didn't understand what she was talking about.'

Marta was by now ready to object and to test Helena's ideas. 'Where did you get this theory from?'

'It was Simon, something Simon said that made me realise. He had read the short stories of Arkadi Novikoff and he told me about one of them; about a man who is jealous of a woman's success and commits suicide. Simon thought it was about Pia and Arkadi. I suddenly saw that it was about Diana and George. That's what the Great-aunt meant when she says something about Arkadi understanding.'

'You mean she knew George committed suicide? Why didn't she say so at the trial?'

'I think it must only have been some time later that she understood. If you remember, she just keeps saying that she can't imagine anyone else doing it. She didn't draw the logical conclusion until later; perhaps she even found some proof.'

'It's true,' Marta agreed reluctantly. 'The problem all along has been to find anyone who could seriously be considered a murderer, apart from Diana, of course.'

'And think of their relationship, Diana's and George's. He wanted to punish her. You know that little incident the Great-aunt mentions, about the gun, on the night of her birthday. It must have been George's first attempt to kill them both. But Diana had faced him down. He decided he could not use his gun; he revolted from the violence of the sound that the gun would make, so he must then have redirected his mind to poison and to the chemicals in the photographic studio.'

'Do you think he intended to give Diana poison before taking it himself? Perhaps he even meant to kill her and not to commit suicide at all,' Marta speculated.

'No, I think he had it all carefully worked out,' Helena went on. 'The messages inviting Diana to meet him, the initial D, the appointments for the next week, were all arranged so that his suicide should not be seen as such, but as murder, and murder by Diana.'

'He asked Diana to meet him in the studio. What if she'd come?'

'Who knows? He'd have had a chance to reproach her once again, a really good row. We know he enjoyed that sort of thing. She'd have been convincingly implicated.'

'But it wasn't Diana who came. It was Jono, looking for his papers. That's what he was writing about in the letter to Winter. He must have spoken to George about the Bois de Lencourt incident.'

'Yes, yes. You can see that must have pushed George over the edge. Even though he had not had his last words with Diana, he had to kill himself. He had already made his plans. Jono merely made him act at once.'

Helena could imagine George listening to the uneven footfall of Jono's departure, pouring the chemicals into his glass with a mad precision and walking out into the garden. What would the summer air feel like when it was the last time? 'Poor man,' she said. 'I suddenly feel so sorry for him, the world growing smaller and smaller, the past closing in on him, no escape.'

'If what you've described is what happened,' Marta said

briskly, 'I don't feel sorry for him at all. It is too ingeniously nasty. How he must have hated her.' She did not want to dwell on it; she had more important things to occupy her. 'Well, it sounds as though you have almost wrapped it up, Helena. At least to your own satisfaction, which was always the object. I can now abandon the murder and concentrate on the wider picture. I must call Ram. See you this weekend perhaps?'

Helena replaced the receiver. Satisfaction was hardly the word for what she felt.

She rang Sophie to announce her illness and in fact, as if the word was the deed, was immediately sick again. Not even she could accuse herself of malingering now. As she crept back to bed she discovered the envelope from France lying on the sheet beside her and opened it.

My dear Helena, she read, *I have now found the letter from Diana which I mentioned to you. It seems unforgivable that I did not think to search for it (that is, get Henriette to do so) while you were with me, as it tackles many of the questions that you wanted answered. My excuse can only be that those questions never seemed important to me. Far more significant was why Diana and I never met again. I cannot really understand it. But her letter, which is precious to me for this reason, made a link at last. And I think she was right in this: understanding is all, more than blame and guilt and forgiveness. She was not, I think, justifying or vindicating herself, she was long past that. She wanted to explain what happened, to know that someone who had witnessed those events at last understood them.*

Helena picked up her great-aunt's letter. Why, she wondered, did she not tell me? and recognised with humility that the young are important to the old because they do not know about such ancient horrors.

She read with recognition. Those moments of insight

when Simon had said, *How he must have hated his wife*, when she had read the word SUICIDE upside down were confirmed.

I had wondered if his death was suicide, wrote Diana, *when I was in gaol. I even suggested it to Hector Wallace, who rejected the idea as another of my evasions of reality. There was no note, he said; there were specific appointments and arrangements made for the next day. George had been in good humour all weekend in the view of numerous witnesses. To present suicide as the explanation would be to invite defeat, he said. But in no other fashion could I account for his death. I did not kill him and if it was not I, how could it have been anyone else?*

It was almost two decades later, to be exact in 1942 after Peter's death and Arkadi's disappearance, that I discovered the truth. I was going through my photographs in order to select an album of Peter from his babyhood onwards, and I found a note from George. He had written it in the studio that night and slipped it among my photographic prints. To read it was like opening the door of an oven which you did not realise was on. A blast scorched me, hatred seventeen years old. Yet if I had found it just after his death it would have saved me. He had left me a chance of being saved, then hidden it so effectively that it was not found for seventeen years. I cannot tell you what it said because I destroyed it and tried to destroy the memory. But it is impossible to forget that someone, your husband, has tried to kill you, by killing himself. Suicide is the ultimate revenge, even without the little extra twist that George added to his. He had a mind for puzzles, making order in a little self-contained universe satisfied him. How pleased and triumphant he would have been that his puzzle was insoluble. Who could imagine the setting up of his own death to incriminate and kill me: truly a suicide mission like the one he got his DSO for in the war . . .

Reading this last sentence, Helena realised she had come to the end of her quest. In her searches and researches she had reached a more complete understanding than any of the participants in the events of George Pollexfen's death. She now knew what Great-aunt Fox had known. She knew what Gaëtan de Cantegnac and Jono had known and she had discovered things which they could not have known. And what was she to do with this knowledge? Her original question about a tainted inheritance now seemed foolish and irrelevant. If Diana was innocent, her husband, from whom she inherited Ingthorpe, was not. He had been a sham, a would-be murderer of his wife. But so what? Even he, in some lights, seemed pitiable rather than evil, unable to live up to his own ideals and unable to reject those ideals when they were shown in the shambles of the Western Front to be self-evidently wrong. She put down the letters of the two old women and closed her eyes. The past was over; she would accept, with some understanding, her legacy.

The future was another matter. She knew that what had just happened to Sara Occam and what she had learned about George Pollexfen had a meaning for the present. At first she had only seen Simon who had been the key to her understanding, thinking he was at risk of killing himself, like George or Sara. Only gradually had she realised that Simon was not a man to commit suicide; it was not there that the meaning lay. It was closer to her, more powerful and more poignant than the loss of a cousin. It was Sara who had taken the ultimate revenge.

Even after meeting her, Helena had thought that the danger came from the direction she had always feared: exposure in the press. She had done Sara Occam an injustice; she had constructed a far subtler plan, worthy of George Pollexfen, a plan which at last, as Helena lay in bed where Sara herself, in her wanderings around the house, had probably lain, Helena understood. Sara had contrived to take from Robert not his career, but Helena herself.

Helena could see two futures, neither of which would permit her Robert. If Sara Occam lived, her knowledge of Helena's existence would prevent any continuation of the relationship with Robert; if she died, she would equally effectively have separated them, for who could live, united by suicide?

She had not valued herself enough, Helena thought, to see that she, rather than his job, was the highest price that Robert could be made to pay.

During the afternoon she heard through her drowsing a knock on the door and staggered down, expecting a biker with an envelope of papers from the office. To her astonishment it was Robert. He came in quickly and closed the door behind him, pushing back his long, grey forelock. His face, drawn and unsmiling, told her at once what he had come to say.

He kissed her on the cheek and said, 'You look dreadful. I've brought back your keys.'

'You won't be needing them now.'

He saw that she had understood everything; there was going to be no need to explain.

She wondered whether he would just turn and go straight away. He hesitated, searching for a way of making the final point, the full stop. They went up to the haunted drawing-room where two days ago Sara had welcomed Helena to her own home.

He sat down, leaning back and closing his eyes. Helena studied the beloved face for the last time. She remembered

Dr Ramasubramaniam describing Pia Novikoff's eye that could not escape the minute details of texture, colour, pattern on every surface that it saw. Pia could recreate those details, Helena thought; Diana Pollexfen took photographs of Arkadi, Pia, Peter, so that even though they lost them, they kept them, too. Like Simon envying Arkadi's power, Helena longed to capture, somehow, what she saw. A lawyer had only her memory to retain the past. She annotated, memorised: thick, grey hair, long grooves running from nose to chin. For so much of the time he had been simply an idea, a presence in her life.

When he had left, she dropped the spare keys into a drawer of the hall table. She was feeling better. In her room her eye fell on the untidy pile of the Great-aunt's diaries. She bent to straighten them and thought, all these can go to Marta now. She found a box and loaded it with the volumes of the journals and carried it to the front door.

Tomorrow she would go to Ingthorpe and ask Mary to stay on.